Enthusiastic praise for Barbara Delinsky

"One of today's quintessential authors of contemporary fiction...Ms. Delinsky is a joy to read. With the incisive skill of a surgeon and the delicate insight of true compassion, she deeply probes the quality and meaning of life...."
—*Romantic Times*

An author "of sensitivity and style."
—*Publishers Weekly*

"Ms. Delinsky has a special knack for zeroing in on the pulse of her characters immediately—we know them and understand what makes them tick within the first few pages.... Well done!"
—*Rendezvous*

"When you care enough to read the very best, the name of Barbara Delinsky should come immediately to mind.... One of the few writers... who still writes a great love story, Ms. Delinsky is truly an author for all seasons."
—*Rave Reviews*

BARBARA DELINSKY

Bronze Mystique

MIRA BOOKS

ISBN 1-55166-423-2

BRONZE MYSTIQUE

Bronze Mystique

1

It was a conspiracy of darkness. What with the gloom of the skies, the heaviness of the rain, the narrowness of the road and a preoccupation with his own somber thoughts, Doug Donohue never saw the motorcycle until it had rounded the curve and skidded sidelong into him. He swerved onto the muddy shoulder of the road and slammed on his brakes, but it was too late.

Within seconds he was out of the car and running back the several yards toward where the cyclist lay. "My God!" he exclaimed, then more softly under his breath, "Damn fool kid!" when he caught sight of the slender form beneath the bulk of the Suzuki. With strong hands he levered the heavy motorcycle up. "Are you all right?"

Setting the damaged vehicle aside, he knelt down just as the cyclist's head moved. "Wait!" he commanded. "Be careful! If it hurts, don't move!" A quick perusal of the prone figure showed neither sign of blood nor the grotesque posture that might suggest a bone break. When the head turned again and a shaky hand moved toward the helmet, he got there first, unhooking the strap, sliding the visor up, then pausing and quite helplessly catching his breath.

The face bared to his gaze had to be the most delicate and feminine, not to mention the palest he'd ever seen. "My God!" he exclaimed again, though in a whisper this time. By sheer instinct he smoothed the thick fall of auburn bangs to the side, to expose gentle features to the rain's ministration. Heart pounding, he watched wide-set eyes flicker, then open.

It took Sasha Blake a minute to focus. Stunned, she blinked. The world was an amalgam of darks and lights, the shadows of trees and hedgerows, a nearby automobile, the contrasting glare of an overcast sky. She'd been riding home. Her front tire had hit something. She'd skidded, then slammed into a car. Now she was on her back on the road. Eyes widening, she turned her head toward the figure kneeling beside her. Then, brought to full sense by the steady patter of rain on her face, she struggled to sit up.

"Wait!" the dark figure by her side commanded, a firm hand at her shoulder restraining her. "Maybe you shouldn't—"

"I'm all right!" she moaned, ignoring small twinges of pain to shift cautiously in search of more serious damage. Her arms worked, as did her legs, though when she tried to curl them sideways to prop herself more steadily, she couldn't suppress a whimper.

"Something hurts?" the deep voice demanded instants before long fingers closed over the taut muscles of her thigh and probed carefully down the slim length of denim. Skipping to her other leg, they repeated the exploration.

"Everything hurts," she murmured, her breath coming faster as the enormity of what had happened hit her. She'd nearly been killed! Had she been inches farther to the left it would have been a head-on collision. Feeling suddenly hot and faint, she mustered as much strength as she possessed to shove the helmet from her head. The rain, her enemy earlier when it had come so suddenly and with such force that her ride home from North Tisbury had become an ordeal, was suddenly, almost patronizingly refreshing. She was only marginally aware of the arms that supported her when she swayed, of the broad chest against which her head was momentarily cradled. By the time she regained her equilibrium, the support was gone.

"It doesn't look like anything's broken," the voice came less gently. "And we'd be a damn sight drier in my car. Can you make it?"

Stunned or not, Sasha was hesitant. The sooner she could be on her way, the better. "No. I mean, yes! I can make it. But I'm fine." Experimentally she flexed the taut muscles of her neck by slowly swiveling her head. "If you could just help me get the Suzuki up—" she gasped as she put a hand down and tried to stand "—I'll be on my way."

It was the strong arm around her ribs that got her to her feet. "You can't get back on that damned cycle. I'm taking you to the hospital."

"No hospital!" she cried, imagining the spate of publicity such a visit would cause. In her three years on the Vineyard she'd successfully maintained a low profile. She wouldn't blow that now. "I don't need a hospital. I'm fine!"

"Fine?" was the harsh retort. "Then what's this?"

To Sasha's horror, her rescuer took her hand and turned it until she could see the raw heel covered with blood. Fighting a flash of dizziness, she struggled to keep her knees from buckling. Her voice was a distant, ragged protest.

"It's a scrape. It doesn't hurt. Really." Even as she whispered the last word she was being lowered out of the rain into the passenger's seat of a plush sports car. "But...my Suzuki...."

"I'll set it off to the side of the road," he growled. "It can be picked up later."

"I want it now! Really! I'm all right!"

Wondering at the stubbornness of the woman, Doug worked his way back through the rain to the disabled cycle. Pulling it erect, he wheeled it to the roadside.

"Wait!" she cried, stumbling after him. "Is it badly damaged?"

"I thought I put you in the car," he snapped, his glower made all the more forbidding by the rain dripping freely from his dark hair.

Sasha managed to tear her eyes from his ominous expression to peer at her motorcycle. "The worst is the front wheel, I guess," she said shakily, then grimaced. "But look at the rest. It's scratched up pretty badly."

"Humph." If she was well enough to worry about damages, he decided, he had a word to add on that score. "You wanna see scratches? Take a look at my car!"

Horrified, Sasha wheeled around. The sudden movement made her dizzy, and she stumbled as she went back to study the jagged tracks marring the Maserati's otherwise smooth flank. Shaking rain from her fingers, she traced the ugly grooves. "I'm sorry," she whispered, then looked up at the man who had come to join her. For the first time she was struck by his height, which was accentuated by the breadth of his shoulders as he loomed above her. His hair and face dripped, his leather bomber jacket was sodden, his hands were clenched on hips covered by denim nearly as drenched now as her own. Slightly intimidated, she took a breath. "I'll cover the cost."

Ignoring her offer, Doug shot an angry glance at the spilling clouds. "This is ridiculous!" he breathed. "Get in the car!" He grabbed her elbow to enforce his command, but she winced. With a soft muttered oath, he released her to place a more gentle guiding hand at her back.

Each step made Sasha more aware of the battering she'd taken as her cycle had skidded those few yards with her between it and the road. Her ankle ached as she walked, her hip and shoulder throbbed. When once again she found herself seated in the Maserati, she dropped her head back and closed her eyes. In delayed response to the shock of the accident, her limbs began to shake. Yet her mind was alert. No sooner had Doug climbed behind the wheel when she spoke.

"I will cover the expenses. I mean that."

"I've got insurance."

"But it was my fault. I was the one who barreled into you."

"Now that you mention it, why in the hell were you racing? In case you hadn't noticed, it's pouring out there."

Feeling her first flare of testiness, Sasha sat straighter. "I wasn't racing. And of course I knew it was pouring. I was *out* in the stuff, or hadn't you noticed!"

He cast a wry look at his saturated clothes. "Oh, I noticed all right. I'd planned on staying dry." His gaze shifted, then narrowed. "Damn. Look at that hand." Reaching across her to the glove compartment, he withdrew a small towel. "Here. This is clean. Press it to your hand while I drive." With a grunt, he started the engine. "Now where's the nearest hospital?"

After no more than a moment's pause, during which Sasha decided that his question made him an off-islander, she gestured stiffly with her head. "It's back that way. You've got to return to Menemsha Cross Road, then cut over to South."

Three deft moves reversed the car's direction. Within minutes Doug was headed back toward where he'd come from. Jaw clenched, he wondered how he'd managed to get himself into yet another sticky situation. Hadn't he left New York in search of peace? Wasn't Martha's Vineyard supposed to have that? It had been bad enough when the skies opened, he mused. Charming as they were, the narrow island roads were treacherous in a downpour, and he'd practically slowed to a crawl. Then, to have this woman plow her cycle into his car.... Peace? Hah!

"What were you doing out there anyway?" he growled.

On the defensive, Sasha raised her chin. "Visiting friends in North Tisbury."

"And you don't have a car, or access to one?"

"It wasn't raining when I left this morning. For that matter, it wasn't even raining twenty minutes ago! It just...came."

"So you decided to speed on home?"

"Look," she breathed unevenly, "I've said that I'll pay for whatever repairs are needed on your car. But please. No lectures. You can take my word for the fact that I didn't run into your car on purpose. You can also take my word for the fact that I'm a responsible person...and that I didn't want, didn't *need* this any more than you did!" The gingerly way she pushed a long strand of wet hair up into the catch at the top of her head illustrated her point. Her voice grew more weary. "Something happened. I don't know what it was. I must have hit a stone or something going around that curve...."

Her voice trailed off and she frowned, staring out the rain-smudged windshield. If only her imagination weren't as fertile. But then, her imagination was her stock and trade. Unfortunately, it did nothing but frighten her now. Of course she had hit a stone. Or a piece of glass. Or a nail. And if the incident was reminiscent of *Autumn Ambush?* Pure coincidence. A simple blowout, that was all it had been. "Make a left here," she murmured, forcing her thoughts along a saner route. Yet the fingers holding the towel to her palm were white knuckled and her expression was grim.

Doug drove in silence, the rhythmic slap of the windshield wipers echoing his vacillation between worry for, then annoyance at his tight-lipped passenger. Hesitant to take his eyes from the road, he saw her from the corner of his eye—her body drawn into itself, wayward strands of hair plastered to her neck, one hand clutched to the other, her eyes straight ahead. She was a soggy water rat; she was a lost and injured lamb. She was a hazard on the road; she was an innocent victim herself. However he viewed it, though, she was the last thing he'd needed in kicking off his new life. He wanted nothing more than to deposit her at the hospital emergency room and be done with it. Actually, he amended, squinting with impatience at the roadway ahead, he wanted nothing more than to *find* the hospital.

"Where is the damn place?" he mumbled half to himself, then cast an anxious eye at Sasha.

"Almost there," she returned. "Go left up ahead."

He slowed at the crossroad, turned left and accelerated. Sasha winced at the slight jolt to her bruised body, but caught herself in time to say, "There's a road coming up on your left." Her voice sounded weak and tired. She felt cold and wet, and wanted only to submerge her aching limbs in a hot bath and stay there forever. "Here," she directed, pointing with her uninjured hand. "Turn here and go straight for a bit. You'll be coming to a fork in the road. Make a right at the fork and we're all set."

Doug turned the small car onto a road even more narrow than the first. As the car jounced over several bumps, he shot a glance at his passenger to assess her condition. Her face remained pale, her jaw tight. "I don't believe this!" he exploded anxiously. "What kind of civilized place hides its hospital down long bumpy roads?"

"You haven't been here long?" Sasha ventured, relieved as the route leveled and smoothed, and the physical punishment subsided.

"Not quite," was the terse response. Attention riveted to the muzzied view beyond his windshield, he managed to spot the fork and bear right onto a road that, though narrow, was well kept. When soon after he found himself in the circle of a dead-end drive, he was forced to stop. "What the...this isn't a hospital!" He turned his eyes from the single-storied rambling farmhouse to see Sasha slip stiffly from the car.

"It's my house," she answered quietly. "Thanks for the ride. As soon as you get an estimate for the repairs to your car, drop me a note. The name's Sasha

Blake." Before he could get in a word, she slammed the door and, head bowed against the rain, started at an uneven trot up the stone walk.

Doug was out of the car and halfway up the walk when the front door closed behind her. Stopping in his tracks, momentarily oblivious to the rain, he stared. She'd tricked him. In her own quiet, insistent way, she'd tricked him! Momentarily indignant, he wondered if he should go after her. Perhaps he should insist she have a hospital checkup. After all, if she'd broken a bone or done some kind of internal harm, she could sue him. That was all he'd need. New town. New home. New lawsuit.

Shaking his head in renewed admiration at how silently she'd bested him, he turned and headed back to his car. He doubted she was seriously hurt; he hadn't felt a thing out of place when he'd touched her. Nor did he truly fear she'd cause him trouble. To the contrary. She seemed more than eager to put the entire incident behind her. There was something quiet, something private, something somehow off limits about her.

Puzzled, he started the car, turned in a wide arc and headed back toward the main road. Sasha Blake. Sasha Blake. Her name had a pretty ring to it. It was pixieish, like her. Small and elusive. And wily. It had been a long time since a woman had sidestepped him as skillfully as she'd done. His lips curved at the corners in a subtle smile of appreciation. If Sasha Blake was an example of what he was to find on Martha's Vineyard, his man-in-control image was apt to be well tarnished before long. Strange, he observed, that that thought didn't bother him as once it might have done. Strange how he felt lighter. Strange how Sasha Blake, accident and all, had knocked those darker, more serious thoughts from his mind.

He did like the Vineyard, he mused as he hit South Road once more. Rain and all, it was what he wanted. Fresh air and space, freedom and privacy. New York had become claustrophobic. And tiring. And boring. He needed a change. Midlife crisis? Perhaps. Or perhaps he had simply begun to reassess his goals. Something was missing in New York, in his career, in his life. Before he could begin to identify it, he needed breathing room. Well, he sighed, casting a skeptical eye toward the skies, he had that. He had the house that he'd built overlooking the Sound; he had rocks and grass and acres of rolling hills. And...he had a side full of scratches just waiting to be itched. Or was it the other way around, a whole lot of itches waiting to be scratched. Sasha Blake was a woman. He'd handle her.

"Ahhhh!" Sssha cried aloud when the leather boot finally relinquished its grip on her swollen ankle. Dropping it on top of its mate with a despairing look, she pushed herself to her feet, unsnapped her jeans and wrestled the soggy denim over her hips. Moaning again, she eased herself back onto the small bathroom bench, carefully worked the fabric down her legs, then tossed it aside and sagged back against the wall. It was from that position that she unbuttoned her blouse and pushed it unceremoniously to the floor.

Removing her inner polo shirt was something else. Sitting forward, she crossed her arms and drew the material up over her ribs, then off with a yelp of discomfort. Half wondering whether she'd cracked a rib, she gently poked around a bit. When she sat still she felt fine—well, not exactly fine. Her hand stung like hell, her side ached, her ankle throbbed. But there was nothing sharp, as in broken bones. For that she had to be grateful.

Slipping from her underwear as gingerly as possible, she hobbled to the bathtub, stepped into hot water laced with scented oil, carefully eased herself down, then sank back with a sigh of relief and let her body float.

It was tense. She was tense. The last thing she'd expected when she'd left the house to visit Janine and Paul had been an accident on the way home. In three years of driving the Suzuki around the island, she'd never had any trouble. She was a good driver. Cautious. Even today in the rain, she hadn't been going terribly fast. But the road had been slick and something had sent her into a skid.

With a slender hand, she reached up to adjust the barrette that held her hair atop her head. Wincing as her muscles rebelled against even that simple motion, she gritted her teeth and slowly returned to her original position.

Thank heavens she'd been wearing a helmet. Thank heavens the man in the Maserati had been there to give her a ride home. She laughed sardonically. Perhaps if he hadn't been there she wouldn't have needed a ride home. Had there not been a car in her path she might have recovered from her skid. On the other hand, had there not been a car in her path she might have gone headlong into a tree by the roadside and been knocked unconscious or worse. Aches and pains were a small price to pay, she decided, in the face of that other possibility.

Absently dunking the washcloth she'd set out on the

tip of the tub, she drew it up over her stomach and between her breasts. Who was he, the man in the Maserati? She'd never seen him before. Was he from Boston? New York? Phillie? He was city; she was sure of it. Wetness notwithstanding, his clothes had that look of designer casual. And his car, well, that was proof of the pudding.

Sighing deeply, she settled more comfortably in the tub and brought the hot cloth over one breast, then the other. Made slick by the oily water, the terry square slid with sensual ease. Eyes closed, she concentrated on her muscles, willing them to relax, letting the moist heat work its magic. Her hand was only scraped. Raw, but nothing worse. It would heal, as would her bruises, though by morning she'd surely have a slew of purple patches to show for her mishap.

Who was he? She didn't know his name, but his face had made an indelible impression on her. Ominous. Forbidding. Yet…gentle beneath his glower? She recalled the hand that had carefully probed her legs for breaks, the arm that had circled her ribs to help her stand. Letting the washcloth sink to the bottom of the tub, she slid her hand to her thigh, inched it back along toned muscle to her stomach.

He was strong, that much she knew. And aside from the occasional brash outburst, he had treated her with care. Care. Her lips thinned. Sam had known nothing about care. He had taken her when he'd wanted her, used her to satisfy his needs. If he was hungry, he'd expected her to cook. If he was tired, he'd expected her to run his bath, turn down his bed, spend the evening alone while his snoring echoed through the house. If he was in the mood for love, he'd expected her to turn on at will. No, Sam had known nothing about care. Did any man?

With a small snort of disgust, she turned to happier thoughts. Her outline was almost done. Tonight she'd put the finishing touches on it. Tomorrow morning she'd begin. She had six months, more than enough time to write this book at a leisurely pace. And actually the six-month deadline was her own. By contract, the book wasn't due on her editor's desk until well after that.

Number six. Would it be up to par? Having been writing steadily now for eight years, she well knew the feeling of insecurity that would hover about her for the next few weeks. Creating her characters. Getting to know them. It was challenging and exciting and infinitely rewarding, if frightening. But she had her setting and her plot outline down pat, and her characters had been brewing for days. It was time to start.

Five o'clock the following morning found Sasha at work, the light of her study cutting a blazing swatch through the predawn darkness. She was sore all over and, as she'd expected, slightly discolored along the side that had borne the brunt of the road's hard fury. But her mind was primed and ready, and her fingers sped over the keyboard, registering line after line on the screen before her.

By nine, though, she was stiff and in need of a break. After another long hot bath she tried to dress, finally deciding that her silk robe was the only clothing her battered body would abide. It was soft and light, slitted at the sleeves and leg and belted ever so gently at the waist. Of a pale apricot hue, it brought out the auburn tint of the hair she'd characteristically parted in back and loosely caught up in matching clips at the crown of her head. Her bangs fell thick and low on her brow. With a dash of blusher to cheeks whose lingering pallor spoke of yesterday's trial, she headed for the kitchen and breakfast.

What to have. As she stood staring at the contents of one open cabinet, preoccupied with thoughts of what she'd written, of what she planned to write when she returned to her study, the doorbell rang. Puzzled, she looked up; she hadn't expected anyone. Her mind ran through the possibilities: her friends knew she was working, she hadn't ordered anything to be delivered, the mail never arrived until early afternoon. When the bell rang a second time, she turned, then flinched when her muscles rebelled. Walking stiffly, favoring her sore side, she headed for the front door by way of the living room. Opposite the window she came to a standstill, eyes glued to the dark green, sun-misted Maserati sitting calmly in her drive. Inexplicably, her heart began to thud.

It was the third ring that set her legs in motion again. She hesitated a final time before the door, her hand on its brass knob. Then, with a deep breath for encouragement, she opened it.

For a moment they simply stared at each other, Doug as stunned as she. He had seen her in the rain yesterday, dripping and pale. Now, though, her skin gleamed. She looked fresh out of the bath, her face warm, her hair damp with escaped tendrils curling ever so slightly. Nothing in his vivid imaginings had prepared him for the vision of gentle femininity before him.

As for Sasha, she'd been aware of ominous and forbidding, even of the softer streak that had broken through from time to time. Today, though, confronted with near-black hair that was well trimmed, newly washed and combed, a straight nose, fresh-shaven jaw and stunning gray eyes shaded by the thickest lashes, she was taken aback. If she hadn't been rendered speechless by the male intensity of those eyes, she might have been by the rich bronze sheen of his skin, warm and bold but infinitely touchable. Raw breathtaking virility was something for which she hadn't been prepared.

"Hi," he said at last, his voice faintly rough in a sensual kind of way.

An awkward smile toyed with her lips. "Hi."

"I thought I'd make sure the hospital treated you well."

Her smile relaxed, though her hand held the doorknob for dear life. "It did."

"You look…fine." The understatement of the year, he mused. It was all he could do to keep his eyes on her face. Her robe clung to slender curves he'd somehow missed yesterday. Pixieish, elusive, even delicately feminine he'd thought her then. Nothing had prepared him for downright sexy.

In an unconscious nervous gesture, she dabbed the tip of her tongue to the corners of her mouth. "I am."

"No…aftereffects of the accident?" he asked, daring a fast once-over by way of elaboration.

She followed his gaze, then, self-conscious, showed him her palm. "It's dried up. I'm sure it'll scab over in a day or two."

He nodded, sensing her awkwardness, feeling his own as acutely and being appalled by it. Where was Doug Donohue, the ladies' man? Where was the playboy of the northeastern world? He could take her hand in his, run his forefinger around her bruises, raise her fingers to his lips and suck each in turn as his eyes seduced hers. He could put her palm to his cheek and then kiss away her hurt. For that matter, he could forget the preliminaries and sweep her into his arms for the sole purpose of feeling her body against his.

He cleared his throat. "Well, I guess I'll be going. Just wanted to make sure you were okay." Pivoting on his heel, he took a step down to the walk, then stopped and half turned back to Sasha, his dark brows drawn together. "I stopped on the way to see your cycle but it was gone."

"I had it taken care of." A call to the gas station was all it took. Hank Rossi had been more than eager to jump to her aid. The only price, above and beyond the cost of repairs, would be the sidestepping of another pass, and she was becoming quite adept at that.

"I see," Doug answered, impressed by the independence of such a vulnerable-looking woman. He wondered if there was a man somewhere in the picture. She wore no ring; he'd made note of that yesterday. At least he'd been on top of *something*. Damn, but he was curious. "Well, see 'ya around."

Sasha gave a half smile and a nod, and watched him resume his walk to the car. Wearing stylish gray cotton slacks and a plaid open-necked shirt with a charcoal sweater thrown across his shoulders, he looked decidedly dashing. A man to admire. A man to avoid.

By some twist of fate, admiration won out. "Uh...!" she called, lifting a hand on impulse. When he turned, she blushed again, and let her hand drop. He stood straight, expectant. Startled herself that she had halted his exit, she wondered what she was doing. But there was precious little time to analyze her motives. "Your name," she improvised. "I—I didn't catch it."

"I didn't say it," he replied with a crooked smile. "But it's Doug."

"Doug." She said it once, then nodded again. As when first she'd opened the door, they stared silently at one another. There was an undercurrent of something Sasha couldn't begin to identify. She'd never felt as simultaneously drawn to and unsure with a man. She knew she should let him go, but she couldn't. She moistened her lips. "I was, uh—" she cocked her head toward the back of the house "—I was just taking a break for breakfast. Would you, would you like something? Coffee? Eggs? Juice?"

His smile spread. "I'd like that."

"Of…course, if you've got to be somewhere—"

"I don't."

She moved back then in silent invitation. Seconds later Doug stepped over her threshold, his tall form nothing less than imposing as it passed. Struck by a wave of trepidation, she hesitated, then half reluctantly closed the door.

"Nice place you've got," he said, taking in the open space of the hall and living room. The house was a Cape, as were so many on the island, actually a "half" Cape, with the door and the chimney to the right and two large front windows to the left. Numerous additions had been added at later points in its history, allowing for an oversized kitchen, extra bedrooms and a study, and lending a sprawling air to the house Sasha had fallen for on sight. "Like white, do you?"

She blushed again and followed his gaze. "You noticed." The walls were white; the furniture was white.

The floors were brightly sanded oak. She'd added color in cushions, rag rugs and artwork, leaning toward the softest shades of beiges and pinks, giving the house the airy quality she'd sought.

"Hard to miss. But I like it." His gaze turned back to Sasha with a warmth that made her tingle. It also made her suddenly aware of her clothing, or lack of it. She shot a glance downward and raised her hand to her throat. Her robe was high necked, with a mandarin collar and small buttons. All in all, she was well covered, though the cover was all she wore.

"Um, maybe I'd better change," she stammered. "I wasn't expecting anyone." Head down, she made for the stairs, only to have her wrist caught.

"Don't."

She looked up quickly, stunned by Doug's quiet intensity. The sooty gray of his eyes was rich and positively riveting.

"You look fine," he went on softly, waiting to hear himself make a more suggestive quip, as was his normal style. Something about the cling of her robe being good for his appetite. Something about his liking his women soft and sleek. Even something as simple as that she looked sexy as hell.

Strangely, those words eluded him. Reluctantly, he released her hand. "I didn't mean to disrupt things. It's enough that I'm imposing on you for breakfast."

"You're not imposing," she said, pink-cheeked as she recalled her body's present aversion to anything that might bind it. Acceding to that fact, and that fact alone, she led the way back to the kitchen. "What'll it be?" she asked without turning as she opened the refrigerator door and made ceremony of peering inside.

"Coffee. Eggs. Juice," came the voice in passing as Doug walked through to the round kitchen table framed by a semicircle of windows. "Whatever you were planning to have. It'll be a treat for me, in any case."

At the lack of pretense in his tone, she looked up. "You don't usually eat breakfast?"

He snickered. "I'm not much of a cook." He'd never had to be. Over the years he'd had an abundance of cooks. All of his women had cooked. He'd left that chore to them. Since he'd been on the Vineyard, though, he'd been on his own and without. If Sasha Blake wanted to take up the slack, he mused—then caught himself. "But I could try to do something to help, if you're in the mood to instruct."

She smiled. "That's all right. I think I can manage. Why don't you sit down. You can talk to me while I work."

Rather than sitting, he circled the table to stand with his back to her at the window. Sasha studied him for a minute, noting the dignity of his stance, the sense of control exuded by his large frame. A controlling man—the last thing she wanted. For that matter, she didn't want a man, period. Then why, she asked herself, had she invited this one in for breakfast?

Clenching her fingers on the refrigerator door, she turned her attention to a carton of eggs, a tub of butter and a bottle of orange juice. After setting each on the counter in turn, she fished a package of breakfast sausages from the freezer. Perhaps she owed the man, after what she'd done to his car. At least she'd make it good. Then he'd be on his way and they'd be even.

"Your view is beautiful," Doug commented, his

voice aimed toward her backyard. "Have you lived here long?"

"Three years."

"That's how long you've been on the Vineyard?"

"Uh-huh."

For as far as he could see there were open fields, broken only by clusters of low shrubs and trees, and crisscrossed at intervals by rambling stone walls. "These were all farmlands once, I'm told."

Pausing to guess at how many eggs to crack, she finally placed half a dozen in a large bowl. A blob of butter already sizzled in the skillet. "I guess so, though there aren't any sheep nowadays. It must have been pretty then."

"It's pretty now," came the voice suddenly headed her way. "I've got an ocean view. Yours represents a whole other aspect of the island."

An ocean view. Janine and Paul had an ocean view. It was that ocean view, wild and white capped, that she'd spent hours contemplating not long before her accident...or whatever. Stifling a shudder, she asked with studied nonchalance, "You live here then?"

"As of two weeks ago."

"Ah. A newcomer." Reaching for the sausages, she struggled to separate the frozen links, hampered by muscles that groaned with even the slightest exertion. Pulling a knife from the drawer, she tried to chop them apart. Her ribs protested.

"Of sorts. Here." He crossed the room. "Let me do that." Effortlessly he separated the links, pleased to see a weakness in the woman, though as yet unaware of its cause. Taking advantage of the excuse to come closer, he simply leaned back against the counter when his job was done. "Don't tell me you have something against newcomers, too?'' he asked, arching a wry brow.

Sasha didn't have to glance up to sense his closeness. It was a warm fact not two feet from her, a line of heat that seemed to sizzle along her side. Frightened, she swallowed hard, then turned to set the table. It didn't occur to her that in denying her guest one source of satisfaction she was supplying another. For each time she moved—slow and easy in keeping with the demands of her bruises—the brush of her robe's silk added stroke upon stroke to a vivid picture of her body.

''You've met Old Willie,'' she observed dryly.

''Old Willie?''

''The big weathered guy at the Menemsha docks who—''

''Who hates the sight of anything from the mainland? I've met him. Charming fellow.''

''Oh, he's not really all that bad. Just wary.''

''Wary? I don't know. He came across pretty strong when I was down there last week. Really lit into me about how things just aren't what they used to be.''

She grinned fondly. ''Old Willie can do that, all right. He's an islander from birth. A fisherman. A tourist attraction in and of himself. I think he enjoys his soapbox almost as much as the sermons he delivers from it.''

Returning to the stove, she turned the sausages, then pulled the bowl of eggs a safe distance from Doug, cracked each egg in turn, and concentrated on beating them. True vigor was impossible; the best she could do, given her stiffness, was to put added wrist action into play. She prayed he wouldn't notice...and question and prod. She felt shaky enough as it was.

"He's got a point, when you come down to it," she resumed, half hoping to distract him with her chatter. "Things *aren't* what they used to be. Each summer is a little worse than the last. Suddenly the population is five times what it's been. There are lines at the markets and banks and post offices. The roads are more crowded, the beaches and restaurants filled. It's almost enough to send a person packing."

"Almost...."

She grinned sheepishly. "But not quite." For a split second her hazel eyes met his. Then she looked away again.

"You didn't leave."

"This is my home," she stated with the force of simplicity. "I choose to live here. I can go to the market early, before the rush. Same thing with the bank or the post office. Summertime is crucial to the island's economy. For us year-rounders, it's simply a matter of accommodating ourselves to the population swell for the few months a year it exists. Besides—" she set the eggs back "—I kind of like the crowds. They're cheerful and carefree and colorful." Her eyes grew momentarily distant. "A place like New York, well, that's different. Crowds there are somber and less personal. They're in a rush. And if you don't hold the pace, you stand to get trampled."

"Tell me," Doug drawled, drawing Sasha's thoughts from herself.

"You're from New York," she stated.

"Not originally. But since my mail's been going there for the past twenty years, I guess you'd have to call me a New Yorker."

Sasha found New Yorkers distinctly threatening. Tearing her eyes from Doug's she took a large bread knife from the drawer. Thus armed, she reached for the loaf of bread she'd bought fresh baked yesterday morning—*before* her fateful trip to Janine and Paul's—and began to slice it. "Are you here to stay?"

"If things work out."

"Things like...?"

"Courier service and long-distance calls. Hey, I hope you're not cutting all those slices for me. Two is my limit."

To her dismay, she saw seven slices of bread on the cutting board. Suddenly the emotion that had inspired her spree was spent and she gave a self-conscious grin. "Guess I got carried away." Was it New York? Or this stranger in her kitchen? Confused, she quickly knelt to ferret a second frying pan from a low cabinet. Her limbs screeched. She clenched her teeth. Rearranging the pots with far more noise than was necessary in hopes of buying herself some recovery time, she finally slid the pan she needed onto the counter, closed the cabinet and, fingers clutching the edge of the countertop, eased herself up.

"You look a little stiff."

"I'm okay."

"You were favoring that ankle when we walked in here."

"I'm okay!"

"You should really see your doctor—"

"Damn it, I'm fine!" Angry at him for pushing, angry at herself for being angry, angry at her body for having put her on the spot to begin with, she impulsively stretched toward a new package of coffee filters stowed on a high shelf. "Ahhhh...!" she moaned helplessly, then whispered, "Damn!" as she pulled her arm back and tried to catch her breath.

Doug was suspiciously quiet. She stood, head bowed, for a minute, then, unable to stand the suspense, glanced his way. His eyes were dark, his bronzed face grim as he focused on her arm. With a touch so light that it might have been imperceptible had she not been watching, he slowly parted the slit of her sleeve, gently eased the fabric up over the curve of her shoulder and stared. Sasha could do nothing but hold her breath, her eyes large, her heart pounding.

When at last he spoke, his voice was low and ominous. "This is quite a sight. I thought you said you were okay."

"I am," she mustered shakily, terrified by something beyond Doug's simple discovery. He was close. Too close. And his fingers on her bare skin.... "It's just ugly," she managed, confused and upset.

"And painful." He lifted his eyes to hers. "Why didn't you tell me?"

"It wasn't your business."

"But I asked. And I'm half responsible."

"You're not! It was my fault! *I* was the one who skidded into you! You were doing fine on your own side of the road. It was my fault! All mine!"

His fingers slid down her arm to her elbow, then inched back up ever so lightly. All the while his eyes held hers. "But I was willing to help."

"I didn't need your help."

His gaze dropped to her lips. "You have someone else to look after you?"

She pressed her lips together as though in an attempt to dislodge his gaze. Her mouth felt dry. Her voice was meek. "I look after myself. I don't need anyone's help."

"Ever?"

"Just about." She would have elaborated had it been appropriate. But she knew this man didn't want to hear about her agent or her carpenter or the bear of an islander she'd hired to plow snow on the rare occasions it fell. He wasn't thinking of that kind of help. And increasingly, as her blood seemed to heat, neither was she.

"You're that self-sufficient?" he asked, beginning a slow perusal of each of her features in turn.

"I try," she whispered and attempted to shrink from the tangibility of his gaze, but it was unrelenting.

His hand crept to her shoulder, then slid over silk to her neck. His fingers curled around its nape, his thumb caressed the gentle line of her jaw. "Any special reason?"

She felt as though she was stifling. Something was building inside. She burned. She throbbed. She'd never reacted to a man's touch this way before. And a stranger's...? "One." She managed to think and speak only with the greatest of effort. "I like self-sufficiency."

If her voice was breathy, his was hoarse. "But why?"

"Because."

His thumb traced her jaw, gliding back and forth as his eyes followed the gesture. "That's a lousy answer," he murmured. "You have to have reasons."

If she did they were her own, but she could barely think of them now. The feel of Doug's thumb on her chin, inching ever closer to her lips, mesmerized her, as did the power of his gaze scouting the terrain.

"Well?" he prodded in a very masculine whisper.

"I guess," she whispered back.

"Care to share them?"

"No."

"Too painful?"

Had Sasha been fully aware of the conversation, she would have been appalled by her transparency...or this stranger's uncanny insight. But she wasn't fully aware. Far from it. She was spellbound. Drugged. Unable to think beyond the fiery crinkles inside, beyond the dark head slowly lowering, beyond the thumb stroking her lips. She couldn't think, couldn't protest, could only wait, wait until, after what seemed an eternity suspended, his lips touched hers.

2

Had she known this would be coming, Sasha would have been terrified. She didn't know this man, his character, his motives. Had she been able to think, she would have balked. But she hadn't known this would be coming, and she couldn't think. Doug had corralled her senses, heated them, primed them, then focused them on his lips.

Firm but gentle, almost hesitant, those lips touched hers. They were warm, tasting her lightly at first, barely sampling. His fingers slid forward on her neck, his thumb easily propping her chin, holding her face where he wanted it. She couldn't move, couldn't breathe, could only experience a new world of delightfully arousing sensations.

Her name was a breeze on his lips, soft against hers, sending gentle flutters to her chest. Eyes closed, she waited as he hovered, waited for something more than the sampling he'd given. For, quite without her knowing what was happening, her appetite was whetted.

When, with innocent allure, her lips parted, he captured them more surely, sipping thirstily, savoring her sweetness. Alive with a rioting awareness of pleasure points radiating outward from his touch, Sasha felt her lips respond, tentatively at first, then with growing conviction as even her slightest movement doubled the pleasure.

Moisture and warmth, with a lining of fire—she'd never known anything like it. She'd heard, she'd read, she'd written, but never known. Oblivious to all but the glory of the moment, she sought to sustain it, opening her mouth to Doug's gentle prodding, drinking in his breath, his heat, the exotically tempting scent of his skin.

"Sasha," he gasped as he drew back to relish her expression of need, as stunned by its innocence as he'd been by the newness of her kiss. He'd expected...he hadn't known what he'd expected. Certainly not the kind of unaffected, spontaneous, utterly guileless response he'd received. Sasha Blake was different. He felt different himself when he was with her. Not that he understood it; his caution and consideration were new to him. Perhaps there was something in the Vineyard air that made a person slow down, appreciate the finer things in life, strive to draw time to its limits and make the lovely things last. Yet the emotions he felt had come in a torrent. Slow? No way.

His hands trembled beneath her chin. His smoky gray eyes absorbed the soft pink of her cheeks, the moisture of her parted lips. A lovely thing—that she was. Lovely and warm and apparently alone.

Bereft without his kiss, Sasha struggled to open her eyes. Her lashes fluttered, then lifted. She saw Doug's face, inches above hers, his hair falling dashingly over his brow, his color heightened in male counterpoint to hers.

"Sasha..." he whispered, then, with a soft groan, slipped his arms around her and, for the first time, brought their bodies into full contact. It was the stunning evidence of his arousal that made its mark.

Surrender. Humiliation. Pain. A world of memories

long suppressed surged to the fore in Sasha's mind. With a groan of her own, not soft as his had been but anguished, she stiffened.

"What—?"

"Let go," she gasped, levering her arms against his chest. "Let go!"

Stunned, Doug did just that. "I've hurt you," he said, his voice thick with self-accusation. "God, I'm sorry! I should have remembered how sore you are. I guess I got carried away."

Braced against the counter, her body trembling with something far removed from desire, Sasha lowered her head. Her breath came in large gulps. She pressed a shaky hand to her brow.

"I'm sorry," he repeated in alarm. "Is it very painful?"

Neither pausing to correct his misconception, nor lying, she nodded.

He swore softly. "Damn, I knew it." He thrust his fingers through his hair, which promptly fell forward again, then hooked his hands low on his hips. His dark brows knit in frustration. His tone held a tinge of reproof. "You really should see a doctor, you know. Something may be chipped or cracked."

"I'm all right," she whispered, slowly regaining control. "I just wasn't prepared...for...." She doubted she'd ever be prepared for what this stranger had so obviously had in mind. Ten years. It had been ten years since she'd felt the force of that particular male appendage against her thigh. Ten years, and yet the memories remained. She'd been seventeen when Sam had married her. Seventeen and utterly innocent. What he'd done to her over the course of two years had been dreadful. And yet...and yet...this man she didn't know had kissed her, and she'd enjoyed it. She'd been oblivious to everything for a few minutes there, and it had been more than she'd ever dreamed.

"Can I get you something?" came the worried voice close by her side. "Some aspirin or something? A heating pad? Maybe you ought to sit down. Or get into bed. Will that help?"

His concern touched her. Looking up, she forced a tremulous smile. "I'm okay. It was just a pang. It's better now."

Oblivious to the hidden meaning of her words, Doug looked doubtful. He was likewise unaware that it was precisely this doubt and its underlying concern that had helped ease Sasha's pain.

This wasn't Sam, she told herself firmly. It was a man named Doug Donohue, a stranger, a man to whom she owed nothing, a man to whom she was in no way bound. He held none of the power over her that Sam Webster had held by virtue of the document proclaiming her his wife. She was her own woman now. Doug Donohue couldn't force her to do anything. And somehow she sensed he wouldn't try, as the other had done with gusto so very many times.

"You're sure you're okay?" he prodded gently. He still felt she should have medical help, but he couldn't force her. She was an adult.

She nodded, feeling better by the minute. "I'm sure." To prove her point, she turned to confront the eggs.

"Hey, you don't have to do that—"

"I want to. I'm hungry."

"Listen, why don't you get dressed and we'll get something in town."

She shot him a pithy glance, then gave a strangled

laugh. "Clothes don't seem to agree with me today."
More awkwardly, she added a quick, "It'll be easier
this way. Besides, everything's out and ready. The
sausages are just about done."

"You must be some kind of masochist. To hell with
the sausages!"

"You don't like sausages?"

"Of course I like sausages."

"And scrambled eggs? And toast?"

"Those, too. But I don't think I can bear to sit here
watching you suffer to cook for me."

"I'm not in pain. Not anymore. I told you—it's better." It was the truth. Having thrust what had happened between them to the back of her mind, she was
relieved of those other memories as well.

Doug reached out to take her shoulders, but let his
arms fall away when she inched back a step. He hesitated for just a minute. "You strike a hard bargain,
babe." He looked down at the bowl of eggs, back at
Sasha, then down again. "Okay—" he rubbed his
hands together "—you'll have to tell me what to do.
I'm not very good at this. I can't guarantee anything."

"Oh, you don't have to—"

"Either you sit in that chair and direct me, or I'll
leave." He issued his ultimatum with quiet finality.
"That's the choice."

Astonished, Sasha gazed up at the figure towering
over her. A man had never cooked breakfast for her.
Sam wouldn't have dreamed of it. She recalled a time
she'd been sick with the flu. Nauseous and weak, she'd
stood at the stove preparing the feast necessary to bol-
ster his lordship for a day on the farm. It hadn't mattered that she'd had a raging fever, a throbbing head-
ache, more aches than she'd known she had muscles.

The only thing that had mattered had been Sam Webster and his empty pit of a stomach.

This man, on the other hand, was offering. He was different, so different it scared her. *Call his bluff,* one part of her cried. *Let him leave!* It would be safer, far more sensible. Bronze-skinned, golden-lipped Doug Donohue wasn't for her. No man was for her. She'd had one once and been ravaged. Now she had all the heroes she wanted, strong men, loving men, men who if they acted up were sentenced to life with a villainness, thrown into bankruptcy, exiled to a Siberia of sorts, or simply written out of her book. She had what she needed. And yet...and yet....

What demon possessed her she was never to know. With an expression of utter helplessness, she meekly took a seat, forearms braced on the table, oddly comfortable.

"That's better," Doug sighed. "Now then." He faced the counter full of breakfast in the works. "First things first. If the sausages are done, I guess the eggs go on."

He was neither helpless nor dumb, Sasha mused as she watched him work. Granted, he was no expert. The eggs were dashed with brown from butter that had begun to burn, the toast bore uneven clusters of jam, the coffee was laced with its own grounds, ones that had missed the filter and gathered on the plastic holder to be washed down with hot water from above. There were dribbles of raw egg on the stove and crumbs galore on the counter. But the juice was poured perfectly. And grounds and brown stuff and blobs of jam notwithstanding, everything tasted wonderful.

"Not bad. Perhaps you've discovered a new talent," Sasha quipped between bites. She paused, then scrunched up her face. "What kind of work do you do, anyway?"

"I'm in clothing."

"You make it?"

"Um-hmm."

"Out of New York?"

"Yes."

She nodded.

"And you?" he asked, spearing a sausage. "What do you do out here all by yourself?"

"I write." She gave a shy smile. "One of the many here on the Vineyard."

"Writers?"

"Um-hmm."

"What kinds of things do you write?"

She wavered. "Oh, short stories, novels."

"Published?" he asked with the arch of a brow.

"Um-hmm."

"Have I ever read anything of yours?"

Her cheeks grew warm. "Oh, I doubt it." She wrinkled her nose and made light of her accomplishments. "Not unless you're into romance."

"No, I've never exactly been into that," he reflected, momentarily pensive. He'd always taken his women at face value, seeking nothing more than light conversation, home-cooked meals, sex. He'd never had cause to be romantic, if being romantic entailed truly sharing himself as a person. He was a selfish bastard. He was the first one to admit it. As a matter of fact, he mused, looking down at his eggs, this was a first. He'd never waited on a woman before.

"No matter," Sasha said to cover the awkwardness she felt. "Most men prefer to read adventures or nonfiction."

"Or thrillers. There's nothing like a book that drives you into a corner on a dark rainy night with the doors and windows locked and every light in the house burning."

"Ahhh, you're one of *those*."

"On occasion. But don't tell anyone I told you. It doesn't do much for the image of a strong, fearless man." He wasn't quite sure why he'd told *her*, but the damage was done.

She chuckled. "So why do you do it? Why do you read things that scare the wits out of you?" She was well familiar with the genre, though the intrigue she wrote into her own books was of a far less nerve-shattering form.

Doug shrugged and gave a decidedly sheepish smile. "I don't know. Maybe for kicks. Or excitement. Maybe to take an entirely different view of the world every so often."

She eyed him thoughtfully. "You're bored with your life?"

She'd hit on the truth. He felt instantly defensive. His gaze narrowed. "Are you love starved? Is that why you write romance?" As soon as the words were out he regretted them. Even more than the words themselves, his tone bothered him. Cynicism seemed totally out of place here in Sasha Blake's peaceful kitchen.

Peace was the last thing Sasha felt at that moment. He'd hit on the truth. She felt instantly defensive. But it wasn't in her nature to snap back as he'd done. Rather, she simply avoided the first of his questions. "I write romance because I enjoy it. It's fun. It's a challenge." She eyed him with quiet conviction. "And it pays the bills. It enables me to be totally independent.''

''Totally? Or simply financially?''

She tipped up her chin. ''Totally. As I said before, I'm a self-sufficient person. Believe it or not, I wouldn't have starved had you not made my breakfast.''

He knew it to be fact, and it disturbed him. Men liked their women to be dependent. The weaker sex. ''Humph,'' he scoffed, scowling toward the window. ''The liberated woman.''

''Yes, liberated!'' she exclaimed, a sudden fire in her eyes. ''And proud of it. I live as I do out of choice. And I've earned the right to it. No man can force me into something I don't want. I made that vow a long time ago. And,'' she added, her thoughts straying back in time, ''if you think that making my breakfast entitles you to a round in my bed, you're mistaken!''

Doug stared at her tense features, then dropped his gaze to her fists clenched on the table. ''You've been hurt,'' he stated softly.

''You said that before.''

''I'm not talking about the accident.'' And well she knew he wasn't. He looked her in the eye. ''I'm talking about a man. You've been hurt. Badly.''

For a minute she wasn't sure what to say. No way would she go into her past with this man who was little more than a stranger. Lowering her voice, her vehemence spent, she murmured, ''Haven't we all?''

It was Doug this time who wasn't sure what to say. Had he hurt his share of women along the way? He supposed he had, though he'd never promised more than he'd delivered. But that was another life and one he'd wanted to escape. Perhaps simply because she was part of this newer life, Sasha Blake was one woman he wanted never to hurt.

"Look," he said, pushing his fork idly around his plate, "I'm sorry. This isn't exactly what I'd planned."

"What had you planned?" she challenged impulsively.

He raised his eyes. "To check up on you. To make sure you were okay. It's not every day that I'm in an accident with a motorcyclist. The least you could do is to give me credit for having a conscience." It was asking a lot, he realized. He wasn't sure he deserved it. His motivations for coming this morning were far more complex. He had been curious. He was still. About this woman. About her life. And now about the man who had hurt her once. He sensed, though, that his questions would have to wait. Very obviously, Sasha prized her privacy.

"I'm sorry, too," she murmured, eyes downcast. "And you're right. It was sweet of you to come by." She looked up. "Thank you."

Their eyes held for an instant, mirroring a strange kind of bond. It was Doug who finally broke the spell with a self-conscious laugh. "Well—" he jutted his chin toward his near-empty plate "—I got more than I bargained for. It was good." He stood. "But I'd better be running."

Sasha gave him no argument. It was for the best...even if he *had* left her with the dishes.

Untitled work number six progressed well that week. As her characters built slowly, Sasha grew fond of them. Her hero was tall and dark haired with sun-bronzed skin. Bold and compelling, he was a man who designed and built race-class sailboats and luxury yachts, a man who had started from scratch armed with equal parts engineering genius and daring, and had gone on to fashion a small empire. Her heroine was a far more private sort, an artist who lived in the small coastal town to which the hero had come for the summer to test out a revolutionary sailboat design. Their life-styles were different, yet from the first they were drawn to each other. True, a strong physical attraction arced between them. But there was something more—a sense of curiosity, of intrigue—that promised to bring them together again and again.

"Dan?"

"Yeah, Doug! Damn it, where have you been? I expected this call two hours ago!"

"I was out." Walking the beach again, thinking. But that was none of Dan Pfeiffer's affair, and Doug had no intention of explaining. "You've got the papers on your desk?"

"Right here."

"Okay. Start from the top. I'm listening." Swiveling his large desk chair around so that he wouldn't have to look at the unpacked cartons of books piled in random stacks around his den, he stared blindly at the ocean. Within minutes, his concentration sped southward, arriving in New York, homing in on the words of the proposed contract his executive vice president was reading.

"Whoa," he ordered after several quiet minutes. "Run that by me again." He paused and listened, then stiffened. "That wasn't what we agreed to."

"They're getting fussy."

"Have them change it."

"I don't know if they—"

"If they won't, drop the whole thing. When we worked this out last month, that clause was very clear. It's in all our foreign contracts. It'll be in this one."

"And if they—"

"Change it. As a matter of fact, take the wording from the Austrian contract."

"Doug, that's stiffer than—"

"I like it. If Perkins won't go for it, he's got a problem. There are other distributors in Sydney. Okay, read on."

Twice more Doug interrupted to have things changed. At the end he took a breath. "Send it to legal for a good going-over and then express it to me." He grinned. "Maybe I can think of some other changes to rock the boat."

"The Aussies may tell you to take a flying leap."

"I'm not all that sure I'd mind it. We've had trouble with Perkins and his crew from the start. What do you think, Dan?"

"I think that they're the best ones to do the job for us. You know that. It's just unfortunate that Perkins is nearly as headstrong as you are. The two of you test each other."

"But doesn't he know I'll win?"

Dan Pfeiffer gave a wry chuckle. "He will soon. Listen, I'll get these up to you by the first of the week. Or do you want me to hold them here? If you're flying in—"

"Send them. I may not be in for another few weeks."

"You like it up there?"

"It's quiet. And restful." He sighed, his thoughts slowly returning to the Vineyard. "I like it."

"You're not bored?"

"Bored? With the piles of papers I get from you guys every day? Hell, the post office knows me. Good thing they're used to prima donnas pestering them about when things are going out. By the way, I sent a packet of preliminary sketches up to Prosser. Tell him to get to work on them."

"Sure. Anything else?"

"Not now. I'll call if there is. You do the same." Doug knew Dan would, though he also knew that his CEO was perfectly capable of handling things in New York. Well trained and insightful, what Dan Pfeiffer lacked in toughness he made up for in sheer business acumen. He'd been a perfect foil for Doug in New York; now he was a perfect right-hand man once removed.

Tipping his chair back, Doug grew pensive. Somewhere along the line he'd grown hard. Had it happened when he'd first started the business, when so many things had seemed to go wrong? Had it happened over the years as a kind of accompaniment to corporate success? Or did its roots go further back, back to a childhood of scrimping and scraping and forever being without?

The jangle of the telephone tore him from his thoughts.

"Donohue here," he barked quite by habit.

"Douglas?"

Recognition of the drawl at the other end of the line brought a twist of impatience to Doug's lips. "Lisa."

"How are you, Douglas?"

"Not bad."

"I've been waiting for you to call."

"I've been busy."

"Busy? Up there?"

"Busy. Up here."

"Work kind of busy? Or play kind of busy?"

"A little of each," he replied in truth, though large hunks of his time during the past three days had been occupied with thoughts of one Sasha Blake. They were serious thoughts, curious thoughts, far from work, yet not carefree enough to be play.

"You must miss the city."

"Not particularly. It was my decision to leave."

"But you'll be back. Janet said she expected you next week."

Janet Mason was Doug's personal secretary, Lisa's sister and the instrument of their introduction. "Janet had no right to say that. Anyway, she's wrong. There's no need for me to rush back."

"But I thought that was part of the deal, that you'd be commuting."

"It is an arrangement strictly contingent on the business, Lisa. You know that. When the business needs me, I fly down."

"I need you."

"I doubt that."

"But I do."

"I'm sorry."

"You're a bastard, Douglas Donohue. A cold-hearted bastard. Do you know that?"

"Yes, Lisa. I do. That's precisely why you need to find someone else, someone who really cares."

"But you could if you tried—"

"Lisa...." The warning in his tone hung in the air for long moments before Lisa finally swore and hung up.

He *was* a bastard, Doug mused, returning to the

thoughts that his ex-lover's call had interrupted moments earlier. He was callous and arrogant, and proud of neither. As a matter of fact, he didn't particularly like himself. Which was one of the reasons he'd left New York. He needed a change, a break from the whirlwind of a life he'd led for twenty years. He needed inspiration.

Like…Sasha Blake. She brought out things in him he hadn't known existed. Patience. Concern. Self-restraint. Even now he could feel his muscles begin to relax. His face, hard and immovable when he'd talked with Lisa, softened at the thought of Sasha's name. His insides warmed. His anger thawed. She was the antithesis of the world he'd known. Bruises, fiery temper, independent spirit notwithstanding, she excited him. He was looking forward to seeing her at the Slater's tomorrow night.

Knowing she'd be there, Doug had an advantage on Sasha, who, having no word from him since their breakfast together, had spent the better part of the week when not lost in her work trying to convince herself that it would be for the best if this intruder simply vanished from her life. She wasn't terribly successful. She couldn't seem to forget the warmth of his expression or, to her chagrin, the heat of his kiss.

The call from Ginny Slater had come at a time when she very definitely needed distraction. Ginny and Rob were having the group over for a spontaneous, last-minute dinner party on Saturday night. Nothing formal. Strictly casual. No, she couldn't come early to help in the kitchen. Yes, she could bring a dessert, but only if she promised not to leave the instant it was served.

Ginny and Rob were two of the first people Sasha had met when she'd first come to the Vineyard. They'd been introduced by a mutual friend, Sasha's agent, Diane DeScenza. As the publisher of a nationally distributed monthly magazine, Robert commuted to New York as did so many other islanders. Ginny spent her time working at home translating manuscripts and research papers from English to German or Spanish, or back, at the whim of scholars at universities in Boston and New York.

The first few evenings Sasha had spent with the Slaters had been quiet ones, just the three of them. Though Sasha half suspected that Diane had warned the Slaters about what an introvert she was, she didn't mind, for those early times she spent with Ginny and Rob were warm, intimate ones, the perfect antidote for the chill she'd acquired while living in New York. Gradually other islanders were invited along, and when they took to Sasha as readily as she took to them, Sasha became one of the group. It was a small group, no more than eight or ten together at any given time, but its members were friendly, and all were drawn to the Vineyard for its peace, its protectiveness and its privacy.

It was therefore in anticipation of a pleasant evening with friends that Sasha bathed and lightly made herself up, gathered her hair softly atop her head, tugging tendrils to fall here and there, put on a silk blouse, wool gabardine slacks and stylish leather pumps, took a wool blazer against the October evening's chill and her chocolate rum cheesecake and drove to the Slaters.

Doug was the very first person she saw. Granted, he was taller than the others and, to Sasha's eye, the most attractive man there, but the fact of his presence had telegraphed itself to her central nervous system the instant she stepped inside the door. Stunned, she simply stood at the entranceway for a minute, knees locked, gaze frozen. She didn't notice the presence of her friends or the gentle hum of conversation. Only when her hostess approached did she manage to tear herself from the hold of the silver eyes across the room.

"Sasha, come on in and shut that door." Ginny hugged her, then set her back. "You look gorgeous, as usual. Here, let me have your masterpiece." Taking the large round plastic container in one hand, she ushered Sasha toward Rob. "Sweetheart, why don't you get Sasha a drink to warm her up."

"How are you, Sasha?" Robert Slater asked with a smile. Taking Sasha's hands in his, he pressed a fatherly kiss to her cheek. "Hmm, you *are* cold." He squeezed her fingers, then put an arm around her shoulders and drew her toward the first cluster of people in the living room.

"Sasha! Good to see you!" This from Tim Carlin, a retired economics professor, whose wife, Susan, chimed quickly in.

"How have you been, Sasha?"

"Very well, thanks. And you two? Tell me about your trip. Was China an experience?" If she was babbling, she didn't care. Anything to be nonchalant, to try to forget the virile presence nearby.

"What'll it be, Sasha?" Rob murmured. "White wine?"

She smiled and nodded, watched her host walk toward the bar, then turned back to the Carlins.

"We were just telling Maggie about it," Tim said,

tapping an older woman on the shoulder, drawing her attention back from the next group.

Margaret Powell was a sculptress who had lived and worked on the Vineyard for more than twenty years. At the age of sixty-eight, she was the matriarch of their group. Sasha had always been touched by the sensitivity of both her work and her person. In her own gentle way Maggie had come to be a sort of favorite aunt to Sasha. Their affection was mutual.

"Sasha," the older woman cooed, a smile lighting her weathered face, "how wonderful to see you." She extended an arm and Sasha immediately met it with a hug.

Though touching and kissing was spontaneous with these people, Sasha had been skeptical until she'd realized it accompanied a genuinely fond attachment to one another. Feeling that fondness now, she grinned. "How are you, Maggie?"

"Not bad for an old lady. But you—" she poked a finger at Sasha's ribs "—you're doing beautifully. Was that *Midnight Rogue* I saw on the *Times*'s list? No, not *Midnight Rogue*. *Raven's Revenge*. Was that it?"

Sasha blushed. "That was it."

"And you're working on something new, I gather."

"Always," Sasha admitted with a dash of self-mockery. "But I want to hear about Tim and Susan's trip." Still holding Maggie's hand, she turned back to the other couple. "Come on. Tell."

Managing by some miracle to look enthralled, she barely heard a word they said. Her mind was at the far end of the living room, on the figure dressed in hunter-green and navy—slim-fitting slacks, turtleneck jersey, Shetland sweater—and the eyes that seemed to meet hers every time she dared glance his way.

When Rob returned to push a glass of chilled wine into her hand, she jumped, managing to recover only momentarily before her host had his arm around her waist again.

"Excuse us, folks," he said to the others. "Sasha hasn't met Doug. She'll catch you later."

Sasha had no choice but to acquiesce as gracefully as possible, a monumental challenge on legs that seemed strangely and suddenly uncoordinated. Doug was standing with Paul O'Hara, her good friend and fellow writer, and Jonathan Macoubrie, the rising young multimillionaire of the group. The two turned to her with smiles of welcome; Doug simply stared intently.

"Hey, Sasha," Jonathan drawled, slipping his arm around her waist for a momentary hug. "How's it going?"

"Okay," she said breathlessly, then offered a hand squeeze and a kiss to Paul. "Hi, Paul. I'm glad you two made it—hey, where is Janine, anyway?" Looking frantically for a diversion, she scanned the room.

"In the kitchen. She'll be right out."

"Maybe I could do something—" she began in Rob's direction, only to have her feeble attempt at escape nipped in the bud.

"Two in the kitchen's plenty. Besides, I want you to meet Doug. He's just moved here from New York. Douglas Donohue...Alexandra Blake."

For a split second, Sasha wondered whether to acknowledge that they'd met before. Douglas Donohue...his name, spoken in full for the first time, was as familiar as his face, and she suddenly wondered whether she should have recognized it from the start. Each member of this group was renowned in his or her way. Douglas Donohue...Douglas Donohue. Stifling tiny frissons of trepidation, she let Doug take the lead.

Without so much as the slightest pause, he extended his hand and enveloped hers in its warmth. "Alexandra." He nodded once. "It's my pleasure." Then, to her perverse satisfaction, he offered a legitimate frown. "Alexandra Blake. Why does that sound familiar?"

"No doubt you've seen Sasha's name in bookstores, supermarkets, drug stores, etcetera," Rob put in proudly. "She's the queen of romantic intrigue. She's written five bestsellers, the most recent of which is on the *New York Times*'s list now."

"Five best-sellers," Doug repeated with quiet concentration. His eyes held Sasha's, his hand gripped hers all the more tightly. "I'm impressed. This is truly an honor, Alexandra."

"Sasha, please," she corrected, her voice weak in response to his imperceptibly sardonic note. Or was it his meaningfully firm clasp of her hand, or her own imagination? Was it simply her own guilt she felt? "Here on the Vineyard I'm Sasha Blake. I—I prefer it to the other."

"No need for excuses—or modesty, Sasha," Rob went on. "Doug, here, is renowned in his own right. I'm sure you've heard of his clothes. The Douglas Donohue label carries its share of clout in high-fashion circles."

It was Sasha's turn to be stunned. Douglas Donohue. Of course! Those gray eyes that sun-bronzed face, the near-black hair falling rakishly across his brow—

Douglas Donohue! How could she have been so stupid! With great effort she tugged her gaze from his and let it fall to the small insignia on the breast of his sweater. Back-to-back D's. Freeing her hand from his, she raised it, lay a forefinger on the initials, then looked helplessly up again.

"I should have recognized the name instantly," she murmured dumbly. She might have, had he not made light of what he did. He was "in clothing," he'd said, and had admitted that he made it. But designing it was something else, and selling it in only the finest men's stores and boutiques in the country and abroad was another thing entirely. "This *is* a pleasure, Mr. Donohue," she said, less able to hide her sarcasm than he had been. Suddenly aware of a fire beneath her fingertips, she pulled her hand away and thrust it into the pocket of her slacks.

"Not that we're hung up on occupations, Doug," Paul felt called upon to explain. "It's more a matter of making the association, then forgetting it. We're pretty protective of one another here. We respect each other's need for privacy. Take Sasha, for example. If she wanted constant adulation, she'd have stayed in the city. The Vineyard is a place where she can come and go without people staring or treating her any differently.

As though to disprove his point, Geoffrey Briggs chose that moment to arrive, offering boisterous hellos to the others in the room but seeming to make a beeline to Sasha.

To her chagrin, though she hadn't expected much less, he came up behind her, slipped his arms around her waist and gave her a sound kiss on her cheek.

"How's my favorite bestselling author? Mmm, you smell good."

"Geoffrey," Sasha pleaded, color rising from her neck. She tried to free herself with as much grace as possible, but succeeded only in endangering the wine in her glass. Not daring to look at Doug, she sent Paul a silent plea for help. Rob had disappeared in response to an urgent wave from his wife, and Sasha needed rescue.

"Geoff," Paul began, "why don't you let go of Sasha and say hello to Doug. Geoffrey Briggs... Douglas Donohue." Satisfied when Sasha was momentarily freed, Paul turned to Doug. "Geoffrey is the island's resident photographer. When he's not on assignment, that is."

His composure fully intact, to Sasha's dismay, Doug shook the newcomer's hand. "Geoffrey Briggs. *LIFE? National Geographic?*"

"Right on, man," Geoffrey said, beaming. "I mean, it's not the kind of stuff you need for *your* ads, but it sells, if you know what I mean."

"I'll say it sells," Doug returned. "It's beautiful."

Geoffrey nodded his thanks, then turned his gaze back to Sasha, who stood quietly beside him, feeling awkward and unsure. "I've done models' portfolios in my time, but this little lady keeps refusing me."

"I'm not a model and I don't need any pictures," Sasha insisted self-consciously.

"Book jackets, publicity—you must need something."

"My publisher takes care of all that in New York. You know that, Geoff. We've been through it before."

"Yeah, yeah, but why won't you humor me and let me photograph that beautiful face of yours?"

Sasha sighed. "I guess I'm not the humoring kind. Sorry, friend."

Geoffrey shook his head and sent the other men a conspiratorial wink. "Shot down again. The woman's a witch. She's got me half in love with her and she won't even let me take her picture. No heart. No heart at all."

A welcome female voice came from behind just then. "Is this lecher after you again, Sasha? Here, guys, have an hors d'oeuvre."

"Janine," Geoffrey exclaimed, taking a toothpick-skewered something from the tray Janine held, "you look great! Hey, what is this?" The last was said with a mouthful of food. "It's great!" Still juggling the item in his mouth to counter its oven-fresh heat, he reached for another.

"That was *rumaki*, these—" she pointed "—are mushrooms rolls, and these are miniature quiches." She extended the plate in one hand, a pile of cocktail napkins in the other. As the men helped themselves, she leaned over to kiss Sasha hello. "How're ya doin', sweetie?"

Sasha raised her eyes skyward and took a big breath. Between Douglas Donohue and Geoffrey Briggs, she felt at that moment squished between a rock and a very hard place. "I'm fine," she murmured, though she shook her head when Janine passed the plate her way. "Did you make all these?"

"Ginny did. Looks like she's been on a cooking binge. I think this party was an afterthought, a necessity to dispose of all she's made. She's outdone herself this time." As the two women inched off by themselves, the men picked up conversation of their own.

"Are you okay?" Janine whispered. "You look a little peaked."

"Peaked? Oh, no, I'm fine." Sasha smiled. "Working on my book, though, I barely step foot outside. Jailhouse pallor, I think they call it."

"How's it coming?"

"The book? Okay. The beginning's always tough. I can never tell whether it's really going to be any good."

Janine drew Sasha farther from the men and leaned closer. "Did you get a look at him?"

"At who?" As if she didn't know.

"Doug Donohue. Gorgeous, isn't he?"

"Janine, you're a happily married woman!"

"And a good five or six years his senior, but that doesn't have to tarnish my eye. You're single. And just the right number of years his junior. *You* take a look. What do *you* think?"

Given good cause by her friend, Sasha cast a glance over her shoulder to find Doug's eye on her. She looked quickly back. "He's dangerous, that's what I think. Looks like the kind to love 'em and leave 'em." He was a slick New Yorker, wasn't he. And *Douglas Donohue* to boot!

"That's what they say."

"They do?" Sasha asked in unbidden dismay.

"Mmm," Janine replied. She looked down, popped a tiny quiche into her mouth, then deposited the plate into the hands of Tim Carlin. "Make yourself useful," she teased, her voice lowering again once he'd moved on. "The word is that he's a pretty hard guy. A tough businessman. An even tougher ladies' man. Strange." She seemed genuinely puzzled. "He doesn't look that bad from here."

Strange, he hadn't looked *that* bad on the two other occasions she'd seen him. "Maybe it's the Vineyard. It brings out the best in people. Maybe he's planning to turn over a new leaf."

"I hope so, for your sake. He hasn't taken his eyes off you."

Sasha scowled. "He must be taken with my work. Men like that assume that a woman who writes best-selling novels with sex in them have to be wildly erotic creatures themselves."

"And you're not a wildly erotic creature?"

"Hardly."

"I wonder...."

"Come on, Janine. You know me as well as anybody does."

"Which is only to say that, woman to woman, I find you a warm and caring person. What you'd be like with a man, if you ever gave yourself a chance, is something else. It's in there, Sasha. I've read your books. You wouldn't be able to write what you do without feeling something."

Sasha sighed. "Dreams, Janine. Not only mine, but those of millions of women. My heroes are ideal, imaginary. They are men who truly love, who care enough for their women to risk everything, to *be* there." Her expression saddened. "I'm not sure I've ever met a man like that...or that I ever will."

"You've never been in love."

"No. I suppose not."

"You never loved Sam?"

Sasha shook her head. "My marriage was more practical than anything else. Love was never an issue."

"But surely you're capable of love."

"Surely," she drawled facetiously. "That's what makes me a bestselling author of love stories."

"Hey, such a sober face," Paul O'Hara quipped, coming up behind his wife and slipping an arm about her waist. "Discussing your latest villain, Sasha?"

"Could be," Sasha mused moments before she felt the warm body behind her. Tensing imperceptibly, she tried to steel herself against its presence, but her pulse already raced, her nerve ends buzzed.

"The lady's dangerous, Doug," Paul joked. "Better watch out for her. She's got any number of evil ways of disposing of unwanted men."

"Oh?" came the deep, faintly smug reply. Obviously, Doug Donohue wasn't frightened. "I'll have to read her books then. Forewarned is forearmed."

Sasha grimaced. "While you boys are having fun at my expense, I think I'll see if Ginny needs a hand." It was the perfect excuse for the perfect escape, which would have been perfectly executed had it not been for the fact that, with a wink to Paul and Janine, Doug followed her.

3

The kitchen was empty. Knees weakened by a world of conflicting emotions, Sasha leaned against the counter, facing the large window above the sink. She took a deep breath, then sucked it steady when she saw Doug's reflection join hers. She didn't turn, simply regarded him warily in the glass, taking comfort in the sense of distance though she knew it to be an illusion.

He took a bold stance, his hands flanking hers on the counter, his long arms imprisoning her. Though his body touched hers but lightly, it was enough to set her blood pounding through her veins.

"So you're *the* Douglas Donohue," she forced herself to say, unable to bear the silence, praying that the sound of her voice would hide the thunder of her pulse.

"And you're *the* Alexandra Blake," he retaliated softly.

"Why didn't you tell me?"

"Why didn't *you* tell me?"

"I had my reasons, and they were probably a lot more sound than yours."

"Try me."

"Privacy, for one thing. I like it. New York takes care of publicizing my books. I don't. For another thing," she raced on, gripping the counter, "I like to come and go without people staring...or leering."

"Why would they do that?"

"They stare if they are curious about a bestselling author. They leer if they are curious about a bestselling author of romance. Don't tell me you aren't curious." Her gaze narrowed with the cynicism of her tone. "Don't tell me those wheels haven't started going round and round in your head. Don't tell me you're not wondering just what's in my books and how juicy it gets. I've been doing this long enough to know your type. New York was full of them."

"So you came here."

"Yes."

"And you wish I'd leave you alone."

"Yes."

"Why, Sasha?" he asked, his voice disturbingly gentle as he talked to her reflection. "What are you afraid of?"

"I'm not afraid of anything," she lied, even then tormented by the manly scent of the body so close to hers. "I just don't *want* anything from you."

"Your mind says that. So why is it you're trembling?"

"I'm...upset."

"About me? About who I am?"

"Maybe. You could have told me, you know. Why didn't you?"

"For many of the reasons you didn't tell me about yourself. I had my motives for moving to the Vineyard."

"Why did you move here?"

"To get away. To break a pattern I didn't like. To

try to think things out, to decide where I want to go in life.''

"Humph. Sounds like you're already there."

"Are you?"

"Yes. I have what I want."

"A man?"

"I don't want a man."

"Is that why you write the stories you do?"

She swallowed hard, unable to take her eyes from their dual images in the glass. Her body, smaller, more slender, fit in front of his perfectly. The top of her head barely reached his chin. "So we're back to that?" she muttered weakly.

"It's a legitimate question." He paused then, lowering his head, closing his eyes to breathe in the lemon fragrance of her hair. "I'm attracted to you," he said thickly. "You know that."

She did. And she couldn't deny the warmth that surged through her at his touch.

Bowing his head until his mouth touched her cheek, he kissed her ever so gently. "Give us a chance, Sasha. That's all I ask."

Mesmerized by the sensual tableau before her, she couldn't move, much less breathe. It was as though after a buildup of hours—no, days—the air was suddenly charged with erotic sparks, a fantasy in the works. Without realizing what he was doing, she relaxed back against Doug, absorbing the strength of his body, giving in to the mindless demands of her own. The fact that she barely knew him was irrelevant at the moment. He seemed so gentle, so caring. And her body responded in ways that were new and infinitely exciting.

"I won't hurt you," he murmured, his breath a

warm caress on her cheek. "Please believe that. It would only be good and filled with pleasure."

"But...." She couldn't remember what she wanted to say, for his hands left the countertop and slid up her hips to her waist. His thumbs inched higher, drawing exquisite circles on her silk-sheathed skin before touching the outer swells of her breasts. She sucked in a breath, but he was speaking again before she could protest.

"You're soft, so soft and delicate." His thumbs moved inward. She watched their progress, his bronzed skin so very masculine against the white silk of her blouse. She felt the betraying hardening of her breasts, and when her breath came faster, she bit her lip. This man was a stranger, an unknown to her, yet he courted her in ways that sent swirls of heat curling from her breasts to her toes. The effect of his touch fascinated her, as did the seeming naturalness of his hands as they came to curve beneath her breasts. By the time his thumbs found their mark, her nipples were already taut. He rubbed them and a burst of pleasure surged within her. Her eyelids slid shut, her head fell back to his shoulder. Fear was in another world, another time. What Doug was doing to her was warm and erotic and too good to be denied.

"So sweet," he rasped. "Oh, babe, it's happened so quickly, but if you only knew how much I want you...."

She did feel wanted and, for the first time in her life, very, very feminine. Her body craved something she'd only dreamed about and had a mind of its own as it leaned toward that dream.

A loud burst of laughter from the other room broke the spell, bringing with it a harsh reminder of where she was and what she was doing. Stiffening, she brought her head forward, eyes wide open, and leaned against the counter once more.

Having heard the laughter too, and appalled that he'd so forgotten the time and place himself, Doug moved to the side, turned his back to the glass and took several great gulps of air. "Damn it, Sasha. I don't know what's gotten into me. I haven't been able to think of much else this week besides holding you again."

"You didn't call," she managed in a whisper, trying desperately to catch her breath.

He looked sideways at her. "I wasn't sure you wanted me to." When she didn't answer but continued to stare down at the sink, he went on. "You're feeling better?" She nodded. "Soreness gone?" She nodded again. "But you didn't drive that damned cycle here tonight, did you?"

"No. It's still in the shop."

"Good. I'll drive you home."

She looked up quickly. "No! I have a car."

"Then I'll follow you home. We have something to work out."

"No!" She shook her head, feeling soft wisps of hair against her cheek. As though he'd felt them too, Doug reached out and fingered one long silken strand. He was about to argue when the swinging door opened and Ginny bounded through.

"Hey, this is *my* kitchen," she exclaimed, smiling as she bustled toward the stove. "You're not supposed to be out here." Slipping her hand into an oversized oven mitt, she pointed toward the living room. "You're supposed to be out there, eating my hors d'oeuvres and mingling with my guests." She gestured with the mitt. "Now, scoot!"

Doug had the grace to give a sheepish smile first to Ginny, then to Sasha. "Yes, ma'am," he said to the former, with a low-murmured, "Later," in Sasha's ear as she passed through the door a breath before him.

He might have yelled it, or plastered it in bright red paint on the wall, for try as she might to forget it, that one word reverberated through Sasha's being for the rest of the night. To her surprise, Doug left her pretty much on her own to talk with her friends. He kept his distance, fitting into the conversation easily but always in a different group. She half wondered if he didn't trust his control; each time she caught his eye it held the same promise he'd made at the door. *Later.* The word grew nearly tangible as the hours passed, and Sasha grew more and more afraid.

Douglas Donohue. *The* Douglas Donohue. From the fast lane, for sure, and certainly not for her. Yet she couldn't help but warm each time she thought of the way he'd leaned into her, the way he he'd kissed her neck, the way he'd held her breasts—so gently, almost worshipfully. Oh, yes, it was a purely physical thing, yet she felt cherished, and to her surprise, she liked the feeling. It was something new, albeit something that frightened her with its sudden force.

Doug, too, was in his way frightened. He'd never met a woman like Sasha Blake before. Amazed at her success, he wondered at her innocence. For that was what he'd felt in her responses, both to his kiss that first morning at her house and to his touch earlier this evening. Innocence. Simplicity. But she was right; though he had no idea what went on in the bedrooms of her books, he was downright curious. Was the innocence all for show? Was she truly a woman of the world?

All week he'd harbored the image of her sitting alone in her house writing, eking out the scant living most authors did, praying that her latest masterpiece would sell. Hell, in advances alone she probably made a million. And here he'd spent hours thinking of the little luxuries with which he might dazzle her. Thinking of giving, a new experience for him. And to find that there was probably little she couldn't buy for herself—it was damned frustrating. As was, he mused, the quiver of arousal he felt each time he looked at her. Damned frustrating! The evening couldn't end fast enough.

Not so for Sasha. Had she not promised Ginny she'd stay, she would have run out the back door right after dessert. But she had promised. And as though suspecting her second thoughts, Ginny seemed to stick close by her elbow until, guest by guest, the gathering broke up. Having missed her chance for an early escape, Sasha waited, prolonging the inevitable. But if she'd hoped Doug would leave graciously with the others, she was mistaken. He, too, waited. The inevitable was, it seemed, indeed inevitable.

When it was only Sasha and Doug and Ginny and Rob lingering over refills of coffee in the Slaters' living room, Sasha finally stood.

"I guess I'd better be running," she said with a sigh of regret that held its share of resignation. "I'm planning to be up at five to work tomorrow."

"It's today," Ginny said, "and you can't do that. It's Sunday. You deserve a day of rest."

The other three had risen with Sasha, who tried to ignore the fact that Doug had taken a step closer.

"Days of rest will have to wait until this manuscript is done. And since I've just started...." What was meant to be a subtle hint to Doug only succeeded in bringing Ginny and Rob down on her.

"You work too hard," Rob said with a frown. "The book will wait. You deserve a day off now and then."

"We were planning on taking the ferry to Falmouth and driving into Boston for the day," Ginny added. "Why don't you join us?"

"Oh, no, I couldn't—"

"Why not? It would be fun."

"Actually," Doug broke in, his voice a deep lure, his eyes echoing the sentiment, "I was hoping she'd show me around the island. Just a few hours. She can't refuse."

"Oh, Sasha—" Ginny grinned enthusiastically "—why don't you? Doug is new to the Vineyard, after all. And if you could get some work done in the morning—"

Sasha sent Doug a withering look and promptly ignored his offer. It was to Ginny and Rob collectively that she spoke, as polite a smile on her face as she could muster. "You're sweet to worry, but don't. I'll be fine. I do love what I'm doing, remember?"

Rob arched his brows, then headed for the closet and her blazer, which Doug took from him and put gently around her shoulders.

Sasha smiled at her host and hostess. "Thanks for a lovely evening. It was great seeing everyone."

"We should do it more often," Ginny said, then leaned forward and gave her a hug. Rob repeated the gesture and stood back, his arm curling comfortably about his wife's waist, emerging only briefly to shake Doug's hand.

"Thank you both," Doug added. "It's a lovely group of friends you've got."

Ginny grinned smugly. "You'll join us again soon, won't you?"

"My pleasure." With a final nod of goodbye, he put his hand on Sasha's back and escorted her out of the house. Only when the door had closed firmly behind them did he reach out to catch her hand in his. "Where're you going so fast?"

"My car."

"Shall I follow you?"

"No."

"I'd like to talk."

"It's late. Like I told Ginny and Rob, I've got to be—"

"What's another hour? Besides, you don't really want to send me home to that big empty house with cartons all over the place."

The darkness hid his expression. Unable to tell if he was mocking or serious, she sent him a quizzical look. "You mean you've been here a month and you haven't unpacked?"

"Not quite a month, and no. I'm not good at that type of thing."

"Don't you have a houseboy or a maid or something?" Surely *the* Douglas Donohue would have help.

"No," he answered curtly, reading her thoughts. "I left the servants back in New York. I would have thought you'd guessed that after my enthusiasm for breakfast the other morning."

"Poor Doug."

"Not really. It's nice to have breathing room for the first time in years." Quite a turnaround, but he meant it. Though he could remember the days when thoughts of having a maid were second only to those of eternal salvation, he did enjoy the freedom.

"You mean that, don't you?" They arrived at her car and she fished in her blazer pocket for the keys.

"Yes." He paused. "Is that yours?"

"Um-hmm."

He choked on a forced cough. "A step up from the Suzuki, I'd say."

The night hid her blush. "You can see why I like the Suzuki," she said in a tiny voice.

"Oh, I don't know. There are many people who'd kill for a little number like this." He whistled and stepped back to admire the car. "A Mercedes two-seater. Not bad."

"Mercedes, Maserati…not much difference," she murmured, opening the door, sliding quickly inside. But Doug wasn't so taken with the extent of her means that he'd let her escape him as easily. Before she could shut the door his hand was on it, holding it ajar.

"I'll follow you."

"Please. You don't have to. I'm sure we'll bump into each other another time." Only after she'd said it did she wince. Doug mirrored the motion.

"Hell, I hope not! My car hasn't recovered yet. Neither have I, for that matter."

"Look," Sasha began with a weary sigh, "this really won't work out. Please, I've got to run."

Doug stared at her for a long moment, the moon just catching the silver of his gaze. Then, with a nod, he shut her door and stepped back. Needing no further encouragement, she started the car, turned around and headed down the long driveway toward the main road.

No more than a minute passed before the Maserati's headlights glared at her in her rearview mirror.

Swearing softly to herself, she tightened her grip on the wheel. There was always the possibility that he was headed home. After all, this was the major road along the north shore of the island, and he'd said that he looked out on the ocean. Any one of the upcoming drives led to private homes with ocean views. Any one,....

By the time she'd turned onto Menemsha Cross Road, though, she'd given up that hope. He was following her, just as he'd said he would. What was she going to do now? The last thing she needed was "to talk" with a man who stirred such new and overwhelming sensations in her. True, she was curious, and excited even as she thought of it. But she'd been hurt so badly once, and in ways above and beyond the physical. She didn't need that kind of hurt. She didn't need Doug Donohue.

Unfortunately, she didn't have much choice in the matter. Doug kept her in sight, turning when she did first at South, then her private road, then the fork. She'd no sooner pulled into her garage when the Maserati drew to a halt outside her front door. Doug was waiting for her there.

Trying to make the best of an uncomfortable situation, she said nothing as she unlocked the door, stepped into the house and flipped on every light in sight. Only then did she turn, interlace her fingers, and eye him guardedly.

"You wanted to talk?"

"Yes."

"Well?"

He glanced toward the chair. "May I sit down?"

"Be my guest." She watched as his leggy frame settled itself comfortably, then, feeling more awkward than ever, she took refuge in a protective corner of the sofa. "Okay, what is so urgent that we have to talk tonight?"

"Your friends are nice, Sasha. I enjoyed them."

"*Urgent*, Doug. There's nothing urgent about my friends." She thought for a minute. "How did you come to be there, anyway?"

"Maggie and I have a mutual acquaintance in New York. He told her I was moving to the Vineyard. When Ginny invited her to the party, Maggie mentioned me. Naturally, consummate hostess that she is, Ginny called me."

"I see."

"It is an interesting group, each renowned in his way." He paused. "Has Geoffrey really tried to photograph you?"

"He's a pest."

"But a talented one, you have to admit."

"I'll grant him that."

"And he's good-looking."

"He's a kook."

"Because his hair passes his collar and his jeans are worn to threads?"

"Because his idea of photographing me is only the first step in a very deliberate seduction scenario. But come on, Doug. There's nothing urgent to discuss about Geoff. What's on your mind?"

Doug took a deep breath, then let it out. He'd hoped she'd relax, even offer him coffee, though he'd had more than enough to keep him up all night. But it wasn't the coffee that would keep him up all night, was it?

"Who was he, Sasha?"

She tensed. "Who?"

"The guy who hurt you."

Expelling a ragged breath, she shook her head and looked away. "You don't mince words, do you?"

"You wanted to know what I thought to be urgent? Well, I'm telling you. Something's happening between us and I think that whoever *he* is, he's standing in our way."

"Whatever gives you that idea?" she snapped defensively.

"You," he said more thoughtfully. "Your reaction to me. Your reaction to your reaction to me."

"This is getting complicated." Her attempt at humor fell flat. Doug wasn't to be deterred.

"It doesn't have to be. Just tell me who he is. Or was. Then I'll have an idea about what I'm up against."

"You're not up against anything...or anyone. I'm me. What I want is what *I* want."

"Look who's playing with words now, Sasha. We're both fairly intelligent people. We know that what we are is a product of a whole series of life experiences."

"Then tell me about yours, Doug," she burst out. "You're an enigma to me. I mean, here you are, a world-renowned fashion designer who's probably had the most glamorous women at his beck and call, and yet you're chasing me. Why? What attraction could I possibly have for you?"

He didn't blink. "You're here. And you're alone. And you seem unbelievably innocent and fresh."

"Innocent? Hah!"

"Who was he?" Doug growled this time, beginning to lose himself to his frustration.

At his tone, Sasha jumped up from the couch and crossed to the fireplace. Fingers gripping the marble mantel, she stared at the compact lineup of ancient mystery books, then raised a hand to one that had been removed from the lot and lay open. When had she taken it out? She couldn't recall. With an impatient scowl, she closed the book and returned it to its awaiting slot.

"Who was he?" Doug asked again, this time more gently and from directly behind her.

"My husband," she said, a note of contempt in her voice. "My husband!"

"When?"

She sighed, regaining control. "A long time ago."

"Couldn't be that long. You're not old enough to—"

She swiveled around to face him. "I was seventeen when we married. But you're right. I wasn't old enough to know better."

"That wasn't what I was going to say."

"It's okay. It's the truth."

"What happened?"

Wondering how she'd let Doug Donohue get further than most people had, she grew self-conscious. Unable to meet the intensity of his gaze, she lowered her head. "Oh, the usual. It was a bad match, that's all."

"So you've turned off to men as a group?"

"Men as a group can be vile. I thought it would be better in New York, but there was only one thing on *their* minds, too." She sent him a scathing glance. "Don't you all think of anything but sex?"

He arched a brow in humor, unable to help himself. "It can be pretty nice to think about."

"Pretty boring."

"Were you bored before?" All humor was gone. "Tell me, Sasha. I need to know. Did you feel anything for those men in New York?"

She dropped her gaze in soft admission. "No."

"Did you feel anything with me before?" When she didn't answer, he curled a finger beneath her chin and turned her face up. "Did you? Or was I imagining it because I wanted it so badly?"

At that moment his expression was one of a longing she'd never seen the likes of before. Something tugged at her, something far beyond the physical. "No," she murmured, unable to lie. "You didn't imagine it."

"Then you felt something?"

"Yes."

"And it frightens you?"

"Yes." Her voice caught on that single word and was further choked by the utter gratitude in his gaze.

"Oh, Sasha," he murmured, his voice velvet soft. "I wouldn't ever hurt you. I've told you that. I think you're...precious."

"A newborn kitten is precious," she whispered, wide-eyed.

"Not precious as in one of a kind."

She didn't know what to say. She'd had compliments before, but none offered in as heartrending a tone from a man whose expression was so utterly devoid of pretense. Her pulse skipped a beat, then raced on double-time.

"Doug—"

He put a long finger to her lips. "Shh. Don't say anything. Just kiss me. I've been wanting you to all night. I've been needing you to all night. Just kiss me. Once.''

There was no way in the world she could deny him, not when he was so close, so warm, so lean and tall and every inch a man. Her lashes fluttered, then fell as his lips touched hers, and as had happened before, she felt herself melt.

His mouth was gentle at first, then opened more hungrily. And she met its demand, giving of herself freely, driven by the unsolved need that sprang from her depths and took control. His arms circled her back, her own crept to his shoulders, then coiled around his neck. He drew away, then returned, tempting her with the tip of his tongue until she welcomed it. She actually welcomed it. Far from her mind were memories of Sam, of men in New York who'd grabbed her and kissed her this way. Then she'd gagged. Now she could only revel in the feel and texture of Doug's tongue as it skimmed across her teeth then plunged deeper. Only when she gasped for air did he retreat, and only then to lift her and carry her to the sofa she'd bounded from in frustration moments before. When she tried to protest, he soothed her.

"Shh, babe. It's all right. I won't hurt you."

"But you…you said…once."

"It's still going on."

And it was. His lips returned to hers, tasting and consuming, exploring and conquering as rational thought became a thing of the past. High on its newness, wanting the delight of it all to continue as badly as he did, Sasha held him closer. Her fingers were in his hair, celebrating its thickness. His own were near her face, caressing whatever was missed by his lips, then moving lower to frame her neck and shape her shoulders. Everywhere he touched she bloomed, arching toward him, seeking an answer to the raging quest of newly awakening sensations.

When his hands moved inward to work at the top button of her blouse, she gave a faint moan, but her protest was lost in his mouth and the moistness of his tongue diverted her. When she felt the cool air on her chest, though, she mustered a frail resistance.

"No..." she whispered against his lips.

"Let me touch you. Oh, Sasha, it's so good."

"But I barely know you. You...barely know me...."

"Let me," he crooned, brushing aside her objections along with the silk of her blouse and deftly unhooking the catch of her bra. Then his hands were on her and she had no idea what she'd fought. "Oh, babe, so soft. Silk beneath silk."

And beneath that, fire. Her body flamed where he touched her, burning, needing. His hands spread over her ribs, her breasts, moving in large sweeps, tracing her fullness as though imprinting an image of her nakedness in his mind. She was devastated with desire. One moment he would caress her breasts, the next he would stroke her shoulders or her neck and her breasts would swell in frustration. And all the while he maintained the mind-drugging kiss that muffled her tiny whimpers of pleasure.

When at last he raised his head to look down at what he'd only felt she was too dazed by passion to demur. Her breasts were of exquisitely molded ivory crowned with firm auburn buds. Stunned by their beauty, Doug shook his head in astonishment.

"You're beautiful, Sasha. Very beautiful."

She bit her lip and felt positively helpless.

"You believe that, don't you?" he asked in a soft but husky voice.

"I never have," she managed somehow to whisper. "But you...you almost make me...believe...."

"Believe, babe. Believe every word." Still holding her gaze he slid his hands to her breasts, capturing them fully, caressing them, straightening his fingers until only his palms manipulated her nipples.

"Ahh!" she cried, stunned by the jolt of heat that shot from her breasts to her loins.

"Beautiful. Soft there. Hard here." His fingers closed in on those twin turgid buds, and unable to bear the sweet pain, she closed her eyes and pressed her face to the cushion. "No, no, Sasha, don't look away. Kiss me. And tell me what you feel."

She doubted she'd ever be able to speak again, but she needed his kiss desperately and met it with an ardor more eloquent than any words. Swept up in the force of his passion, she drifted higher and higher, sighing her delight at the continued play of his fingers, aching for the something more that her insides demanded.

"Is it good?" Doug whispered against her lips.

"Oh, yes," she answered in kind, eyes closed, arms wound tightly around his neck.

"Do you feel it here?" He rolled her nipples between his thumbs and forefingers in waves of gentle eroticism.

"Yes," she breathed.

"And here?" One hand pressed against her heart. It's thudding was a visual thing.

"Mmm."

"And here?" His hand fell to her trembling thigh, then slowly slid upward.

"Oh, yes…yes!" Her voice was little more than an airy rasp as his hand found her warmth and caressed her tauntingly. "Doug!" she exclaimed, her senses aflame.

When his mouth covered hers, he quickly released the button of her slacks, lowered the zipper and slid his hand along the warmth of her abdomen beneath the band of her panties. He found her unerringly, his touch a silken brand on her feminine heart.

"Doug…no!" she whimpered in a moment's fright. "Please, no!" She clamped her legs together, succeeding only in holding him closer. No man had ever touched her there since Sam, and he had pawed her and mauled her such that she'd been in pain. The pain she felt now was different, though. It was hotter, sweeter, more fluid and demanding.

Doug caressed her face with his free hand. "I need to, Sasha. I need to pleasure you. Please let me. Please."

Eyes still closed, she moaned softly, for already his hand had begun to move in a slow, rhythmic lilt that calmed her, excited her, eradicated all thought of pain as though it had never been. Caressing her gently, his fingers stole deeper. Never in her life had she imagined the pleasure of such intimacy. She gasped, tried to hold back, then arched up against the rising of a deep, deep heat. It was all new. All new. She'd never felt….

His pleasure inexplicably interwoven with hers, Doug sensed her bewilderment as though it were his own. "It's all right," he murmured thickly. "Don't fight it. Let it come, babe. It's good." Brushing the weight of her bangs free of her brow, he moved up against her to kiss her forehead while his fingers brought her ever higher.

Reaching, reaching, she gave a breathless cry. "Doug!"

"Oh, yes," he crooned hoarsely. "That's it. That's it, Sasha."

"Oh—" She caught her breath and her body stiffened. Then, as she clung frantically to his shoulders, her being exploded into a myriad of sun-burst spasms that went endlessly and gloriously on and on.

It seemed forever before she could breathe again, and even then her lungs labored for what seemed an eternity of gasps and sighs. Only slowly, as the trembling of her limbs yielded to a kind of lethargy and the high haze of passion began to dissipate, did Sasha realize what had happened.

Stunned, she opened her eyes. Doug's were warm and waiting, but his face held a subtle tension. "Was it good?" he asked softly.

She stared, then covered her eyes with her hand and whispered, "My God!"

"Was it good?"

"Oh, yes!"

Within seconds he'd scooped her up and had sat on the sofa, hugging her to his side. "Then what's to be shy about?"

She buried her face in the wool of his sweater. "I've never...I've never...."

"Never climaxed like that?"

"Never...."

"Never climaxed *at all?*" It was his turn to be stunned, though in hindsight it explained the bewilderment he'd felt in her. She'd been married. She wrote stories of love and passion. Yet she'd never experienced this pleasure? Feeling strangely awed, he sucked in a ragged breath. "Ah, Sasha, what a gift that is."

"A gift?"

"To me. To know that I was the first to show you...and there's so much more. So much more. It's beautiful. Not painful or ugly or something to be ashamed of." He turned her face up with a gentle hand and was startled by her look of doubt. "You didn't know that, did you?" When she didn't answer, he swore softly. "You must have been married to a jackass!" He paused, frowning. "But what about other men, Sasha? Surely there were—"

"There weren't—"

"In New York?"

"No."

"My God," he breathed, "you're practically a virgin." When she tried to push herself away, he simply held her more tightly. "What is it, babe? What's the matter?"

Eyes downcast, she tugged at the edges of her blouse. "I feel foolish."

"But why?"

She thought for a minute, struggling to gather her wits as her pulse rate steadied. "Because you're practically a stranger and that was so...intimate. Because you're...very experienced. You knew what was happening to me before I did."

"Oh, you knew," he chided, his tone velvet and soothing. "And I'm no real stranger, not in my heart or yours. You let me pleasure you because it felt good and right. You were just frightened by its force. It's like that sometimes."

"For you?" she asked with an upward glance.

"Sometimes," he said, but he couldn't recall when he'd enjoyed it as much as he'd enjoyed pleasuring Sasha just now.

His eyes spoke to her, reaching out. It suddenly occurred to Sasha that while she was physically sated, Doug could not be. He'd been so good, so gentle, so generous. She'd been trained.... She was frightened, yet it seemed her role.... "Doug?" she began unsurely. "You haven't...I mean...." She shot a pointed glance downward by way of elaboration. "If you want..."

He was very quiet for a moment. "Why?"

She shrugged and told herself that he was right, that he wasn't really a stranger anymore. "It—it's only fair."

"You mean you'd make love to me just to even things up?" When she looked away in agony, he studied her sadly. Then, very slowly, he began to set her clothes to rights. "No way, Sasha Blake," he said softly. "When we make love—when we *really* make love—it's going to be because we're both positively burning with need."

"But aren't you...." Again she faltered. This time, Doug stood and drew her up with him, then took her face in his hands.

"Believe it or not," he said, faintly incredulous himself, "my satisfaction came from yours."

"Then your need isn't...."

"It's there, all right. And I'll probably have all hell to pay for my nobility when I get home. But for now—" he lowered his voice "—it's enough for me to know that you've felt good."

Unbelievably touched, Sasha could think of nothing to say. There had to be something very special about a man who could defer his own gratification this way. While the heaven he'd taken her to had been one kind of awakening, this self-control was another. *The* Douglas Donohue—or *any* man, for that matter—putting her pleasure before his own? It had to be pure fiction....

The sound of a steady, distant ringing tore Doug's eyes from hers. "What's that? Not the telephone. An alarm?"

As puzzled as he, she made for the stairs, to return moments later with silence restored. "Strange, I must have flipped it on by mistake."

"It's nearly two in the morning. That's quite some mistake. I thought you said you got up at five."

"I do." She frowned a minute longer, then shrugged and forced a smile. "I must have been really out of it yesterday when the stupid thing went off. Lucky thing I wasn't sleeping just now."

"I'll say," Doug drawled, then threw his arm around her shoulder and swung her toward the door. "How about if I pick you up, oh, say, twelve hours from now?"

"Pick me up?"

"You were going to show me the island."

"You've been here for days," she argued, feeling more than a little awkward. "Don't tell me you haven't already seen the island. It's not that big. Besides, I really do have work to do."

"Then do it in the morning."

"I'm not sure how early I can get up."

"I'll be here at two."

"Four."

"Two-thirty."

"Four."

"Two-forty-five."

"Four."

"Come on, Sasha! Give a little! Three o'clock is my last offer." He released her and opened the door. "Three o'clock. Take it or leave it."

As he turned to await her decision, Sasha felt the weight of it. After what she'd just experienced, she reeled in uncertainty. On the one hand, if she agreed to go out with Doug she was admitting to wanting to further the relationship. True, he'd opened her eyes in several respects tonight. But there was far more to a relationship than sex. And in spite of the delirium he'd produced in her, there were memories too harsh to ignore. Yet, if she did refuse his invitation, what was she to do about the strange and unbidden curiosity she felt?

Take it. Leave it. Take it. Leave it.

"Well?" he asked softly, all banter forgotten.

"Three o'clock," she murmured softly. "See you then."

The purr of the Maserati had long since faded when she double-checked her doors and put out the lights. Starting up the stairs, she paused, then looked back at the sofa. What had happened there still stunned her. And frightened her. And made her blush. What was the hold Doug had over her? What was it that made her quiver when he came near, that made her melt in his arms and come alive, that made her accept an invitation to drive around the island when she knew her time was better spent at work?

She shook her head. It was a mystery—a mystery, involving this dark-haired, bronze-skinned man of the silver eyes and the golden touch. Just last week her life had seemed well-ordered and relatively complete.

Suddenly things had changed. Doug Donohue challenged her; he fascinated her. And her own curiosity after all she'd been through and had sworn to avoid—therein lay the mystique.

Loath to agonize, she sighed and climbed the stairs, entered her room, idly stepped from her pumps and reached to remove her earrings. Suddenly she stopped arms midair, and stared at the bed. Her hairbrush lay there. But she'd left it in the bathroom, hadn't she? Puzzled, she skimmed the room, only to have her eye catch on the dresser and her favorite perfume, it's glass stopper lying uselessly by the side of the bottle. How could she have been so careless?

Crossing the room in annoyance, she replaced the stopper, turned and, frowning, leaned back against the dresser. Within seconds her gaze was on the small alarm clock that had gone off earlier. The alarm, the hairbrush, the bottle of perfume—had she been that distracted lately? She recalled the book downstairs on the mantel, the book she could have sworn she hadn't touched in months. A shiver coursed through her. Her eye crept slowly around the room as though in search of a presence lying in wait.

Then she straightened and took a deep breath. Coincidence. That was all. There was nothing to fear. She'd been careless and forgetful, but then, who could blame her, with a new book in the works and a man the likes of Doug Donohue toying with her peace of mind? It'd be perfectly understandable for her to displace a book or a brush or accidentally twirl the alarm setting of her clock to an ungodly hour. If it was *Autumn Ambush* again, that too was chance. Life didn't mirror fiction; it was the other way around. Wasn't it?

4

The Sunday Times lay forgotten on the kitchen table, the instant coffee remained dry powder in his cup. After no more than three hours' sleep, Doug spent the morning walking the beach.

Reliving the party and the hours immediately after, he felt stunned. Sasha Blake had to be the most intriguing woman he'd ever known, and he realized it not for the first time. Rather than being satisfied as, one after another, the pieces of the puzzle fell into place, he was more curious than ever...about himself as much as her.

Self-control. He'd never, never experienced the likes of it before. To have held her, kissed her and brought her to the heights of passion and then held back...it was mind-boggling. She'd even offered to complete the act, and he'd refused! But he'd been honest with what he'd told her, though even now it confounded him. He *had* found satisfaction in hers, more so than he'd ever imagined possible. Was he going soft in his old age? Oh no, not soft, he mused, shifting his hands in the pockets of his jeans to alleviate a pressure that had even now begun to build. Not soft, but gentle? And considerate? Or was it simply his ego that screamed against having a woman offer her body out of duty?

He wondered what her husband had done to her.

Beaten her? Taken her with brute force? Indeed, when she'd offered herself to him in the wee morning hours there had been a look of resignation in her eyes. The whore selling herself for the money she needed? No, the wife accepting her dismal fate in life.

Swearing softly to himself, he kicked at the sand with his booted foot and walked on. Her body was beautiful. He couldn't imagine any man wanting to hurt that. And her passion was something to behold. But that was new, perhaps well hidden even to herself over the years. She'd been startled by the pleasure she'd felt, the pleasure he'd given her. And yes, his own pleasure had been nearly as great as if he'd taken her fully. Nearly...but not quite.

He wanted to make love to her. But how, and when? She was frightened. He couldn't do anything to add to that fear. From what she'd told him, it had probably been close to ten years since a man had touched her as he had earlier. And things were happening so quickly now....

He'd have to take it slow, another first for him. But he'd meant what he'd said. When they made love, he wanted her to burn for it as he did, to ache so badly that the past was nothing.

It could be very easy. He already knew that he could produce near mindlessness in her by his kiss alone. But that was *too* easy, and he resisted its lure. Perhaps it was a sense of total conquest that he needed. Or perhaps, just perhaps, he wanted more from her than sex. Perhaps.

As he took refuge atop a cluster of rocks and stared out at the sea, he wondered what she was thinking just then.

Her work forgotten along with the Sunday paper
and the super breakfast she'd promised herself, Sasha
paced the floor. She didn't understand what had gotten
into her that she'd allowed Doug Donohue, a man
she'd known less than a week, the freedom she had.
It could only lead to pain of one kind or another.
Hadn't she had her fill of that years ago?

After he'd left, sleep had been slow in coming and
even then, brief and filled with troubled dreams. Now,
tired and unbelievably keyed up, she had to face an
afternoon with Doug. How could she? She felt confused and frightened and not at all comforted by the
memory of what she'd let him do. It had felt good.
Oh, yes. And though she fought it, she couldn't deny
the speck of eagerness she felt at simply seeing him
again. He was a man, through and through. But would
he turn on her when passion seized him? A relationship with him might prove a magnificent illusion
around his leanly muscled frame, his dark face and
hair, his warmth and his gentleness. An illusion
built...only to be crushed? She wasn't sure if she
could bear it.

The clock ticked irreverently on, minutes into hours
as she wandered, distracted, from one room to another
of her house. She couldn't work. She couldn't read.
The only thing she seemed capable of doing was taking one outfit after another from her closet, studying
it critically, then discarding it as all wrong. By two-
thirty she could delay no longer. Finally choosing a
faded pair of jeans and a comfortable sweatshirt in
hopes of blending namelessly with the islanders, she
dressed, piled her hair on top of her head, applied a
trace of mascara and blusher, and went downstairs to
wait.

She prayed he'd be late, but he wasn't. On the stroke of three her doorbell rang. She pressed her dry lips together and rubbed her clammy palms against her jeans, then answered the door.

His jeans were as faded as hers, his shirt a dashing plaid wide open at his neck. He wore the same leather bomber jacket she'd first seen him in, and boots as weathered as her own, he looked gorgeous.

"All set?" he asked eagerly. She gave a jerky nod as his gaze skimmed over her. "Will you be warm enough? There's a breeze off the ocean. Maybe you should bring a windbreaker or something."

She cast a glance at the swaying grasses on the moor, so much more serene than she felt at that moment. "I guess so," she murmured, bypassing more chic jackets to ferret from her hall closet a simple corduroy one that Doug promptly threw over his elbow. They walked to the car in silence.

"So where should we start?" he asked. "You're the guide."

She sent him a look of skepticism before refocusing on the scenery. "South Road is fine. It's a pretty route into Edgartown." She was safer in a crowd, she reasoned, and even this late in the season there were bound to be day-trippers galore.

Sensing her awkwardness, he didn't speak until they hit the main road. "How do you know the Slaters?" he began, trying a less personal approach in hopes of settling her.

"My agent knew them. She introduced us when I first moved here."

"Your agent has a place here?"

She shook her head. "In New York. She knows Rob

professionally. She's submitted things to him from
several of her other clients from time to time."

"Have you been with her from the start?"

"Diane sold my first book, but only after I'd written
several smaller things and sold them on my own." She
gave a shy laugh. "I wasn't sure I'd sell *anything* way
back then. It was a shot in the dark. I wouldn't have
had the presumption go get an agent at that point."

"How did you finally get her?"

"A mutual friend." For the first time she smiled.
"Seems to be the way things work."

"This friend was a writer too?"

"Uh-huh. He'd had a mystery published and was
forever working on his second." Her eyes took on a
look of fond remembrance. "Simon was a character.
I think his efforts were misplaced. He should have
been in the theater. The man had a way with makeup
and disguises, not to mention accents and physical de-
formities he could put on at will. There were any number of times he put on a show to cheer me up."

"You needed cheering up?"

Awkward again, she looked down at her hands.
"When I first moved to the coast, I was kind of
down."

"The coast?"

"Maine. It was soon after...soon after my marriage
broke up. I was very alone and pretty unsure of myself."

"He filled a void?"

She glanced up quickly. "Oh, not in that sense. He
was a friend. That's all. And I needed one badly."

"You don't have family?"

"I have family." Her gaze returned to the passing
landscape.

Doug waited, then dared prod. "You don't sound thrilled."

"They're the ones who aren't thrilled. I was a disappointment to them. I was supposed to marry and raise a family and be a good, loyal, obedient wife." Her bitterness was ill-hidden.

"But you didn't."

"No. I wanted something more."

"Like...?"

"Like—" Like love. And romance. And trust and caring and loyalty. "Ach, it's not important."

Doug knew it was. He also knew, though, that he could only dig so deep at one time. She was talking. She was opening. It would come, all that deeper stuff, in time.

"Your family must be proud of you now."

"Not particularly. They're potato farmers. Not," she hastened to add, darting a glance his way, "that there's anything wrong with that." She took a breath. "Sam is a potato farmer too. They all work hard. But they're not terribly sympathetic toward a dreamer."

Doug took his eyes from the road for a minute to study her grim expression. "Is that how you see yourself? A dreamer?"

"That's how *they* see me. Head in the clouds. Eye on the stars. Me? I suppose I am a dreamer of sorts. Even more so an idealist. What I write expounds on an ideal." She sighed, her voice tainted with defeat. "They can't understand that."

"Do you ever see them?"

"No. They live in Aroostook County. Inland Maine. I haven't been back since I left."

"Not even since you've become famous?"

"I'm not famous, at least not in my mind. I'm a

writer who has been very, very lucky. I feel good about myself, self-confident at last. To go back there and have to deal with *their* image of success, well, I don't think I could stand it.''

"Do you...miss them?''

She looked at him and let out a short laugh, then pressed her fist to her mouth and stared out the side window. There was something comforting about the windswept moors, the ripening of wild apples, the brilliant color of the huckleberry thickets.

"I suppose I do,'' she admitted softly. "There are some good memories, memories of when I was a child, memories of my mother holding me after I'd had a nightmare or my father carting me around on his shoulders.'' The warmth of her tone faded. "But times changed. Money grew tighter. The weather didn't cooperate. And the expectations of a child were very different from those of an adult.''

As they approached Edgartown, Doug slowed the car to accommodate the growing traffic. Brought back to the present, Sasha felt suddenly self-conscious. She brushed a strand of hair from her cheek and frowned.

"What is it?'' he asked softly.

"I shouldn't have gone on and on like that. It's all really irrelevant.'' And startling given the fact that the story she'd held in for years was now spilling itself for this compelling newcomer.

"Not at all,'' the compelling newcomer replied with sincerity. "I think it's fascinating.'' It was, though he'd never been particularly interested in a woman's history before. Now he couldn't seem to hear enough. "Did you always want to write?''

"Me?'' She coughed. "You're talking to the

woman who practically flunked English in high school."

"Those teachers must be dying now."

"I hope so. They gave me lousy grades on one paper after the next because my ideas were impractical, so they said."

"Ah. Potato country school."

"You bet."

"So when did you start? Writing, that is."

For some reason, astounding given the fact that she'd never revealed as much about herself to a living soul in years, the words flowed. "Actually it was Simon who got me going. I was working as a waitress at one of those little lobster places on the coast. I was reading everything I could get my hands on. He suggested I take a course at the state university."

"So you did?"

She nodded. "English literature. Then creative writing."

"Did your teachers think your work...impractical?"

She chuckled embarrassed. "No. They liked it."

"And encouraged you to submit for publication?"

"No. Simon did that. At first I thought he was crazy. Then I realized that I had nothing to lose. I did love to write. And if a few rejection slips were the price of satisfying my curiosity...well, it seemed a small price to pay."

He brought the car to a halt in a parking space near the center of town and turned to face her. "And you sold instantly."

"Not quite. There were rejections at first."

"Were you devastated?"

"Not really. After all, it was only a short story, and I hadn't expected anything."

"Then..."

"Then that first acceptance came, and..."

"And the rest is history."

She blushed and averted her gaze from the silver eyes that so bound her. "Pretty much." She sat silently for a minute. It was Doug's gentle voice that finally made her look up.

"Thank you."

"For what?"

"For telling me all this. You don't tell many people, do you?"

"No."

"Then I feel honored." When she blushed again, he squeezed her hand. "Come on. Let's take a walk."

The streets of Edgartown were as delightful as ever, small shops and eating places intermixed with large houses of the Georgian and Federal styles set flush to the street in the old-English fashion. People browsed idly along, islanders and off-islanders alike with their jeans and sweaters, shoulder bags and sneakers. Occasionally they passed a more colorful character, a young woman in trendy peasant garb, an old-timer decked out in wing tips and bow tie, a bearded, slightly surly looking cad who stared at Sasha until she was pulled by Doug into the nearest bookshop. There Doug proceeded, to her mortification, to buy a copy of her latest book.

"Doug!" she protested, turning beet red and tucking her chin to her chest.

"What's wrong?" he asked with an innocent grin.

"You don't want to buy that," she chided in a hushed whisper.

"But I do. I want to see what juicy things you've put in it. See, you've piqued my imagination."

Her high color persisted. "You won't like it."

"Of course I will. You'll autograph it for me, won't you?"

"I'll write something lewd," she scoffed.

He lowered his voice, the eager wolf. "All the better to get me going on a cold and lonely night, my dear."

Sensing he'd best her in any further repartee, she simply stood by the door examining the magazines, pretending not to know him while he paid for his choice. Then, with the book tucked safely in the back pocket of his jeans, they started out again.

It was a glorious day for a walk. The sun was warm to counter the breeze that gave the air a fresh salt tang. Wisps of Sasha's hair fell to wave down her neck; Doug's hair was likewise windblown and infinitely attractive. As they wandered through the town, he threw his arm around her shoulders. She couldn't protest. The fit was ideal.

They passed the courthouse and the town hall, then strolled farther, past the newspaper office, then a museum. "Hey, there's the library," Doug teased. "Shall we go in and see if they've got a copy of your book on their shelves?"

"It's closed. And they don't."

"You've checked?"

"In Chilmark. I go there to do research. Let me tell you, that librarian would just as soon I move back to New York. She made it very clear that she doesn't particularly care for my brand of literature."

"Snobbery? On the Vineyard?"

"A little." She smiled, amazed at how relaxed she felt. "But not often. Besides, it's all a matter of taste."

Doug squeezed her shoulder and they ambled on. Their hips knocked together, then meshed again and their easy strides were well mated. Sasha found herself wondering whether Doug often walked down streets with his arm around a woman, found herself wondering about the kind of woman who had last come under his spell. For she was, without a doubt, under his spell. All her forewarnings were for naught when he was as amiable, as innocently companionable beside her.

Retracing their steps, they found themselves headed for the waterfront, where they stopped to quietly watch occasional fishing boats return from an abbreviated Sunday outing.

"Hungry?" he asked her. The sun had lowered dramatically on the horizon.

"Um-hmm. All this walking and neither breakfast nor lunch must do it."

He smiled, a broad, endearing, man-of-the-world smile that tickled her all over. "Let's get something to eat. Okay?"

"Okay," she said, returning his smile with a warmth that made Doug wonder whether he'd simply missed the boat all these years. Perhaps the way to a woman's heart was through her stomach.

Hand in hand they turned and began to walk. Lost in a world of momentary pleasure, Sasha barely heard the slow roll of a dull thunder. Doug heard though, looked up and tensed, then with lightning speed crushed her close and dragged her back several paces. He was just in time. A contingent of large barrels fell from a roof to the pavement, pounding the very spot where they would have been standing at just that moment had his reflex not been as fast.

Both round-eyed, they stared in horror as the barrels rolled to a halt. Sure concussion, if not skull fracture or worse—they'd missed it by seconds.

"Holy Moses!" Doug exclaimed, holding Sasha tightly against his own trembling body. In anger he looked toward the roof. "Where in the hell did those come from? My God, you could have been killed!"

"Your head is harder than mine?" she teased shakily. Had she been alone she might have panicked. But Doug had saved her from both harm and panic. Burying her face against his shirt, she soaked up his strength.

For a minute they simply stood clutching each other as the impact of what might have been hit them. "That was close," he breathed at last, then growled, "Damn it, how could something like that happen?"

"Very simply," she stated. "Those are empty oil barrels, the kind the old whalers used to use. They've probably been piled up there for years, slipping slowly. Maybe a gust of wind did the trick, maybe a gull."

Doug looked down at her. "How do you know so much?"

She grinned, liking the fact that he hadn't seen fit to let her go just yet. "I used it once in a book. *Midnight Rogue.* It can be real spooky, especially if the heroine suspects that someone is out to get her." In *Midnight Rogue* it had been a jealous stepbrother who had given the barrels that final push. But that had been fiction, and a very convenient ploy. Things like that didn't happen in real life.

"Did the heroine survive?"

"Oh, yes."

He arched a brow. "How?"

"Her true love was there to pull her out of the way in the nick of time," she responded smartly, then swallowed hard when she realized what she'd said. "It's all make-believe," she added quickly. "It's what romantic intrigue is all about."

Her belated attempt at rationalization fell flat. Doug's gray eyes held hers with uncompromising heat as the words echoed in his mind. *Her true love.* He wondered if he could ever be that to Sasha, wondered if that was what he wanted. He'd never been in love before. Was there an explanation for the protectiveness he felt, for his sudden willingness for self-sacrifice? When he'd hauled them from the path of the barrels, he'd thought only of her. Was it love? Or simple chivalry?

"Doug?" she whispered, unable to stand the tension a moment longer.

The sound of her voice, the look of fear in her eyes drew him from his trance. He raised his eyes to passersby who bystepped the barrels and cast curious glances toward the roof. He followed their gaze. The roof was empty, marked only by the darkened shingles where, as Sasha had suggested, for years the barrels must have lain.

Stifling an eery feeling at the pit of his stomach, he muttered a sober, "Let's get out of here," and fixing an arm firmly around her shoulder, led her around the barrels and away.

He walked briskly, staring straight ahead. Sensing his need to work off the fright they'd had, Sasha pushed herself to keep up. They were nearly back to where he had parked the car when he finally relaxed and recalled their original intent.

"I'm sorry, babe," he said, looking down at her in surprise. "I forgot. You're hungry—"

"I'm okay," she was quick to assert, but Doug quelled her protest by ushering her across the street toward a small restaurant.

"Well, *I'm* hungry," he informed her, the corner of his mouth twitching in mockery. "Heroic acts take their toll, you know. I'll have to keep my strength up if I'm to rescue you from future calamity." True love or not, he recognized his need to do that. It was a very pleasing thought.

To Sasha as well. "My knight in shining armor?"

He opened the door to the restaurant and let her pass through. "Maybe a little rusty around the edges," he mused only half in jest, "but nothing that a little oil won't cure. Look, there's a table just waiting for us. Come on." Taking her hand, he led her there, then leaned down as he seated her to whisper in her ear, "They've got terrific fish chowder here. And fresh zucchini bread."

"Hey, I thought you were the newcomer to the island," she protested in fun and was rewarded by an appealingly crooked smile.

"But a noncook. A man has to survive," he drawled, and for a minute, with his bronzed skin, his windblown hair, his shirt open to reveal dark tufts of very masculine chest hair, he was pure rogue.

When push came to shove, she'd known all along that Doug hadn't sought a sightseeing guide when he'd asked her out for the afternoon. He'd wanted her company. And, in truth, she'd wanted his. The dinner they proceeded to share convinced her that, whatever the consequences, she'd been right in yielding to that whim. Their conversation was light and relaxing, focusing mostly on the Vineyard and each of their experiences living here.

It was only later, long after Doug had dropped her at her house with a gentle kiss to her cheek and a promise to call during the week, that Sasha realized she'd done most of the talking. Yes, she'd been a guide of sorts, but a guide to her background, her occupation, her everyday life as an islander. Other than his attentiveness, his wit and the occasional hint of a passion held strictly in check, he offered nothing of himself, of who he was, where he'd come from, where he was going. Not that she'd asked. It stunned her to realize that she'd been so blinded by his engaging presence that she'd simply followed his lead, and he'd led right back to her time and again.

Alone in her bedroom that night, propped against the pillows on the bed with a red pencil in her hand and the latest printout from her word processor in her lap, she realized how little she knew. Here at home once more, though, she wondered if it was for the best. True, she'd enjoyed her time with Doug today; demanding nothing but her company, he'd managed to put her fully at ease, a remarkable feat given the awkwardness she'd felt when he'd first picked her up. He'd made no mention of the little episode on the sofa. Perhaps he'd sensed she'd be having trouble coming to terms with it herself. Which she was. Even now the thought of it brought a faint flush to her cheeks.

But she couldn't dwell on it. She wouldn't dwell on it. Doug hadn't seemed to, nor had he thought less of her for it. It had happened, and she had enjoyed it far too much for self-castigation. She was also too realistic to deny the fact that, while their outing today had been an outwardly innocent one, the biological attraction between them was as strong as ever. She'd been vitally aware of him from the start, aware of the strength of his arm about her shoulders and the muscled cord of his thigh as it bumped hers. She'd been fascinated by the way he arched that dark brow of his, by the compact movement of his lips when he talked. His hands, his hands had tormented her—sun-toasted skin, the faintest sprinkling of soft dark hair, long strong fingers manipulating his fork when he ate. And the memory of what those fingers had done to bring her such intimately exquisite joy…she sucked in her breath and shook her head, but there was no way she could deny what she'd felt. She was a woman, convinced of it for the very first time in her life.

And Doug was a man. He'd want to make love to her. He'd promised as much even as he'd rejected her immediate offer of satisfaction. What had he said— that they'd make love, *really* make love—only when they were both burning with need? One week before she would never have imagined a day such as that ever coming. She'd never burned for a man in her life, yet now, after such brief exposure to Doug Donohue, she felt an insidious ribbon of smoke curling its way through her system. A smoldering? The first step toward that "burning" Doug had predicted? Or an invitation to disaster?

Bewildered, she picked up pencil and paper. How much safer writing romance was than living it, she mused, her brow furrowing in frustration. Regardless of what happened, she was always in full control. If her hero did something she didn't like, she simply took her red pencil and crossed it all out. If her heroine took a wrong turn and found herself in an untenable situation, there was similar recourse. And there was always a happy ending, a guarantee that the trials and tribulation in a particular plot would be to good avail.

Yes, writing was safer, safer yet nowhere near as titillating as what she'd felt in Doug's arms last night....

Doug didn't call on Monday. Immersed in her work, Sasha told herself that she didn't mind a bit. When the phone rang on Tuesday morning, though, she jumped a mile. She counted to ten as the second ring came and faded, reached for the receiver, drew back, then finally answered it in a voice schooled to calmness.

"Hello?"

"Sasha? It's Diane."

Her disappointment was curbed by the pleasure of hearing from her agent. In the three years Sasha had spent in New York, Diane DeScenza had come to be like family. It had been Diane herself who, having seen Sasha's unhappiness in the city, had suggested she think of moving out.

"How are you, Diane? Gee, it's good to hear from you."

"I'm fine. Wondering how you are. Everything all right?"

"Great. The writing's going well. No name yet for this thing, but then it never does come until later in the book."

"Are you pleased with the characters? They sounded really good in the proposal."

"I'm pleased with them, now that I'm finally getting into them. The hero is very special, I think."

A spirited chuckle came from the other end of the

line. "So are all your heroes, if your sales figures are anything to go by. You've heard about *Raven's Revenge* making the list, haven't you?"

"Uh-huh. That'll please M.P.I." Madison Publishing had handled all of her books.

"To say the least. In fact, that's why I'm calling. They're going back to press with re-releases of *Devil Dreams* and *Autumn Ambush.*"

"No kidding? That's great!"

"Um-hmm. But they want another tour."

Sasha's face fell. "Oh, Diane. You know how I hate those things. Twenty cities in as many days, with every hair in place and a smile plastered on my face. I end up with bleary eyes, sore feet and writer's cramp. By the time I'm done, I need a month to recuperate, and then when am I going to write?"

"Calm down, Sasha," Diane said gently. "It wouldn't be that bad this time. They're talking about ten days. That's all. Major cities. Television spots, media interviews, a few signings."

"But I've just started a book!"

"And you've got a whole load of time to finish it. Besides, the tour wouldn't be for another three or four months. By then you'll be needing a break, if you haven't already finished the thing," she cajoled.

"I never need a break in the middle of a book," Sasha declared perversely. "It ruins my concentration." Strange how her concentration had been broken repeatedly in the past week, and still she'd managed. Doug Donohue was a stimulant...in many ways.

"Well," Diane said with a sigh, "I'll try to hold them off. Or at least keep it to a minimum. Maybe we can limit it to a week. Does that sound fair?"

"Fair?" Sasha echoed in resignation. "I guess so.

After all, I should be grateful that they're doing what they are. New covers?''

"Yup." Diane lowered her voice to simulate bold typeface. "By the author of the bestselling *Midnight Rogue* and *Raven's Revenge*."

"Poor *Demon Woods*," Sasha teased, thinking of the one of her children that hadn't been mentioned. "It's being left out."

"Maybe not. They're...oh, I shouldn't tell you...."

"Diane...." When a silence persisted on the other end, Sasha raised her voice. "Diane, tell me!"

Her agent hesitated for just a moment more. "They're talking of trying to sell *Demon Woods* for a TV movie."

"You're kidding! When did this come up? You've never breathed a word!"

"I've never *known* a word until this morning. And it's purely in the talk stage, which is why I probably shouldn't have opened my mouth at all. You'll have your hopes up, and then nothing may come of it."

"I know," Sasha breathed in awe. "But still. Just to be considered!"

Diane laughed then, a warm, affectionate laugh. "That's what's so wonderful about you, love. You're as innocent and enthusiastic today as you were the day I sold your first book. Fame hasn't gone to your head, that's for sure! And it's a relief. You should see some of my other clients. Speak of un-bear-a-able...!"

Mention of her other clients touched a gentle cord in Sasha, whose mind homed in on that one in particular of whom she had coincidentally spoken to Doug two days before. "Have you heard from Simon, Diane? I feel really badly. I haven't spoken with him in months."

"As a matter of fact, I got a call from him a few weeks ago. He was his old beguiling self, regaling me with stories of his latest adventure. He's diving for deep-sea treasure. Did you know that?"

"I didn't. Is he really doing that?"

"Ach, who knows. With Simon, spinning the tale is half the fun."

"Has he written anything lately?"

"Not that *I've* seen. He talks about it…but no cigar. He asked about you. Wanted to know all about your latest book."

"Raven's Revenge?"

"No. This new one you've started. I told him about the proposal. He was excited." She paused, momentarily unsure. "You don't mind my telling him, do you?"

"Of course not. He was right with me on those first few books, reading my proposals, discussing them with me. I feel guilty losing touch with him like this. With you as a go-between, it's not so bad."

"Why don't you give him a call? He'd love to hear from you."

For the first time Sasha grew hesitant. "Oh, I don't know. I feel awkward."

"Because of your success? Sasha, you shouldn't. Simon of all people is pleased for you."

"But he tried so hard there for a while, writing and writing, selling nothing."

"Maybe he only had one book in him. That's true of many writers. He may have realized it, if he's into diving for sunken treasure."

"Sunken treasure." Sasha chuckled. "That does sound like Simon. I miss him. I really do."

"Then call him. Just to say hello. Uh-oh. There's

my other line blinking. Gotta run. Listen, I'll talk with
you some time next week. Okay?''

"Sure. Take care, Diane.''

"You too, love.''

Sasha hung up the phone feeling infinitely grateful
to have a friend like Diane. From the first, when
Simon had introduced them, Diane had taken her under her wing. When, with two bestsellers under
Sasha's belt, it had seemed the thing for her to move
to New York, Diane had been the one to help her find
an apartment, to show her around, to introduce her to
people. That Sasha had hated New York was no fault
of Diane's. Despite lavish dreams of dash and glamor,
Sasha was a small-town girl at heart.

Emboldened by Diane's urging, Sasha flipped
through her Rolodex, picked up the phone and dialed
Simon's number. When there was no answer after
eight rings, she hung up, vowing to try again another
time.

Returning to work, she put in another two good
hours, then paused for a light lunch before attacking
her keyboard again. It was late afternoon when the
phone rang this time. She looked up sharply. Her heart
skipped a beat. Pressing her hands to her thighs, she
took a long steadying breath, then lifted the receiver.

"Hello?''

A faint but telling static forewarned her that again
the call was a long-distance one. Not Doug, Sasha realized, but her disappointment took a back seat to uncertainty at the sound of her sister's voice. "Sasha?
It—it's Vicky.''

It had been several months since Sasha had spoken
to any member of her family, and then too it had been
to Vicky, her senior by three years and the only one

of her four siblings who'd been even marginally tolerant of the path she'd chosen.

"Hi, Vicky." Sasha's voice was tinged with wariness. Over the years she'd been hurt once too often by her family's lack of understanding and interest, which was why she rarely called home. "How are you?" she asked, her thoughts skipping ahead to the reason for Vicky's call. It was Tuesday, not yet five o'clock. The telephone rates would be at their prime. Sasha experienced a ripple of apprehension.

"I'm okay," her sister answered, but there was obviously something on her mind.

"Is John well? And the kids?" Vicky had a hardworking husband and four growing children. Her parents were pleased.

"They're fine. But," she took a breath for courage and raced on, "it's Mom."

Sasha felt a silent pang. "What is?" she asked quietly.

"She's sick."

"Sick...how?"

As though still debating making this call and then suddenly realizing that it was too late to turn back, Vicky sighed. "She's in the hospital." When Sasha remained silent, she elaborated. "She went to the doctor for a regular checkup and he took her in to do more tests. She's got a tumor. They're going to do a hysterectomy." She paused and lowered her voice to an apologetic murmur. "I—I just thought you should know."

Sasha stared at the floor in anguish. The silence was deafening, yet she didn't know what to say. Finally she cleared her throat. "When? When are they doing it?"

"First thing next week. They want her to get some rest before that. You know how hard she works."

"I know," Sasha said with a glimmer of anger, but it was an anger directed as much at her father, who'd allowed a woman to bear such a tremendous physical burden, as at her mother for having borne it as her lot in life. As Sasha thought back on it, her mother had always been tired. That fatigue had taken the form of impatience with others in general, and in particular with one not quite as prone toward martyrdom, in a word, Sasha herself. "Is she very uncomfortable?"

"No. But she's worried about not being home. She feels guilty. And I'm sure that behind that stony facade of hers, she's probably scared to death."

Sasha was as stunned by her sister's tone as by her words. It was the first time, the very first time, she'd ever heard criticism on Vicky's part of her mother's stoicism. True, as a child Vicky had complained with the rest about the endless string of chores their mother seemed always to have up her sleeve, but Vicky had been a true Blake, marrying young, working beside her husband, bearing and raising the children just as her mother had before her. Sasha had always wondered just how like her mother Vicky was. Vicky's criticism was a sign of hope.

"What do the doctors say, Vicky? Are they hopeful that...that the surgery will take care of it?"

"They don't know. They won't know until afterward. They're talking of the possibility of some follow-up treatment, but it's all so undefined right now."

"I see."

"Well, uh, I just thought you ought to know. I didn't want you to be upset later." She began to stammer, "You know, with whatever, with whatever happens."

"Sure, Vicky." Sasha paused. "Does Mom know you've called me?"

"No. I didn't want to upset her anymore than was— Oh, God. That came out wrong. I mean she's been upset and trying not to show it and I didn't want her to get her hopes up or think I had called you because she's dying."

"Is she?" Sasha heard herself ask in a small unsure voice. The hand she raised to her forehead trembled. "Is she dying, Vicky? Tell me the truth."

"I don't know," was the quiet reply. "We'll know more next week. But listen, there's no need for you to run up here. I mean, she's all right for now. The surgery itself is no more dangerous than any surgery."

Sasha bowed her head, eyes closed for a minute, then looked up. Her voice was as gentle as could be in announcing her decision, though she took no pride in it. She was a coward. Despite what Vicky had said about the lack of immediacy of the situation, Sasha knew she should get on the first plane and fly up to Maine. She knew it, yet she couldn't go. She just couldn't.

"Can I call you…after the surgery?" she asked at last, then waited cautiously for Vicky's reaction.

"Sure, Sasha." There was a touch of resignation…and relief. Vicky had done what she'd felt she had to do in alerting her sister to the situation. Anything beyond that was up to her.

"Well, then, I guess I'll talk with you next week," Sasha began. She half wished Vicky would fight her, would tell her in no uncertain terms to come home. In the absence of such direction, though, she could only make a graceful exit. "What hospital is Mom at?" When Vicky named the one, Sasha nodded. "Do they need any help? I mean with money? I'd be glad—"

"It's okay, Sasha. Insurance will cover it."

And Jerome and Natalie Blake wouldn't want to touch her ill-earned money anyway, Sasha realized bitterly. "Well," she said with a sigh, "if there's anything I can do—"

"I'll let you know. Bye-bye, Sasha."

Sasha stared at the phone for an age before she pushed herself from her desk to wander aimlessly around the room. Hands thrust in the back pockets of her jeans, she stopped before the window and looked out. The surgery wasn't really risky. Vicky had said so herself. And after that, well, her mother was a woman of iron. She'd make it. There was nothing to worry about.

Returning to her desk, Sasha reread the last paragraph she'd written. But her mind wandered and she had to read it a second time. Finally she typed one sentence, then another. She read them over, deleted the first, substituted something she liked even less, deleted it as well. She returned to read the page from the top, added a new sentence in place of the one erased, stared at it and shook her head. It was wrong. All wrong. With a soft oath, she stabbed at the button to save what she'd written, waited until the machine had finished its work, then turned it off and stood up.

It was unfair, damn it, she reasoned unreasonably. Things had been going along so well. She'd come to terms with the estrangement from her family long ago. Between her work, her new life and friends such as Diane and the Vineyard contingent, she had everything she wanted. Now her mother's illness stirred up a host of unwanted feelings, not the least of which was guilt, and second to that regret. But why should she run back to Maine? Had her mother stood beside her when she'd needed her? Had she been there with sympathy and understanding? No! She'd been no more supportive than Sasha's father or her brothers or sisters or her oaf of an ex-husband, Sam Webster!

Angry and hurt, Sasha stormed from her room. In the kitchen she filled the kettle, set it down hard on the stove and turned on the gas. Crossing her arms over her chest, she leaned back against the counter to scowl at the crisp white ceramic tile underfoot.

The tea did little to settle her. She tried to push thoughts of Vicky's call from her mind, to concentrate instead on her storyline, or Diane's earlier call, or even the prospect of hearing from Doug, but it was useless.

Doug. Hah! And what could *he* give her? He'd string her along, toy with her, imply a kind of security that in the end he'd rob her of without a second thought at all. Wasn't that the way it worked?

Plunking her half-empty cup of tea into the sink, she headed for the front door. Her hand was on the knob when the phone rang. Stalking back into the kitchen, confused and annoyed, she snatched up the receiver.

5

It was a startlingly impatient "Hello!" that Doug Donohue heard.

"Sasha?" he asked cautiously. "It's Doug."

As if she didn't know. She'd recognize that voice anywhere. Its deep vibrancy was firmly etched on her brain. Had he called an hour earlier, she might have been pleased. But he hadn't called an hour earlier, damn him. He'd let her down. Now he'd have to endure her sour mood.

"Hello, Doug," she stated coolly.

There was a brief silence on the other end of the line, then a controlled query. "Is everything all right?"

"Of course. What could be wrong?"

"You sound angry."

"Me? Angry? I don't get angry," she snapped. "I'm just a sweet writer sitting here in all her innocuous glory. Nothing fazes me."

"What happened?" There was no hesitancy in his voice this time. Doug had never heard her sound this way and he was genuinely worried.

"Nothing at all."

"Sasha..." he warned.

Feeling shaky all over, she took a deep breath. "Look, Doug. Maybe I should speak with you another time. I'm going out." Without giving him a chance to respond, she hung up the phone and made good the escape she'd begun moments before. She needed fresh air. A brisk walk would be just the thing to work off some of the tension she felt.

All but running from the house, she headed for the moor. The distant burr of the telephone was quickly swallowed up by the whistle of wind through the grass. It was nearly dusk, that gray, eerie time that came earlier and earlier as fall progressed. And it was cold. Protected by nothing but the jeans and sneakers, turtleneck jersey and wool sweater she'd worn in the house all day, she welcomed the chill. Anything to take her mind from that other…

Maintaining a steady pace, she half walked, half ran up a hill, then down the other side. When she was out of breath, she stopped for a minute, tossed her head back and breathed in the sharp night air, then resumed her step more sanely.

Darkness fell quickly. By the time she had turned and headed back in the direction of her house, the moor was enveloped in a murky shroud. Passing close by a clump of pines, she nearly stumbled over an exposed root. Swearing softly, she shoved her hands into the pockets of her jeans and steered toward more open spaces.

In the distance the light from her study blazed into the night. With a sigh of defeat she propped her hip against a rambling stone wall and turned her back on the warmth. She wasn't ready to go in yet. There was still an anguished tugging in the vicinity of her heart that had been only marginally eased by her walk.

Lowering her head, she closed her eyes and put her hand to her brow. The tightness in her throat was something else. She hadn't cried in months and months, certainly not about things that were over and done. Swallowing convulsively, she gulped the cold air, but it didn't dislodge the images that flitted through her brain. Her mother, her father, Sam, Doug—one face was as painful a vision as the next. If only she could blot them out.

As though in answer to her silent plea, the sound of footsteps broke through her brooding. The crisp grass crunched rhythmically. The occasional fallen leaf, dried and waiting for the wind to carry it to a more sheltered spot, crackled as the footsteps neared.

Sasha stiffened. She raised her head, too frightened to turn, a rabbit sensing imminent danger and counting on sheer immobility for its salvation. For a split second her imagination ran away with itself and she wondered whether *he'd* come to get her. In place of those other images that had haunted her moments before came ones of a motorcycle sabotaged, of barrels pushed from a roof, of the gardener's shed whose door had stuck, of personal belongings picked up and rearranged. Someone seemed to be after her. But why?

Heart pounding loudly, sure to give her away, she huddled into herself. The footsteps neared, then came to a halt. The darkness—was it friend of foe? Would it hide her from her pursuer?

"Sasha?"

The sound of Doug's voice, unsure and concerned, sent shafts of self-disgust through her. She'd done it again, imagination and all, the creative urge gone awry. She was a fool!

Several more steps sounded on the crisp grass. He stopped. "Sasha? What are you doing?"

She shook her head and tucked her chin to her chest. With the dispelling of her wildest fears, those other sorrowful thoughts returned. She squeezed her eyes shut against the moisture that gathered.

"Sasha?" His voice was softer, closer. Several more footsteps and he was within arm's reach. "What's wrong?"

Had he been angry or impatient, as he had a right to be given her curtness and the fact that she'd hung up on him, she might have been able to muster some sort of defense. Instead, she merely tucked her chin tighter and wrapped her arms about her middle. One by one, slow tears worked their way down her cheeks.

"Oh, Sasha," came the heartfelt sound behind her. With a single step, Doug absorbed the distance between them and threw his leg over the low wall to straddle the stone. Then, with one hard thigh against her backside and the other bracing her leg, he put his arms around her and tried to draw her close. When she resisted, recoiling into a self-contained knot, he grew adamant.

"Damn it, you're freezing." Unbuttoning the front of his dark pea jacket, he forced her body against the warmth of his, wrapping her in his arms and holding her tight. "Where's your common sense? You'll catch pneumonia!"

"I won't," she murmured, though the sudden warmth was as welcome as anything she'd ever known. "I can take...care of myself."

"Could've fooled me," he scolded with all the sympathy of a dictator betrayed. "You get yourself into a stew about something and don't even have the guts to talk about it, then you storm out into the night hell-bent on self-destruction! What's the matter with you, Sasha? Don't you know who your friends are?"

"Don't yell at me," she rasped against the seeping warmth of his sweater.

"Then don't do anything to give me reason!" he growled. When he shook his head, his chin rubbed against her hair. "Damn it, that was quite a welcome! Here I'd had to spend two days in New York—much against my plans *and* will—and all the while the only thing keeping me marginally civil is the thought of seeing you when I get back, and what happens? You hang up on me! Then pull this crazy stunt! I searched every inch of that damned house for you before I headed out here!"

"Don't yell," she whimpered, touched by an emotion she couldn't explain. And the tears came then, faster and stronger, accompanied by the softest, most heart-wrenching sobs Doug had ever heard.

Burying his face in her hair, he pulled her closer. His arms circled her back and held her to him with a fierce possessiveness, offering her a warmth and protection she simply didn't have the strength to refuse.

"It's all right, babe," he crooned throatily. "It's all right. Let it out. It's good for you."

What was good for her was the sure comfort of his embrace. Slipping her arms around his lean waist, she clung to him as though he were the only stable thing in her existence. He wasn't, she knew, but she went along with the illusion nonetheless. It had been so long, so long since she'd truly leaned on another human being. With his words of reassurance and the sturdiness of his body supporting her when she felt so weak, she was helpless to resist.

Very slowly her tears ebbed. Eyes closed, cheek flush against the commanding beat of his heart, she took long drags of his clean male scent. Gradually her strength returned. It was only with reluctance that she finally pulled her head back and withdrew her hands to blot from her cheeks the faint wetness his sweater had missed.

With the same reluctance she'd felt he released her, but only to take her face in his large hands and turn it upward. "Better?" he asked, very gently kissing away the last of her tears.

She smiled, suddenly embarrassed. "Yes," she whispered and lowered her eyes. "I'm sorry."

"For what? For being human?"

"Crying is a wasted emotion."

"Not if there's no other way to express what you feel. And you obviously weren't about to talk. You must have been holding that in for a good long time. Hmm?"

"Actually, no," she murmured. "Just for an hour or so."

"Like fun," he scoffed, but with an exquisite gentleness. "Something must have happened to trigger it, but it's deep down inside you simmering for far longer... Want to talk?"

She raised her head and took a last hiccuping breath. "I don't know."

"Well, while you're deciding, what say we head for the house. They didn't tell me about this November chill when I agreed to come live here." He feigned a shiver. "It's cold."

At the moment Sasha felt strangely warm, oddly content, as though in the protective cushion of Doug's arms she might forget the ills of the world. But it was dangerous, very dangerous to grow dependent on this type of support. She should know.

Doug drew her up, helped her over the low stone

wall and tucked her inside his jacket again. As they walked to the house in silence, she savored those last moments of warmth. Once inside, he released her, tossed his jacket on a chair and looked toward the fireplace.

"Mind if I light it?"

"Be my guest." Sinking into the nearest chair, she watched as he lay first kindling, then logs on the grate. When he looked wordlessly around, she bounded up and headed to the kitchen for a match. Within minutes a warm fire had taken hold.

"There." Standing, he rubbed his hands together, "Now, where's the brandy."

"Brandy?"

"To take off the chill." He scanned the room for sign of a bar. "And if you don't need it, I do."

She tossed her chin toward the alcove she called her dining room. It was simple but elegant, a white table, four chairs upholstered in pink and ecru, and behind them a long buffet. "In the cabinet on the right. Way back."

He had no trouble finding the spot, hunkering down to remove a bottle and two snifters. Sasha made no move to help, finding that she enjoyed watching the movement of his body. He wore jeans, a rust-colored sweater and a shirt whose rust-and-gray plaid coordinated both the sweater and his eyes. There was a fluidity to his walk, a natural grace. That the narrowness of his hips made his shoulders look all the more brawny was simply frosting on the cake.

"Here," he said softly, handing her a half-filled snifter. "Drink."

"I'm really okay."

Before she knew what he was up to, he'd taken one

of her hands in his. "Your fingers are like ice. Now, drink."

As a form of diversion from the unguarded sensuality of his touch, if nothing else, she raised the snifter to her lips and let the amber liquid warm its way down her throat. She kept her eyes downcast as Doug settled onto the sofa, his long legs stretched before him, crossed at booted ankles. He took a healthy dose of his own drink, frowned at the swirling amber stuff, then looked up.

"I'm really sorry I couldn't call sooner. There was something urgent in New York that I didn't find out about until early Monday morning. I just about had enough time to pack my things and catch a plane and, well..." He'd thought of calling so many times while he'd been in the city. But then he hadn't known what he'd say. Miss you. Wish you were here. When I get back we'll do naughty things together. One was worse than the next. Besides, he hadn't been ready to confess his fascination with this auburn-haired waif with the deep hazel eyes. Not yet. Things had happened so fast. But soon. It was bubbling inside, near to overflowing. If only he knew she was ready. Even now, though, there was a wariness in her. He could see it in the way she sat, in the way she avoided his gaze. She regretted having leaned on him before. She wanted so badly to be self-sufficient....

"Is it—did you work everything out?" she murmured, taking another sip of brandy.

"Oh, yeah. It's all set. They're just having a little trouble getting used to my being away." In another man there might have been arrogance. In Doug there was none. Feeling a shaft of admiration, Sasha looked away.

"You're very successful," she stated.

"I wasn't always."

He had her interest. She met his gaze. "You mean, when you first started the business?"

"That...and before." When she frowned, he explained. "I came from nothing. My parents were dirt poor. My father was a laborer in a textile mill. I worked there after school as soon as I was old enough. When I began to balk and talk of something better, he was furious. We didn't see eye to eye there for a while."

"He didn't want you moving up?" She couldn't understand that, any more than to this day she could understand her own parents' resistance to her success.

"Oh, yes. He wanted better for his son than he'd had. But I was talking on a grander scheme than anything he'd ever envisioned. He was frightened. Frightened that I'd dream, then fail and end up right back there at the mill."

As Doug described it, it made such sense. She had to hear more. "What happened? How did you break out?"

"I was lucky. I won an art scholarship. Without it, college would have been the first of those dreams to fall."

"Did you go right into designing when you graduated?"

"Slowly. I free-lanced while I got a graduate degree in business. Then I took out every possible loan I could get and opened shop." He offered a grimace of a smile as he remembered those earliest days on his own. "It was tough. The rents in New York were staggering and anything I earned by way of profit was poured back into repaying those loans plus interest. Several times I came close to folding.''

"What kept you afloat?''

He looked at her hard. "Pride. And sheer grit. I was determined to make it, if for no other reason than to show my father he'd been wrong.''

"You did.''

Doug's eyes softened and he looked down sadly. "Yeah. Too late. He died just when things were beginning to look up. My mother lasted a little longer, but I was never able to do the things for her that I might have been able to do today.'' He didn't want to go into the frustration he'd felt at being robbed of giving to those he'd loved. Perhaps it had been that anger that had made him so hard. He'd never know.

"I'm sorry,'' Sasha said softly. She was struck by the depth of feeling the man had, a depth etched now over each of his rugged features. "You must have been...disappointed.''

He nodded, leaving it at that. "Anyway,'' he resumed with a sigh, "things went well, and here I am. Oh, there were setbacks here and there, but for every step backward there have been two forward. I can't complain.''

Nodding, she studied the brightly blazing fire. "It sounds as though you've got a very satisfactory life.'' For the first time since he'd found her outside, she recalled her own frustration. In that instant she felt an irrational twinge of jealousy spiked with the self-pity she'd bordered on earlier.

Had he been truly caught up in his tale, Doug might have missed the shadow of bitterness Sasha was unable to hide. But he was looking at her, studying her delicate features, attuned to the moment when her jaw hardened so slightly, when her lips grew faintly tight. He hadn't been truly caught up in his tale because there had been a purpose in the telling. He'd wanted her to know about him, though he'd been miserly with every such bit of information in the past. He wanted her to hear him, to trust him, to open to him.

"Professionally I'm satisfied," he offered invitingly.

Sasha bit. She'd been curious since the day she'd met him. If he was talking about himself, there was far more she wanted to know. "And personally?"

He shrugged. "Personally…leaves something to be desired."

What had Janine said, that he had the reputation for being a tough ladies' man? "Come on, Doug," she chided. "Don't tell me you haven't had your share of fun."

"Fun is one thing, but even then there are different kinds of fun. There's the fun you have when you're eighteen and experimenting, the fun you have when you're twenty-eight and rather high on your own success. By the time you reach thirty-eight," where he was, "fun is a little more elusive." This wasn't quite the direction he'd anticipated the conversation to take, but he was helpless to stop the flow of his words. Suddenly he wanted Sasha to know where he stood, what he needed, what he wanted. Suddenly *he* wanted to know.

Sasha eyed him doubtfully. "The women are still there."

"Oh, yes," he admitted grimly. "Eager and empty."

"Empty? I can't believe that."

"For me, at any rate." His silver gaze caught hers

on a thread of intensity. "Which was one of the reasons I left New York. I've just about had it with making small talk, with abiding by jokes that aren't funny, with being bored. And with being judged, above all, a 'good catch.'" His snarling of the words waxed eloquent on his legitimate disdain. "I even had a paternity suit slapped on me last year." At her look of surprise he went on, though his gaze grew distant, his voice hard. "Oh, I wasn't the father, as the courts easily decided. But the ugliness of it all churns my stomach to this day. To use a poor child…" He made an angry gesture with his hand. "It left me with a pretty lousy taste in my mouth."

Pausing for a breath, he refocused on Sasha. "I want something more. Something deeper and longer lasting." His voice lowered with menacing calm. "I want a future with a woman who's as intriguing as she is adoring. I want someone who will be impeccably loyal and infinitely understanding. I want a home. And I want kids." He made a disparaging sound and shifted the force of his gaze to the window and the bleak darkness beyond. "My…friend in New York just got herself in trouble, then tried to capitalize on her mistake. Most women today, though, are either more concerned with their careers or their waistlines to figure children into the bargain." He looked back at Sasha, his message clear. "But I was an only child and I want kids. Three, maybe four or five." He took a breath then, egged on by the look of astonishment on her face. His voice gentled and he bid his muscles relax. "Didn't you ever want kids?"

It took Sasha a minute to register his question, so swept up had she been in the force of his declaration. This wasn't the man she'd expected to find in *the*

Douglas Donohue. Was he putting her on? Could he be, given the undercurrent of vulnerability she sensed in his every word?

"Hmm?"

"Children. Have you ever wanted them?"

Had she ever wanted them? Her breath caught in her throat and she swallowed the knot that had formed there. Pushing herself from her chair, she crossed to stand before the fire, then knelt, seeking its heat to combat the sudden chill that stormed her insides.

"I wanted them," she said in a very small voice, her thoughts drifting back to those days so long ago. "I almost had one, too."

The fire chose that moment to spark, its loud crackle covering Doug's approaching footsteps. When he squatted by her side, she was startled. "What happened?"

She stared at his face, all bronzed and intent with the firelight playing over its manly terrain. Sam had been handsome in his way, though there hadn't been a touch of softness in him. As though being soft was to be unmanly. Yet Doug was as manly as ever, even more so, with that glimmer of concern flaring from within.

Her lips were dry and she moistened them with her tongue, then looked down at the fire and let herself recall. "I lost it," she stated baldly. "Or rather, it died at birth. I was seven months pregnant." Her voice softened with remembered yearning, and she tipped her head and turned pleading eyes to Doug. "I wanted that baby. Oh, how I wanted a baby to love. It was a boy. A little boy." She gasped for air. "When you have a miscarriage early on, you never know. But I knew. It was a boy. A beautifully formed boy—" her brows met and she struggled, as she had so many times in those days, to understand the justice of it all "—who was strangled by the umbilical cord when his mother didn't know what to do."

Doug raised a hand to lightly touch the hollow of her cheek. Though the fire burned hot before her, the chill within her seemed to have taken possession. "My God, Sasha. You can't actually blame yourself. Surely the doctors—"

Pulling from his grasp, she stared blankly at the flames. "There weren't any doctors. It all happened so quickly. The baby wasn't due for ten weeks. He was so tiny and weak and I was nineteen and scared and at home all alone."

"Your husband—"

"Was out celebrating with his buddies. The harvest had been good that year." She snorted. "Fat lot of good it did me. Pregnant and all, I'd beat my tail helping him, then he wasn't there to help me. He wasn't there when I'd needed him. He was *never* there when I needed him."

"But your parents—"

"It was too late," she said stonily. "By the time I could get to a phone, it was too late." Her voice sank to a whisper. "I couldn't help him. God, I tried, but I didn't know what to do."

Before she could resist, Doug shifted until he was behind her on the stone before the fire, his thighs on either side of hers, his arms drawing her back against his solid frame. Her limbs were stiff and unyielding, but he persisted, fitting himself to her taut form, wrapping his arms around her middle as though to protect the child she'd lost so long ago.

"It wasn't your fault, Sasha. Things like that happen."

Her hair slid against his sweater as she shook her head. "Not where I came from, they didn't. Births weren't complicated. You had your baby and, bam, went back to work. I was a grand disappointment to them even in that."

"Then that was *their* problem," he said, feeling anger that anyone should be so unfeeling, particularly toward Sasha, who deserved so much more. "And you're just as well without them."

She sucked in a breath and tried to control herself, but her emotions were strung tight, too tight, and snapped. "But now she's sick, and I don't know what to do!" Her wail was an anguished one and her eyes flooded anew.

They'd come full circle. Doug realized that in her own way and time, and, he was sure, quite without intending it, Sasha had answered the question he'd first asked when he'd found her outside in the cold. "What happened, Sasha?" he asked gently. "What happened today?"

Taking a staggered breath, Sasha spilled her heart out of sheer necessity. "My sister called to tell me that my mother's sick. She's got a tumor. They're operating on Monday."

"Do you want to go to her?"

"Yes. No! I can't!"

"Why not?" he asked in that same gentle tone.

"I just can't!" Unconsciously she clutched Doug's hands as they crossed her stomach. "There's so much anger and hurt and I haven't been there in so long, and the last thing I want to do is to see her lying all pale and weak in some hospital bed."

"You do love her."

"She's my mother!" Her voice broke into a pitiful moan. "And it hurts...."

"I know, babe," he crooned, rocking her gently, wishing only to relieve her of some of the pain. "And it'll be all right."

"But how? If she dies..."

"What did your sister say? Is it as serious as that?"

Sasha sniffled and blotted her cheek with the back of her hand. "No. Not yet. Maybe not at all."

"So there. Then it's not that bad."

"But the issue's still there. And if it's not today or tomorrow that I have to face it, it'll be next week or next month or next year or the year after that." Running short of breath, she gasped, then quieted, sagging back against him in despair. "Don't you see? I've avoided the whole thing for years. I want to go on avoiding it. But can I? If it's not my mother, it'll be my father. I don't know...I don't know if I have the strength to face them."

"You, Sasha, have the strength. I do believe you've got the strength to do anything you want. Hell, look what you've done—starting from scratch, all alone, building a career and a home. If that's not strength, I don't know what is. There must be millions of women out there who stand in awe of you."

She snorted. "The grass is always greener..."

"Life is never perfect," he argued softly. His breath warmed her temple, stirring her bangs ever so slightly. "It's a question of finding the best compromise."

"I don't want to compromise!" she cried bluntly. "I want it all. I want peace and happiness, love and success and respect."

"Perhaps that's fiction though. An ideal. It may be

fine to write about, but—hey, wait a minute!'' Sasha
had wrenched herself from his hold and was on her
feet, fleeing to the other room. "Sasha!" He took off
after her, nearly running head-on into the swinging
door to the kitchen as it closed in her wake. Pushing
it angrily, he forged ahead. "Listen, Sasha, I wasn't
criticizing." She sat huddled in a chair by the window,
her defeated form a wrenching sight. Crossing the
room, he knelt by her side. "I can understand those
ideals. Don't you think I haven't wrestled with them
myself? And I'm not saying that I've given up. Hell,
I want all those things, too. Wasn't I the one who
presented some pretty firm demands just a few minutes
ago? It's just that, well, to be miserable because one
or another of them elude us…" His voice trailed off
as he gazed into her face. Her cheeks were moist, her
eyes downcast. "I read your book," he coaxed softly.

For a minute he feared she'd say something smart
and bound up and away from him again. But she sat
very still. Then her eyes flickered, not quite meeting
his but signifying that she'd heard.

"You did?" she asked timidly.

"Cover to cover. It was wonderful."

She scowled and darted him a brief, skeptical
glance. "You're just saying that."

"Would I do something like that?" He frowned in
puzzlement, then thought aloud. "Actually, I might
have…before. If it suited my purposes, I'd have been
patronizing as hell." But he raised his eyes to hers
with a candor she couldn't doubt. "I'm not being patronizing now. I could very easily have said something
bland about understanding why women like your
books. But I said it was wonderful, and I meant it. Not
only was it well written, but the characters were real

and thoughtfully drawn, and the intrigue was a very potent thread. But the emotions, those were the key. And as for the idealism of love, well, to tell you the truth, I was envious as hell of your hero. To have found a woman like that, a woman who trusted him with her life, who adored him, who believed that her future would be nothing without him…''

Very slowly, the warmth that had eluded Sasha began to seep into her being. The need in Doug's eyes was a tangible thing, reaching out, aching. Patronization? Not possible. Could it be he truly understood?

Deeply touched and unable to express it in words, she reached out to brush his cheek. It was warm and glowing, its beard-shadowed roughness a heady contrast to the softness of her hand. In that instant she felt closer to him than she had to anyone in her life. Her eyes must have mirrored the feeling, for he smiled then, an endearingly vulnerable smile. When his long fingers closed around the back of her neck and he drew her head forward, she didn't resist.

He kissed her gently, expressing the overwhelming reaction she inspired in him. His lips sucked hers and his tongue filled her mouth, all with that same exquisite care, that same tenderness that had been so lacking in her life until now. For the first time she responded in kind, offering her moist warmth by way of a thank-you for his understanding. To her astonishment, the pleasure she felt in the giving returned the thank-you tenfold. And stirred a desire that shocked her. She suddenly wanted to run her fingers through his hair, to explore the strength of his shoulders, to feel the warmth of his flesh beneath his sweater, beneath his shirt.

When he drew back, she was disappointed, but the

huskiness of his voice suggested that she hadn't been the only one stirred. "I think maybe," he cleared his throat, "that we ought to get something to eat." He slapped her leg in a gesture of nonchalance that didn't quite go over. "Come on. Let's go out."

"Oh, Doug," she whispered, reeling still from the power of his kiss. Then she brought her hands to her tear-ravaged face. "I don't know. I'd be a sight to take into a public place. I look awful!"

"You look beautiful," he said, and meant every word. She looked soft and vulnerable and very much in need of him. He liked that.

"Why don't I just make something here? I've got some steaks in the freezer. And some potatoes and salad makings."

"But that's a lot of work."

"I don't mind." The thought of cooking for him somehow appealed to her.

He reflected on her evident enthusiasm, then cast her a sheepish glance. "A home-cooked meal. Pretty tempting."

"And I'd do it all," she coaxed, recalling the morning he'd waited on her. It was her turn. And she was eager.

"You would?" he asked with a little boy smile. "I could just sit back with my legs up and watch?"

She met his smile with a soft one of her own. "If you wanted."

He stood quickly. "You're on, woman." Then he stretched lazily, looking all the more massive and appealing. "I could stand a little pampering. This living alone bit is harder than I imagined."

Feeling strangely in her element and suddenly more sure of herself, Sasha stood and bodily ushered Doug back to the living room. "Sit," she commanded, then relented momentarily. "Would you, uh, would you like some music or the newspaper or something?"

"Music would be fine. Something quiet and appropriate for daydreaming in front of the fire."

In light of their talk of ideals, he could have said nothing to make Sasha more comfortable. With a lighthearted smile on her face, she flipped on the radio to her favorite FM station—always quiet and appropriate—and returned to the kitchen to make dinner. As the microwave defrosted the steaks, she made salad, then exchanged the steaks for potatoes and grilled the steaks on the Jenn-Air. As she set the dining-room table, with an occasional glance at a closed-eyed, thoroughly relaxed Doug, she marveled at how successfully he'd rescued her from the grip of so many troubling thoughts. Somehow they seemed more in perspective now. At least she was determined not to brood on them, not tonight, when she had more pleasant things to keep her busy.

Dinner was a resounding success, eaten in island elegance with two tapering candles and the bottle of wine she'd prevailed upon Doug to open. Stomachs replete, they sat before the fire finishing the wine, talking softly and of nothing at all in an utterly comforting way. Sasha felt more relaxed than she'd remembered feeling in far too long, and she didn't delude herself into thinking it was the full stomach or the wine or the music. It was Doug, sitting beside her in such undemanding, companionable fashion.

When, thanks to the early hours she'd risen to write and the tension that had taken its toll later in the day, her eyes grew heavy and her head nodded, she very happily curled against his shoulder and fell asleep. He woke her gently several hours later.

"Sasha?" he whispered, brushing a feather kiss to her cheek. "Babe, it's time to go up." Lingering in a half sleep, she cuddled closer.

"What time is it?" she murmured groggily.

"It's nearly one. I fell asleep myself, but if I don't get you to bed and get home, I'm not sure I'll ever make it." Slipping his arms beneath her, he lifted her carefully.

"The fire, Doug," she murmured, struggling to think straight. "Is it out?"

"Cold." He took the steps two at a time.

"And the...lights in my study? I think they're...still on."

"I'll check them before I leave." Only one door was open, very obviously her bedroom. He turned in to it, not bothering to flip on the light, guided by the slice of illumination from the hall to her bed. Freeing one arm, he flipped back the covers and laid her down on the sheets. Knowing he should simply kiss her good-night and leave her, but utterly incapable of such sanity, he began to undress her. He drew her sweater up over her head, then her turtleneck. The sight of her full breasts sheathed in delicate wisps of silk and lace made his hands tremble. But he steadfastly attacked the snap of her jeans, then the zipper, and turned to remove her sneakers, then tug the denim from her legs.

When he turned back, his eyes were drawn to hers, which were suddenly wide open and very much alert. She said nothing, simply stared at him, her gaze questioning his in the shadowed room. His heart hammered. He told himself to leave while he could, but her pale, slender length was too much of a lure.

Her name was a trembling hosanna on his lips, and somehow his hands found their way to her legs and slid up their smoothness, over her hips to her waist. Then, bracing himself on arms less than steady, he leaned toward her lips and worshiped them with small, pleading kisses until her mouth opened in helpless invitation.

He took all she offered, but ever gently, exploring her lips and their soft insides, tracing the even line of her teeth, sampling the deeper, darker warmth. He kept his ardor leashed, though the strain was huge. He simply couldn't get enough of her. He wanted to strip the wisps of silk from her body and feel naked flesh against him. He wanted to throw off his own clothes and bury himself in her. He wanted her body, her soul, her everything, but his greed frightened him as much as, instinctively, he knew it would frighten her. Things had happened so fast...so fast. But as he'd told her before, it was a matter of compromise. For now he would only kiss her and hope that the fire he kindled would bring her to him in time.

Sasha felt his lips on hers, so warm and sensuous, and her lashes fluttered down as she yielded to the sensation. There was a dreamlike quality to his lovemaking that made her weak and pliant in such a feminine sort of way that thought of anything real or practical had no hope for existence. She liked the gentle coaxing of his mouth, the tempting moisture of his tongue, so different, so tender, so new. A hunger grew within her and she opened to him happily. If this was what caring was about, she knew what she'd been missing.

Almost hesitant, as though fearful the dream would be shattered, she raised her arms to his shoulders, letting them rest on the sinewed swells. Then slowly, curiously she began to knead. When he deepened the kiss, she was with him, reveling in the way he filled her mouth with his breath, his tongue, his moistly erotic essence.

Her hands crept to his neck and wove through the thickness of his hair to hold him closer. She felt the tremor that passed through him and marveled that she might stir him so strongly. But it was only fair, she reasoned dizzily. Her own body felt suddenly alive and strong and needing something from his as it had never needed anything before.

And she wanted to touch. Bidden by a strength of their own, her hands fell to his waist and worked their way beneath his sweater, pushing it up, flattening over his shirt in frustration.

"Take off your sweater, Doug. I need...I need to touch you." Was that really her own voice, a whisper, true, but making demands nonetheless? Did she have the right to be forward? Sam would have punished her all the more for it, not that she'd ever ached to touch him as she did Doug. For a minute she wavered, fearing what Doug would do. When he leaned back and whisked the sweater over his head, she sat up and watched him tremulously.

Then he was back before her, his silver eyes glittering. "I need that too," he rasped, his tone and his gaze quelling her fear, the promise of his broad chest replacing fear with desire. Thinking only of satisfying the urge to touch him, she reached for the button of his shirt and, fingers stumbling but intent, she released it, then another and another.

For the first time his bare chest was before her. Even the dim light couldn't hide its utter perfection. Firm muscle corded his shoulders, then swelled even more before tapering to the leanness of his middle. His skin was firm, its dark pelt of hair an irresistible lure. She touched him and felt the echo of the shock that sizzled through him. He was warm beneath her fingertips, then strong as she opened her palms and began to move them up his vibrant torso with innocent expertise.

Doug moved closer, spreading his thighs to bring her kneeling form against him. He whispered her name, burying his lips in her hair, and his hands floated over her flesh as though he, too, were afraid she'd simply disappear in a cruel cloud of smoke.

"Sasha, Sasha," he murmured, eyes closed, body afire. When her hands brushed his nipples, a shaft of sweet pain shot to his loins. His own hands slid down her silken skin to the small of her back, and he arched his hips and pressed her closer.

Sasha couldn't believe the tension she felt. Where she'd thought to find satisfaction in finally touching his skin, the hunger only grew, feeding upon itself. For a fleeting instant she wondered if she was truly sex starved. But no, there had been men who'd made passes over the years and she'd felt neither curiosity nor desire. Geoff Briggs had fairly broadcast his eagerness, yet...nothing. Only Doug stirred her. Only Doug.

Driven by womanly instinct, she lowered her lips to his shoulder and tasted him, her tongue lapping gently, then sensuously. He was clean and fresh smelling with a tang of salt from the sheen of perspiration that had crept to his skin. It was an aphrodisiac to her untutored senses, sending her into a mind whirl of ecstasy from which only his shaky fingers on the thin straps of her bra brought relief.

She sat back then and met his gaze, aware of the race of her pulse, of the rapid rise and fall of her breasts. Speaking his need through his simmering gaze, he haltingly eased the straps from her shoulders. He had no way of knowing that his near-timidity inflamed her all the more. Her memories were of roughness. This tenderness was something new and wondrous.

The straps rasped softly against her arms in their downward glide. With their descent, the cups of her bra slowly lowered, baring her by inches to his lambent gaze. When the bra was at her waist, he lifted her arms free of the straps, then held her hands to the side as, swallowing hard, he stared at her. It wasn't the first time he'd seen her, though well it might have been for the raw electricity that charged his senses. Her breasts were full and aroused, their peaks taut and eager. The chill of the air was nothing compared to the heat engorging her.

Bolstering himself higher on his knees, Doug slipped his hands down her bare back and brought her forward until the fullness he'd feasted on was pressed to his chest. A low moan of elemental pleasure escaped his throat, and he closed his eyes to savor the sensation to the fullest. Had he never taken the time to enjoy a woman this way? Had he always been too greedy, too anxious to satisfy his own primal urge? But it was beautiful, this slow torment. And it was Sasha, Sasha who began to move against him, Sasha who held the key to this exquisite heaven.

When she raised her arms and coiled them tightly around his neck, he thrilled to the rise of her breasts against his chest. With his hands at her back, he gently shifted her body in a rhythmic way that rubbed her against him with excruciating sureness. He moaned again and murmured her name, then slowly eased her back to the sheets. Hands free, he placed them on the silky skin of her thighs, spreading them apart and lowering himself against her. Then, taking her hands in his and anchoring them by her shoulders, he took the taut nub of her nipple into his mouth and sucked hungrily. When she strained upward and moaned her delight, he began to move against her, slowly but inexorably telling what he needed, what he wanted.

Though brought from her haze by the blatancy of his thrusts, Sasha wasn't frightened. Rather, this time his tumescence aroused her all the more as it temporarily eased the ache she felt inside. His shirttails flared to the side as he adored her body. The heavy fabric of his jeans was abrasive against her in a most erotic way. She dug her fingers into his shoulders and arched, that he might have more of her.

And suddenly she wanted everything. If there would be pain, she wanted pain. If there would be fury, she wanted fury. She wanted Doug. She needed Doug. And she wanted to know, or she was sure she'd positively die with this agonizing need unsalved.

"Make love to me, Doug," she whispered roughly, rolling her head from side to side in torment. "Please, make love to me. I need you. I need to know. I need to forget. To forget everything." Her short bursts of speech were punctuated by a tortured moan when he went suddenly very still. The tension in his limbs was of a different sort now and it terrified her. Catching a ragged breath, she waited, half expecting him to erupt and take her with the callous force she'd known from Sam. He was a man, wasn't he? Could she have been so stupid as to expect anything else?

But he didn't erupt. He simply held himself still, then sagged to the side, his face on her stomach. She looked down, only vaguely registering her own knee bent near his outflung arm. He took several long staggering breaths before finally meeting her gaze.

Sasha was stunned. Never before had she seen such raw pain on a person's face. What had she done? God, *what had she done?*

"I didn't mean this to happen, Sasha," he began, his voice hoarse, his dark hair falling damply over his brow. "I swear to God, I didn't. I wanted to give you time. Time to get used to me, to get to know me. Things have happened so fast, maybe too fast. I wanted you to need me."

"But I do!" she cried, her throat tight.

"I want you to need *me*," he said more forcefully, then lowered his voice to a sorrowful murmur. "Not as an escape, Sasha. Not to wipe out whatever horrid memories you may have of the past. But *me*. I want you to want me, and me alone. That's what I meant by a burning, babe." Very slowly he pulled himself up and began to button his shirt while she watched, dumbstruck and incredulous. When he scooped his sweater from where it lay on the floor, he turned to her one last time. "I won't sell myself—or you— short, Sasha, or we've lost it all." Shoulders burdened by the weight of his ideal, he left Sasha in darkness to ponder what he'd said.

6

Sasha thought long and hard, frightened to believe, terrified not to. What kind of a man would leave her high and dry this way? A cad? A playboy? Or a man who cared, very deeply, that there should be something very special to their joining?

She'd been wild with passion, begging him on. Yet she knew neither embarrassment nor regret. For Doug had been fully aroused and in dire need himself, and had it not been for the depth of a certain ideal, he'd most certainly have taken her there and then.

But he'd wanted more than a simple roll in the hay. He wanted her to want him. Him, and only him. Did she? Oh, no, it wasn't a question of her wanting other men. But did she want him as an antidote to the venom lingering from Sam, or did she want him solely for the unique sustenance that was Doug, and Doug alone?

As her frustration wore off she thought back upon the evening. It had been unbelievably lovely, despite its inauspicious start. She'd enjoyed making dinner for Doug. When was the last time she'd cooked for a man? Strange, after Sam's unrelenting demands she'd sworn off her role as chief cook and bottle washer. But she'd enjoyed it with Doug, *for* Doug. And the quiet companionship they'd shared before the fire had been the nicest dessert possible.

When sleep finally came that night, it was deep and relaxing. She awoke in the morning filled with a strange sense of hope, and sat down to write with an abundance of words at her fingertips. If she was aware that the hero she'd created smacked strongly of one Doug Donohue, she ignored it. If she realized that she was imbuing her character with the most idealized form of the qualities she'd glimpsed in Doug, she chose to call it coincidence, or habit. Quite quickly she was falling in love with her hero, as was her heroine, and if things were moving far faster than normal, she simply called it poetic license.

Doug, on the other hand, couldn't work. He couldn't read. He couldn't sketch. He could do nothing but think of Sasha and how wonderful he felt by her side. When he was with her, he liked himself. Once before he'd thought it, and he'd more or less chalked it up to chance. Continually now, though, he was pleased, pleased with his patience and consideration, pleased with the kind of decent and devoted guy he was in her presence.

And he was pleased with her response. From the woman he'd first met who'd seemed wary of his slightest move, she was more confident, more comfortable. And passionate. He still couldn't believe how she'd writhed beneath him. He still couldn't believe how he'd stopped in the nick of time! He'd been prudent, if cruel, given the states of both their arousals. Hell, if a woman had dared do that to him he'd most probably have taken her by force. But Sasha wasn't him. In physical strength alone she'd have failed without his cooperation. He recalled her slenderness and experienced a surge of protectiveness. She was so small, so vulnerable. Had he gone ahead and made love to her, without doubt she'd have had regrets the morning after. He didn't want that. Thank heavens he'd pulled back. Twice, now. Incredible!

Also incredible, to himself as well as perhaps to her, was what he'd told her with such vehemence. But it was true. He wanted a home. He wanted kids. And he wanted a woman, to have and to hold. He wanted Sasha. It was as simple as that.

Now all he had to do was to convince her that she wanted him as much. Not only in bed, but forever. All he had to do was to work through that final barrier. True, the bricks were crumbling one by one as her story came out. He knew that neither her family nor her husband had understood her, that she'd felt unwanted and unloved. He knew that she'd lost a baby she'd desperately wanted in part because her husband hadn't been there, because no one had been there to help her. She'd been all alone. Perhaps, used to being alone now, she was frightened to commit herself to another person. Perhaps she feared that she'd be hurt again.

In a million years he could never hurt her. Had she been his wife expecting his child, he doubted he'd have left her alone at all. Hell, though she wasn't his wife and certainly wasn't pregnant with his child, he still had trouble leaving her! With a snort of amusement, he glanced at the papers on his desk awaiting his attention. How to concentrate? How to earn a living with a woman such as Sasha Blake monopolizing his mind? Perhaps the years he'd spent in total devotion to the corporation had been well spent after all. The company was a strong, going concern, with a staff carefully chosen and perfectly capable. They could do with only his halfhearted attention for a bit. What the hell—they wouldn't have any choice!

And his time? It would be spent dreaming dreams of Sasha, planning the hours they'd spend together, plotting the best way to reach her. He had his direction for the first time in months. With the vision of a future without her strangely bleak, he had nothing to lose.

Thus determined, the first thing he did was to go into town, ball out the librarian for not carrying Sasha's books, then march to the nearest bookstore and buy a copy of each of those that were in stock. He wanted to know everything about her, and her books spoke volumes. Having already read *Raven's Revenge*, he managed to pick up *Midnight Rogue* and *Demon Woods*, then had special orders placed for *Autumn Ambush* and *Devil Dreams*. Returning to his house, he sat down with *Demon Woods*, from which he stirred only to call Sasha at midafternoon.

"Hi, babe," he said in soft response to her voice. "How's it going?"

"Not bad," she acknowledged with enthusiasm. "I've written fifteen pages already."

"Is that good?"

"You bet. Some days it's a struggle to eke out four or five. Fifteen, just rolling off my fingertips...." She gave a self-satisfied grin. "It's good."

"I'm glad. Wanna take a break?"

Did she ever! And with Doug? But...maybe she shouldn't. Temptation was a potentially dangerous thing. "I'd love to, Doug. But I don't know. The juices are flowing. Maybe I shouldn't trust fate and run out just yet. They may be all dried up by the time I get back." There were creative juices and there were creative juices. The type she had in mind at that mo-

ment had little do do with writing and everything to
do with Doug. The vivid memory of what she'd felt
in his arms was slightly overwhelming in the light of
day. She needed a little time to adjust.

"But you'll have to stop some time," he reasoned.

"I will."

"When?"

"It's...hard to tell." She looked from her computer
screen to the clock, which read nearly three-thirty,
then back to her screen, as though to convince herself
that her hesitancy was indeed work induced.

"By dinnertime?"

"Probably."

"Want to go into town for something light? Really
fast. Just an hour or so. Then you can get back to
work."

If there had been sign of his resenting her work,
Sasha would have heard it. She was looking. Oh, she
was looking. Over the years, as her career had taken
hold, she had wondered how any man might want to
share his wife with a career such as hers. Not that
she'd ever consider remarrying, for she truly hadn't.
But in theory she wondered. Her work took such time
and energy. A man would surely never stand for that.

Doug, however, seemed to be standing for it. She
was amazed. "You—you really wouldn't mind something quick like that?"

"Well," he drawled, "I'd prefer more time, but if
it's an hour or nothing, I'll take what I can get."

She hesitated only a minute longer before smiling.
"You're on."

"About six-thirty?"

"Fine. See you then."

She hung up the phone still wearing a smile, feeling

lighthearted and warm all over. She cast a glance at her computer screen, grinned smugly, then saved what she'd written and turned the machine off. In the kitchen she made a fresh cup of tea, sat with her legs up on a chair and sipped it slowly, thoughtfully.

She wanted a bath, but first there was something she had to do. Returning to her study, she extracted a piece of her personal stationery and began to write. The pen moved slowly. She wondered if she'd simply gotten so used to the word processor that her thoughts didn't come as well this way, then she caught herself and put the blame where it belonged. She just wasn't sure what to say. Sorry to hear you're ill? Get better soon? An apple a day...?

She spent a good long time at the task, writing and crossing out, then finally copying the finished product over from scratch. But in the end she was pleased...well, relatively so. Addressing the envelope, she put a stamp on it and set it by her purse, to be dropped in the mail while she was in town.

She took a bath then, long and hot and relaxing, and finally dressed in a pair of clean jeans, a bulky turtleneck sweater and boots, and hoped that she'd look as though she'd just come from work. Her cheeks were flushed. The ends of her hair were damp from the steam. She used no more than a touch of makeup around her eyes. With a final look in the mirror, she headed downstairs and edited what she'd written that day until Doug arrived.

They ate in Oak Bluffs at a small fish place overlooking the harbor. The food, though fresh and good, was incidental to the company. At Sasha's urging, Doug talked about his work, about plans for upcoming shows, about expansion into foreign countries. At

Doug's urging, Sasha talked about her work, about her characters, about the friends she'd made in the field, even about the exciting news Diane had given her the day before.

"A TV movie? Sasha, that's great!" The genuine nature of his enthusiasm was a relief to Sasha, who had half feared he might resent her success. Many another man would, she knew, and she had memories to prove it. More than once in New York she'd been the subject of snide remarks, and though she hadn't cared a whit about the men making them, she'd been stung.

"It's really nothing," she said quickly, looking down to find her hand in Doug's, which echoed the warmth of his tone. "I mean, it may not amount to anything."

"But to be considered…!"

She laughed shyly. "That's what I told Diane. I was pretty excited myself."

"I should think so!" As a new thought struck, his expression sobered some. "If it does go through, will you have to supervise things? To leave here?"

"Not if I can help it," she vowed. "I may write the books, but I don't know the first thing about script writing. I'd leave that to the experts, though I guess I would have some say in the final product. But that can all be done by mail. I won't go on location. As it is, Diane says that M.P.I. wants me to tour when they re-release *Devil Dreams* and *Autumn Ambush*." She scowled. "I hate those things."

"They're not that bad," Doug chided gently.

"You can have them." Even as she said the words, she realized that he did. "Don't you do a certain amount of traveling, celebrity status and all?" He was the handsome fashion designer. Though she wasn't a television watcher herself, she was sure he'd gone the talk-show route.

"I've done it."

"And liked it?" If she was subconsciously looking for a source of incompatibility between them, it was to be soundly dismissed by his reply.

"No. I've never liked them. But—" his fingers began a slow caress of hers "—if I had someone with me, someone special, the whole thing could take on a different light. Like a second honeymoon, or a third or fourth." His eyes glittered, their silvery beams ricocheting into Sasha. "You have to admit that for people like you and me who had none of the advantages growing up, traveling has its excitement."

She grew thoughtful, lulled by the gentle stroking of his thumb against hers. "I thought it would. And I suppose it did at first. Then it…it lost its glamour."

"But *with* someone…?"

For a split second, her eyes held captive by the smoldering in his, she let herself imagine what it would be like to tour the country, even travel abroad, with Doug by her side. A second honeymoon, a third or fourth? It sounded…nice. Without realizing what she was doing, she moved her fingers to hold his tighter. They were firm and strong and warm, just right to give her a boost when she was tired or lonely. Quite helplessly, a tiny smile emerged to match the softness of her voice. "Yes. That would be different."

Without releasing her gaze, Doug brought her hand to his mouth and whispered a soft kiss against her knuckles. "I think we could both survive it," he murmured thickly. "Late-night dinners, breakfast in bed." Uncurling her fingers he sucked on her pinky and was rewarded by the burst of flame in her gaze.

Sasha held her breath. Breakfast in bed...breakfast in bed after a night of... She wanted it, she didn't, though her senses flared wildly even at the simple gesture he made next. It was highly erotic, the movement of his cat's tongue up and down her pinky. She felt drawn in, ready to drown and quite happily so, but...

"Please, don't," she whispered, unable to fathom the power of what she felt.

Sensing her sudden bewilderment, Doug removed her finger from his mouth and enclosed her hand in the cocoon of his fists. "Why not?" he murmured a trifle tautly.

"It's...it's too much."

"Too fast?"

She nodded.

His hands tightened around hers and, eyes closed, he bowed his head against them. He stayed that way for several minutes during which Sasha agonized at her response. She wanted to please him, more than she'd ever thought to please a man. She wanted to give to him, and she'd tried. But he'd turned her down, and he'd been right. Given what he'd told her, Doug deserved to have only the best. And the fullest. Yet at moments like this, in a place that could not help but remind her of what she'd made of herself and how far she'd come, she was still...frightened. Too much, too fast.

Eyes pleading for his understanding, she waited for him to look up. He didn't at first, simply spoke with his eyes shut, his brow creased as though he was in pain. "I know, I know," he muttered, trying to convince himself as he spoke. "It's scary, after all these years, to find someone...and feel so much...so fast." Then he opened his eyes with a look of dire determination and spoke through gritted teeth. "But it's right, Sasha. I know it is. We'll be good together in every way. One day you'll see that yourself. I'm not giving up. I can wait."

Stunned by his vehemence, Sasha needed a moment to recover. He was talking about a future together. A *real* future together, not simply some whimsical imagining. But she'd signed on once before for a future with a man, and it had been a disaster.

"Good together?" she echoed shakily. "You look like you want to throttle me."

Her accusation brought a slow relaxation to his features. He lowered her hand to the table, though he didn't release it, and the far corner of his lip quirked. "Throttle you for sitting there turning me on, throttle me for being so susceptible and disgustingly noble—how could I choose?" His voice became a sensual drawl and he leaned intimately forward. "Throttle you? Oh, no, my lady. What I'd *like* to do is—"

"Doug!" she pleaded, fully serious.

So was he. In point of fact he was tired of being noble. He wanted to spend the night with Sasha, to make love to her until she nearly died of the pleasure and then named him her bona fide savior. And that day would come. He'd make it come, by hook or by crook. "What I'd *like* to do," he resumed, but forced a more casual smile, "is to be like Sean."

"Sean?"

"You know. Sean—in *Demon Woods?*"

She went beet red. Of course she knew Sean. She'd created him. Yet he'd been the last man on her mind at the moment. "How did you know about Sean?" she asked guardedly.

"I'm more than halfway through the book."

"Do-ug," she drew his name to two syllables in protest, "wasn't one enough?"

"You're embarrassed. Why, Sasha?"

"Because...I don't know, because..."

"Because there's so much of you in those books? But I know that, babe. I discovered that early on in *Raven's Revenge. Demon Woods* is very different in its way, but the same depth of feeling is there. Sean is a saint. And it seems he's well on his way to satisfying Nicole's needs."

"You've read the love scenes," Sasha intoned sternly. "Douglas Donohue, don't tell me you're one of those who skims around looking for sex?"

He beamed. "Skims around looking for sex? Hardly the phrase I'd have used, and not at all appropriate when you consider my recent self-restraint—"

"In *books*," she scolded. "In *books*."

He took pity on her discomfort. "No, I don't skim the pages for hot spots, but I have reached that first big love scene in *Demon Woods*. It's quite something. Strong. Highly passionate. But tender. And very emotional...."

Sasha shot him a challenging stare, only to find the most gentle expression on his face. In that instant she believed him; he did envy Sean. And he obviously wanted Sasha to be his Nicole.

Suddenly they were back where they'd been moments before, eyes locked, air sizzling. Sasha felt Doug's pull far beyond the physical. The need in his eyes spoke of an even deeper commitment, one she was no more ready for than the other. But she'd barely opened her mouth to protest when Doug gave a sigh of resignation and spoke.

"Anyway, I think the book is every bit as powerful

as *Raven's Revenge.* When Nicole found that snake draped around the hanger in her closet...." He gave Sasha a pointed stare and asked, "Where *do* you get your ideas?"

She smiled and shrugged. "Sometimes from the newspapers. They often report weird things like that. Sometimes from other books or television. Mostly, I guess, from imagination." She cleared her throat. "Mine is fertile."

"Why the grimace? You've certainly managed to channel it along very productive lines."

"I suppose," she began thoughtfully. "Unfortunately I sometimes get carried away with it. I begin to imagine things like that really happening."

"Really happening to *you?*" His brow furrowed. "What do you mean?"

When Sasha realized what she was about to say, it occurred to her to quickly laugh and pass it all off. Doug was apt to think her positively paranoid. On the other hand, she half wanted to air her fear, to share it, to be told how foolish it was.

"I mean," she spoke hesitantly, keeping her voice low, looking up to make sure the waitress wasn't around, "that there are times when little things happen to me and I begin to imagine that it's not all by chance." She blushed. "It's really awful." She crinkled her nose. "And silly. I guess I'm so used to writing scary things into my books that I grow suspicious of very innocent occurrences."

"Things like what?" Doug asked quietly.

Sasha looked down at her plate and pushed crumbs around with her fork. "Like things out of place in my house. Like barrels rolling from a rooftop. Like the accident with my Suzuki." She forced a chuckle and sheepishly met Doug's gaze. "I even got stuck in the gardener's shed a month or so back. The door hinge jammed. For a minute I couldn't get out."

"What happened?" Doug asked, eyes wide.

"I panicked and hit the door with what had to have been either superhuman strength or sheer luck. It opened."

He let out a breath. "But you wondered, in that minute, whether someone was trying to trap you?"

She nodded and laughed. "Silly, isn't it? That's what I mean by a fertile imagination. It can work for me...or agin' me."

Doug didn't laugh. "Yeah, and when it's agin' you, you're probably miserable. I hope you're not worried now."

"Right now? Of course not. I'm with you." What had emerged on impulse made a very special statement. Doug acknowledged it with a warm smile.

"Maybe you're getting there after all," he mused softly, then tossed his head in the direction of the door. "Come on. Let's get out of here." He left money enough for their food and a tip on the table, then ushered Sasha to the door, throwing his arm around her shoulders when the dark of night enveloped them. "I hope you know that if you're ever frightened you're to call."

"It's only my imagination. Vivid and bothersome."

"But still. Call. Do you hear me, Alexandra Blake?"

She returned a mocking, "I hear you, Douglas Donohue."

He reached into the inner pocket of his jacket and took out Sasha's letter. "Now, let's walk over to the post office to mail this, then I'll get you home. Okay?''

"Okay." Though Sasha was sure he'd have to have seen its address, Doug had been tactful enough not to ask questions about the letter she'd written to her mother. And she was grateful. She was still in a turmoil on that particular issue. Though she felt better for having written it, the letter had been little more than a stopgap measure. For the moment, though, she was simply unable to do more.

Presumably as a consequence of their discussion of vivid imaginings, Doug brought Sasha into the house, turned on the lights and saw that everything was well before he turned to leave. Sasha found comfort in his consideration.

"I'm fine," she laughed after he'd asked a third time. "And as soon as you leave I'll double-latch the door. Have I warped your imagination too?"

"Oh, yes," he drawled, reaching out to take her into his arms. "My imagination has worked overtime since the day you ran into me in the rain." He frowned and studied each of her features as though trying to understand it himself. "Hard to believe it was less than two weeks ago. I feel as though I've known you far longer."

So did she. His long lean body had a familiar feel now. But, she chided silently, that was beside the point. "You're stealing the lines from my books, Doug Donohue!"

"Am I? Naw, I've never read that one in yours."

She thought for a moment, cocking her head to the side. "Come to think of it, you're right. That line was from *Devil Dreams*. Humph! Maybe you're just catching it from me."

"Catching what?"

"Romanticitis," she announced with a sly half grin. Doug's arms were coiled around her waist. Her hands settled easily over his shoulders. She felt comfortable and secure with his compelling presence towering above her, with his bronzed skin aglow and his silver eyes brilliant.

"Is it serious?" he asked, suppressing a grin.

"Sometimes."

"Painful?"

"On occasion."

"Terminal?"

"Only once in a great while, as in Romeo and Juliet."

"I see," he said with an exaggerated nod. "Then there is hope?"

All pretense gone, she returned his soulful gaze. All along she'd known they were talking about themselves and the ailment that had seized them by storm, rather than some fictitious illness. Doug's final question brought it all home.

"I think so," she whispered.

"I know so," he said moments before he kissed her. What started as a gentle brushing of lips, though, quickly evolved into something far more heated. Doug hadn't intended it, any more than had Sasha, but the need had been building all through dinner and could be denied no longer. Their kiss was thorough and soul shaking, leaving them both breathless when Doug finally disengaged his lips.

He moaned thickly and his long limbs quivered. "Oh, God, I'd better leave or I won't be responsible for my actions. Call you tomorrow?"

Unable to speak, she nodded, watched him walk to

his car, then put a hand to her lips as though to pre-
serve the heat of him. But when the Maserati disappeared from view, she felt chilled. Closing the door,
she double-latched it as promised, then returned to her
study to finish editing what she'd written that day.

She was good for all of ten minutes. Suddenly she
wanted simply to be in bed, buried beneath her heavy
down quilt, dreaming. It had been a long day in so
many respects. She was exhausted. And the sooner
tomorrow came...

Sasha was still thinking of Doug when she awoke
at five the next morning. She brushed her teeth and
threw cool water on her face, then made a fresh pot
of coffee and nestled in her study to work. The love
scene she proceeded to write was as steamy as any
she'd ever composed. She half expected to shock her
computer, but it took it quite gamefully, with nary a
curl of smoke. She, on the other hand, was trembling
from head to foot when she sat back to reread what
she'd written.

Her hero and heroine, boat designer and artist re-
spectively, were very definitely in love. It had happened so quickly as to stun them both, and Sasha, too,
for that matter. Usually she spent far longer building
her love story, weaving the web of love and intrigue
slowly and carefully around her characters, establish-
ing side characters and subplots. This book was different, more simple in some respects, but unbelievably
intense. She had a hero and heroine who had been
attracted to one another from the start. Their relationship, growing from acquaintance to friend to lover
stage, had dominated these first eighty pages, leaving
neither room nor energy for awareness of other people,
other happenings. Theirs was a pervasive, all-

encompassing attraction that had grown and grown until its only proper outlet was in lovemaking.

Sitting back in her easy chair in the corner to the left of her desk, Sasha reflected on the cataclysmic scene she'd written. From page one it had been inevitable. The hero and heroine had been fascinated with each other, intrigued, aroused. Neither of them had ever experienced such instant and overwhelming attraction before, and it had been only the force of it all that had, ironically, held them off so long. But it had to be. The craving of their bodies went hand in hand with a mental craving that cried out for fulfillment— a oneness that, when it came, was devastatingly joyous and incredibly electrifying. It was a true merging of bodies and souls, a mind-altering experience, taking man and woman and producing far more than simply the sum of their parts. It was, quite breathlessly, magnificent.

Sasha closed her eyes and took a long breath. Her body tingled. It was Doug's face she saw. Her hero? She wondered. If only she could be a fly upon the wall of the heavens, looking down at the plot outline of her life as she looked down now at the outline of her book. What was in store for Doug and her? Would they be going through a trial by fire, as her hero and heroine would be soon?

For not everything was rosy in her book. While her hero and heroine had been totally engrossed in each other, a sinister force, unbeknown to them, had arrived on the scene. The archrival of the hero, his one-time mentor, a man now half-demented by dreams unfulfilled, was in residence, convinced in his warped mind that the hero's latest design was a copy of one of his own, stolen quite unconscionably years before, only

now put into construction and tested. How to get back
at the hero for stealing one's true love? It seemed obvious. Tit for tat.

Sasha shivered as she pictured the villain. He was
a large burly man with a full beard, one eye that
tended to wander, and a perpetual scowl. He reminded
Sasha of the man who'd glowered at her when she'd
been with Doug in Edgartown the past Sunday. Perhaps she'd even modeled him after that one. He'd
seemed angry, his beard unable to hide the rigid line
of his jaw, his eyes hard, his chin set in a pose of
uncompromising resentment—the perfect villain, the
man with the long-standing grudge, the embodiment
of dementia.

Another shiver brought Sasha from her seat to stand
before the window and open the shutters. She'd been
working, totally absorbed, for nearly four hours. It was
almost nine-thirty. Looking out on the day for the first
time, she saw that it was raining, dark and gray. How
lovely—and meaningful—that she'd produced such a
beautifully strong love scene wrapped in her own private world on such a potentially gloomy day. Now that
the day was exposed, though, she couldn't escape
it...or, strangely, escape the more somber trail her
thoughts had taken moments before.

Before the next chapter ended, the heroine would
be earmarked as the villain's prey. Oh, there would be
nothing sudden, no instantly terrifying event. That
would be too fast for the villain, who, mindful of the
years he'd felt slighted, then betrayed, wished to build
the torment slowly and prolong it for both hero and
heroine.

Sasha tugged her shawl more snugly around her
shoulders. Could it really happen? Could a person set

out to slowly and steadily terrify another? *Could,* of course. But *would?* What kind of perverted mind would want to hurt Sasha. And *why? Had she ever hurt someone that badly? Who?*

For all her skill, she couldn't begin to imagine who might be after her. Certainly no one related to Doug. Weird things had started happening to her well before she'd met him. Coincidence? So she'd tried to convince herself. But it was getting tougher and tougher with each little occurrence, because there was a pattern. Whoever was after her had read her books. Either that, or she was a seer herself.

On that very interesting possibility she stepped away from the window and padded to her desk. If it was true that what she wrote could come true, would it also hold that if she wrote what she wanted the future to hold, it would? So much of what she felt for Doug was embodied in her heroine's heart. Doug Donohue, in even the short time she'd known him, had aroused thoughts and cravings she'd honestly given up on in real life. At this moment she realized that she desperately wanted Doug to be her hero, to be there for her always. But the question remained as to whether he would be. Fiction or reality—was she asking too much?

The lights flickered. She looked up and froze. In *Devil Dreams* the phone lines had been cut, the electricity had mysteriously gone off. She held her breath. But after that momentary wavering, the lights were steady. Just the wind or the rain whipping at exposed wires? Very possibly. Then again...

Shaking her head, she left her study, showered and dressed, then made herself some breakfast. Wandering through to the living room, she stared out the front window at the drive. It was empty, its gravel glistening beneath a steady patter of rain. It was a gloomy day, indeed. She wrapped her arms about her middle, then shot a glance behind her. The fire. She'd work in front of the fire for a while. That would warm her up.

After setting kindling atop the cold ashes on the grate, she reached for several logs, only to realize that her supply in the copper basket was low. She stood and crossed to the cellar door, flipped on the light and started down. She'd barely put her weight on the third step when the plank gave way. Had she not been holding the open rail, she would have fallen. As it was, she stumbled and twisted around, held from a fall by the reflexive grip of her fingers on the steadying wood.

It took her a minute to recover. Heart pounding, fingers relaxing their grip on the rail only when she was sure her seating was firm, she pressed her hands to her knees and took a long ragged breath. From where she sat more than halfway down the steps, she stared back up at the plank that had yielded. It lay innocently if lopsidedly atop the stair frame, very obviously relieved of the nails that should have held it in place. With a shaky hand she touched the wood, raised the plank, tipped it up. Then she dropped it as though burned and stood quickly.

This was no accident. Someone had been in her house. But when? Her nervous eye skimmed the dank cellar, but nothing else seemed out of place. There were storage cartons piled as always in one corner, the furnace and hot-water heater in another, the washer and dryer side by side against the concrete wall. Atop the latter lay the white cloth that Doug had pressed to her hand that day in the rain. She'd washed it; it was clean. Scrambling from the stairs, she grabbed it, then retraced her steps, cautiously lest there be another plank out of place, stepping gingerly over the one designed to trip her.

She had to get out of the house. No longer could she simply imagine that someone was after her. And there was no doubt in her mind as to where she wanted to go. A quick call to Maggie gave her the information she needed. Within minutes she was in her car, speeding over the rain-slick roads en route to Doug's.

Someone had been in her house. More than once? But she worked at home. She was there for most of her waking hours. Lately though, there had been times out with Doug. She recalled the book on the mantel that had been taken from its place, the alarm clock reset, the brush misplaced, the perfume stopper set aside—now her cellar stairs sabotaged. Tallying the signs, she realized that she had indeed been out of the house for a span of several hours before each of these small incidents. Someone was watching her, aware of her comings and goings. It was a terrifying thought and one from which she was still trembling when, as per Maggie's instructions, she turned off North Road, found the private driveway marked by a bright red mailbox, and approached Doug's house.

Only her periphery vision absorbed the ultramodern structure with its pervasive glass and its commanding ocean view. She just wanted to see Doug. Then she'd relax.

He was on his phone in the den, carrying on a heated discussion with his West Coast distributor, when the doorbell rang. His first impulse was to ignore it. The mailman would leave whatever he had at the door. When he realized that most probably his signature would be required for at least one of those pieces of mail, though, he relented.

"Damn it, Frazier, hold on. That's my doorbell." Frustration bade him slam the receiver onto the desk, irritation marked his step as he made for the door. His face was a mask of aggravation when he hauled it open, then his pulse careened when he found a startled Sasha Blake before him.

"Sasha!" She looked much as she had when he'd first seen her, when she and her motorcycle had run into him in the rain. Though only spattered with drops this time from her dash from the car, the same damp tendrils stuck to her cheeks, the same pallor dominated her skin, the same look of fright filled her eyes. "My God, Sasha, come on in." He reached for her and tugged her out of the rain, shut the door behind her, then stood for a moment staring at her, unable to believe she was here on his doorstep. Without thought, he brushed the wisps of hair from her cheeks and ran his fingers around the back of her neck while his gaze devoured her features one by one. Then, as he hadn't done that first day in the rain, he lowered his head and kissed her. He couldn't help but feel the tremor of her lips or the way she seemed suddenly to cling to him. When he raised his head once more, she sagged against him and breathed a great sigh of relief.

"Thank heavens you're home," she murmured against his shirt, taking courage from the solidness of his arms around her back. "I was so worried you'd be out and I needed to see you." Her voice sounded as weak as she felt. Doug set her back.

"What's wrong?"

"Oh, Doug..." Meeting his gaze, she let her voice trail off. He'd think her crazy. Absolutely crazy.

But...he hadn't that other time. He'd been concerned. Even now she could see that same worry in his eyes.

"What is it?" he whispered hoarsely.

"I'm—I'm—" She lowered her gaze and, in a moment's cowardice, reached into her pocket and drew out the white cloth. "I wanted to return this," she murmured, unable to look up.

Doug stared at the cloth. "You're not trembling over a stupid cloth, babe. What's wrong?"

She looked at him then, her eyes filled with trepidation. But she needed his comfort too much to hold back. "I'm—I'm scared, Doug."

"About what?"

"Something happened this morning. And I'm probably imagining it all, but I'm scared." The words came in a rush as her limbs began to shake. Doug took her into his arms and held her tightly for a minute. Then, an arm firmly about her shoulder, he held her beside him and began to walk.

"Come on." Returning to the den, he grabbed the phone with his free hand. "Frazier? I'll have to get back to you. There's an emergency here. You'll be in later? Fine." Without another word he hung up the phone.

"Oh, I'm sorry, Doug. I didn't mean to interrupt. This is really foolish of me—"

One long finger stilled her babble, touching her lips, sealing further apology within. "Nothing is foolish where you're concerned, Sasha. Didn't I tell you to call?"

"Didn't quite expect me at your door, though, did you?" His presence had taken the initial edge off her fear, allowing self-consciousness to peek through.

"How did you find me?"

"Maggie."

He nodded, then leaned back against the desk, brought her between his legs and hooked his hands at the small of her back. "Now, will you tell me what's wrong? Another...accident?"

She swallowed hard and nodded once. "Almost. I was going down to the cellar to get more logs for the fire and I nearly fell. One of the wooden treads had been unnailed. If I hadn't been holding on to the railing..." Her voice faded, replaced by the image of her toppling the length of the hard wooden steps.

Doug swore softly and hugged her to him. He pressed his cheek to her hair and drew reassuring circles on her back with his hands. "It's okay," he murmured, "you're safe here. It's okay." Perversely her body shook uncontrollably for several minutes, during many of which he repeated his whispers of comfort. It was only when Sasha began to relax that she noticed the corresponding tension in Doug. At that moment he set her back and looked at her hard.

"The cellar stairs? As in *Raven's Revenge?*"

She shrugged, momentarily embarrassed. "It's a common enough occurrence—"

"But one too many. Now, I want you to tell me everything that's happened. Everything. Do you hear me, Sasha?"

7

There was to be no compromising. Doug's stern expression stated as much. Not that Sasha wished it, for she desperately needed to air the extent of her fears. When she'd first broached them the night before at dinner, she'd simply tossed them out as examples of her overactive imagination. Now, though, they seemed totally legitimate.

"I'm not sure where to begin," she murmured.

Doug coaxed her softly, patiently. "How about the beginning. Tell me the very first thing that happened, and when."

She frowned, trying to think back. It was hard, since at the time she hadn't thought much of it. "I guess about five or six weeks ago. That was when I thought I was stuck in the gardener's shed. I mean, I got myself out quick enough, and it was a perfectly understandable thing. The shed is nearly as old as the house and not as well kept. Wood swells. Hinges rust."

"What next?"

"My lights have gone out once or twice." She tried to rationalize that too. "It happens a lot on the Vineyard. The wind blows, lines get tangled, conformers shake."

"Did anyone else lose their electricity at the time?"

"I'm not really sure. I didn't check. The lights came back on after five minutes or so."

"Was this during the day?"

She shook her head and shuddered. "At night. Always at night."

"Leaving you in the dark and afraid."

"I'm not that bad," she drawled. "I've got plenty of candles and flashlights. And, like I said, it didn't last long."

"You never called the light company?"

"No. Had the darkness persisted, I would have, I suppose. Once the lights came back on, though, it seemed unnecessary. I assumed they'd had plenty of calls and wouldn't need another one."

Doug sent her a punishing glare. "You may have been too thoughtful for your own good." He sighed. "Okay. What next?"

"I suppose the bike accident was next."

"But it was rainy. You skidded," he argued, playing the devil's advocate.

"That's what I told myself. And I'll never really know for sure."

"The bike's repaired, I take it." She nodded. "Did the repairman have anything to say?"

"I didn't ask. I may have simply skidded, for all I know. Then again it may have been—"

"—a tiny bullet piercing the tire."

Sasha looked at him in alarm. "I guess I *did* do something to your imagination."

"No," he stated baldly. "I'm just anticipating what I might read in one of your other books." When she continued to stare at him, he elaborated. "I've already finished *Raven's Revenge* and *Demon Woods*, and I'm three-quarters of the way through *Midnight Rogue*."

"You are?"

"Uh-huh." For the first time since she'd arrived, he

cracked the semblance of a smile. "Couldn't seem to
concentrate on much else after you left last night.
Couldn't seem to sleep, either. I read for most the
night." The smile, what there had been of it, faded.
"*Raven's Revenge* takes care of the cellar stairs, *Midnight Rogue* the barrels toppling off that roof in Edgartown and, if we exchange wine cellar for gardener's
shed, the incident there. Nothing from *Demon Woods*
yet, though."

"I hope not! That's the slimy one, with snakes and
muddy pits and wild wolves!" Her expression was one
of revulsion. She was trembling again.

When he smiled this time, it was with affection.
"How did you ever write that one if you have such
an aversion to creepy, crawly things?" He ran his fingers up and down her spine, though if he was trying
to scare her, he hadn't a chance in the world. His touch
never failed to affect her, but not in creepy, crawly
ways.

She wriggled in response and mustered a half grin.
"I had plenty of nightmares through that one. I think
it was my own terror that made the book."

"I doubt that," he growled, just imagining the
wealth of love held in that book too. Pushing himself
from the desk, he led her to a chair and sat her down,
then pulled a matching one closer and sank into it,
leaning forward, his hands clasped between his outspread thighs. "There's a definite pattern here. Anything else? What about things in your house being
misplaced. You mentioned that last night."

Sasha sat stiffly. "Do you remember that alarm
clock that rang at two in the morning? I may have
misset it by accident, then again I may not have. The
same night there was a book lying open on the mantel,

but I don't remember taking it out. After you left, I went upstairs and found my hairbrush in the middle of the bed and my perfume bottle left uncapped.'' She sighed and shrugged. ''In all fairness, I may have just been careless. But I'm not usually.''

''Which book?'' he asked pointedly.

''*Autumn Ambush.*''

''And the motorcycle?''

She averted her gaze. ''The same.''

For a long time Doug said nothing. When he finally broke the silence, it was in a voice taut and controlled. ''Have you called the police?''

Sasha's eyes shot to his face. ''No!''

''Why not?''

''Because this is absurd!''

''Is that why you came to me—because it's absurd?''

''I needed reassurance.''

''Because *you* believe it all.''

''I'm beginning to,'' she said meekly.

''Then why not the police? Surely if someone's on your trail—''

''The police are apt to think I'm daft! Either that, or they'll think it's a publicity stunt I've dreamed up!''

His silver gaze held hers steadily. ''But you've told me. And I don't think you're daft. Nor do I think you'd do anything for publicity, least of all this.''

''That's because you know me.''

''Thank you,'' he said a trifle stiffly, then reached for her hand and took it in his to counterbalance his tone with the warmth of his touch. ''But I do think we should call the police.''

''No,'' she declared firmly.

Not quite giving up, Doug took a different tack.

"Okay, then, who could it be? Who could possibly be out to hurt you?"

"That's the bizarre thing!" she cried. "I don't have the slightest idea! I mean, I'm not a cruel person. I haven't exactly raced through life leaving a trail of injured parties in my wake."

"People can be sick sometimes."

"Tell me," she quipped rigidly. "My present villain is a jealous maniac hell-bent on revenge for something he imagined happening."

Doug scowled. "Your present villain?"

"In the book I'm writing." She waved aside the divergence. "But I don't have any enemies. And I can't imagine who could possibly hate me that much."

"Think."

She did, studying her hand wrapped in his larger, stronger one, trying to concentrate on whom she might have clashed with on the Vineyard. Finally she sighed in bewilderment. "I suppose there are those people who may be annoyed with me."

"Such as?"

"Ruth Burke, the librarian who thinks I write trash, Hank Rossi, the auto mechanic I turn down every time he asks me out, Joseph Marovich, the postal clerk I pester—I mean the list can go on and on. There's old Willie Dunton who hates everyone. But this is ridiculous. I've never really argued with any of these people. And I've never been rude—"

"I know, babe. I know," he said kindly, squeezing her hand reassuringly. "But if we're dealing with a sick mind, you never know. Who else?"

"I suppose you'd have to add Geoff Briggs to the list. You heard *his* complaint."

"Yeah. I heard."

"But I can't go to the police, Doug. These are all decent people, despite what insignificant differences I may have with them."

Releasing her hand, Doug sat back thoughtfully and pressed his fist to his chin. "What about your ex-husband?"

"Sam? Oh, no! Sam would never do something like this!"

"You are divorced. That has to leave some kind of hard feeling. Maybe the guy's jealous of your success."

"Sam jealous? Hah! He's too wrapped up in his spuds to even notice," she sneered. "Besides, he would never take the time away from his work to come down here to haunt me. And whoever is doing this has to be nearby. The incidents are spread out pretty far time-wise."

"But getting closer," Doug suggested. "Most of those things have happened during the past ten days."

It would have been a sobering thought had not Sasha already been stone-sober. "I know," she whispered frantically. "I know."

"Then the police it'll have to be."

"No!" she exclaimed once again, then lowered her voice to a pleading murmur. "At least, not yet."

"You've got a better suggestion?"

If only she had. She shook her head in misery. Then she sprang from her chair and whirled in the direction of the door. "I shouldn't have come. I'm sorry."

Doug was behind her in an instant, grabbing her, drawing her back against him. He wrapped his arms around her and bent his head until his lips grazed her cheek. "Never say that again to me, Sasha. You did the right thing. I want you here." Very slowly, he turned her in his arms until she was facing him. "This is where you belong. With me. Don't you realize that yet?"

Suddenly the air changed and all thought of danger receded. In its place was the spark that had been there from the first. It was both sexual and emotional, binding them irrevocably closer. Looking up into Doug's eyes, Sasha knew then.

"I guess I'm beginning to," she whispered, timidly lifting her arms to his shoulders. "There had to be some reason why the only place I thought to run to was here."

"Then you admit that the cloth was a ploy?" he asked, his firm male lips curving crookedly.

She studied them and moved a finger to trace their strong lines. It felt right. Everything felt right just then—his hard, lean body against hers, the whipcord strength of his thighs, his enveloping arms. She felt safe and secure and warm and excited. She felt that strange knot of desire forming beyond the pit of her stomach. Oh, yes, everything felt right.

Standing on tiptoe, she replaced her fingers with her lips, tentatively at first, then, feeling Doug's welcome, with greater conviction. His arms tightened around her back, practically lifting her off her feet, and she knew she'd come home. This was what she wanted, this sense of needing and being needed, of cherishing and being cherished, for that was what came through his kiss. She was a woman, needing this man and only this man to make her life complete.

At his probing, her lips opened fully, but the hunger was mutual, a sparring for depth and possession. She trembled for more, arching her back, thrusting her fingers into his hair to hold him closer. She'd never imagined such wanting, such aching to be part of another person. And it was Doug who inspired it, only Doug.

The hands that had been holding her lowered her gently, then slid around her waist and rose to her breasts. She moaned into his mouth and felt herself swell, loving the moment he found her hard nipples through the layers of clothing, wanting more, always more.

Suddenly a thought intruded on her heaven, though, and with a strength born of pride she pushed herself back. "Oh, no, Doug Donohue!" she cried, staring at his stunned expression. "If you think you're going to do this to me again, you're the crazy one! Twice now you've taken me to near-forgetfulness and then left me unfulfilled." Her breasts rose and fell sharply with the raggedness of her breathing. "But I won't have it this time! Do you hear? I don't know what's happened to my life in the last two weeks, but you've turned it topsy-turvy! I thought I was satisfied! Hah! I didn't know the meaning of the word!" Her voice lowered to a beseechful tone. "But, God, I want you! You, damn it, *you!* And if you're leading me down some primrose path only to abandon me at the last, you can forget it!" Her hand shook as she raised it to her mouth and whimpered, "I don't think I can take it, Doug. I don't."

For what seemed an eternity Doug simply stood where he was more than an arm's length away, staring at her. Then, as she watched warily, his stunned expression took flame. His eyes glowed, their lambent gleam spreading to the bronze of his skin. Neither saying a word nor releasing her gaze, he kicked off his deck shoes. Tugging his shirt from his pants, he ignored buttons to whip the soft fabric over his head.

Hooking his fingers beneath the elastic band of his trendy cotton sweats, he pushed them and his shorts over his hips and stepped out of them in one fluid move.

Still trembling from her heated monologue, it was Sasha's turn to be stunned. Doug stood before her naked, as gloriously masculine as she'd imagined, as strong and lean and proud. Her eyes dropped from his face to his corded shoulders and then to his chest, covered with its dark brush of hair that was as broad at the top as were his shoulders before tapering to a thinner line below. His waist was slim, almost indistinguishable from the virile narrowness of his hips. His thighs and calves were carved of sinewy twists, his feet well formed and planted firmly in the thick brown carpet.

He was a bronze god, his skin a teak treasure broken only by a paler swath across his loins. It was to this paler swath that Sasha's gaze was drawn, to the essence of Doug's masculinity, long and strong and quite helplessly responding to her visual caress.

He made no attempt to hide from her, but stood his ground with the realization that for Sasha this was something new, this slow admiration of a man's bare body. He saw her pleasure in the flush of color on her cheeks, saw her arousal in the flash of hazel in her eyes, saw her need in the rapidity of her breathing, the clenching of her fists, the tautness of her stance.

And he felt utterly exposed. For aware as he was of his own body and of the fact that Sasha admired it, he was abundantly aware of the broader implication of what was happening. In offering himself so blatantly he was asking a corresponding commitment of Sasha. She may have been the one to stand back and dare him to deny her this time, but with these slow moments' perusal of what he offered, she was being offered a chance to refuse him. It was her turn. Standing before him neither held in his arms nor drugged by his kiss, she was being given a choice. Awaiting her decision was perhaps the hardest thing he'd ever done in his life.

By the time Sasha's gaze returned to his eyes, he wore a look of infinite vulnerability. In view of the beauty of his body, she marveled at his lack of arrogance, his lack of pretense. It was as though the tables had been turned, as though it was he who now feared she'd leave him. He had no way of knowing that it was precisely this fear, this vulnerability that bound her to him as nothing else might have.

Feeling suddenly shy, she spoke in an unsure whisper. "I don't know what to do, Doug. I mean, I've never had a choice before."

For a split second his expression hardened. "You want to leave."

"No!"

"What do you want?" he asked cautiously.

She bit her lip and allowed her gaze to fall once more along the manly contours of his body. "I want...to touch you," she whispered.

He spoke one word, no louder than hers and held out his arms in invitation. "Well?" But he didn't move. She was the one who would have to take those last few steps.

In that instant Sasha knew how truly different Doug was from what she'd known in the past. He saw her as a woman with a free, if heavy, choice to make. He'd meant what he'd said before, that he wanted her to want him and only him. And she realized that he was purposely forcing her to move that last distance simply because he had to know.

With one step the distance was halved, with another it was obliterated. Only when she reached up and put her hands on his chest did he touch her, and even then it was with the lightest grasp of her shoulders. She was to lead the way, to do what she wanted, to show him what she needed most.

Swallowing once, Sasha fought a rising fever. She wove her fingers through his hair, finding his chest beneath to be strong and warm. She lowered her hands and traced his hips, trailing her fingers up his thighs to his groin, settling her palm against the rock hardness of his indrawn stomach, moving it slowly down.

She'd never touched a man this way before. Intermingled with awe was a tiny surge of power, dizzying yet self-perpetuating. Her fingers drifted lower, tangling in a more coarse thatch of dark hair, feeling beneath it a softness, a hardness, a throbbing.

Doug was the one who trembled now. It was all he could do not to thrust against her, and the force of his restraint coiled his muscles all the more. But he waited, his breath laboring as her fingers crept lower, finally touching him timidly, experimentally, measuring his length in airy strokes of silk, at last circling his thickness and holding him as he needed to be held.

A deep animal sound escaped his throat and she released him in alarm. But he grabbed her hand and returned it to him, his own fingers holding hers firm.

"Oh, no, babe," he rasped. "Don't let go. I've waited so long. Don't let go."

His urgency was all the encouragement she needed. Bowing her head to his chest, she closed her eyes and pressed her lips to his warm blanket of hair as she stroked him steadily. Her hand fed on his turgescence, delighting in its strength. Her thumb found the silk of its tip and marveled at its butter smoothness. Was this the instrument she'd once thought to be a tool of pain and degradation? It seemed impossible, for there was nothing but beauty in the full rise of Doug's manhood.

As though sensing her astonishment, Doug called her name. His voice seemed to come from a distance at first, from the far reaches of arousal. On second calling, it was stronger.

"Sasha?"

She looked up, her eyes dazed in admiration. "Yes?"

He took her hand from him then and held it against her other on his chest where she could feel the drum of his heart. His voice was thick. "I need to know, Sasha. I need to know what he did."

"He?" she asked blankly. At that moment there was only one "he" in her world and it was Doug.

Pleased, Doug offered a gentle smile and brought her hands to his lips for a kiss before returning them and holding them tightly to his chest. "Sam. I need to know what he did so that I can make it really good for you. I'm frightened, babe. So afraid of hurting you. Of doing something that may remind you—"

"Shhh," she whispered, loving the feel of his hard length pressed intimately to her body. "I'm not thinking of him, Doug. Only you."

"But tell me Sasha. I need to know."

For an instant she resented the intrusion. Sam was of another world, an alien being to this new heaven. But she saw that same look of urgency, of vulnerability in Doug's face and could deny him nothing, least of all this glimpse of her past. He cared. And if his knowing everything would set his mind at ease, she cared in turn.

Letting her head fall forward until it was cradled atop their entwined hands, she gently kissed his fingers, then took a deep breath. "He was rough. That's all."

"He beat you?"

"No. He just took me without care or consideration." Momentarily reliving the humiliation, she couldn't look up. Her words spilled forth with a will of their own. "He was little more than a rutting animal. When he felt the urge, I was his receptacle. I was a virgin when we married. My wedding night was a nightmare. Over and over again. Oblivious to my pain, my bleeding."

Doug freed his hands to hold her in his full embrace. "It didn't get better after that?"

"It might have had he ever tried to arouse me. But he didn't. My pleasure wasn't part of his definition of the act. He was only concerned with relieving himself." She looked up then. "It sounds dirty, doesn't it?" When Doug nodded she went on, holding his gaze unwaveringly. "Well, it felt it too. When I was embarrassed or humiliated he only pounded all the harder. When I was dry—which I always was—he seemed to take pleasure in my cries. It was his way of exerting his authority over me, I suppose. I half wish he *had* hit me. If I'd been unconscious I wouldn't have had to feel what he did to me. Not once was I proud to be a woman. Not once."

Running out of breath, she fell silent and awaited Doug's response. That he was appalled was obvious. But there was something else in his expression that snagged her pulse. "Oh, God," she cried softly and covered her face with her hands. "I *feel* dirty! And I've turned you off!"

"You could never turn me off!" Doug declared, taking her face between his hands and gently forcing it back up to his. "Never, Sasha! It's just that...just that I feel...guilty."

"Guilty? You?"

"Yes, me." He sighed and sent a pleading look over her head. When he returned his gaze to hers it was with humility. "I've taken women that way. Too many times. And I'm ashamed of it! You know, before I met you I didn't like myself very much. I've used people, men in business, women in bed. Since I've met you, I feel different. With you I'm different. I think that for the first time in my life I truly respect myself as a man." A fine tremor shimmered through his limbs. "Maybe...maybe that's what love's all about."

Sasha's breath was caught in her throat. "Love?" she warbled.

"Yes, love." Suddenly it was in his eyes, in the fingers that stroked her finely sculpted features with wonder. "I love you. Is that so hard to believe?"

"No one's ever said that to me before," she whispered.

"And I've never said it to anyone before, so it's a first for us both."

Sasha's heart swelled until she felt it would burst. "And you mean it?"

He gave a crooked smile. "Would I be standing here naked as the day I was born, exposed and unprotected, and lie?" The smile waned, yielding to a more sober set of his mouth. "I need you, Sasha, in ways I've never needed another human being. Oh, I've taken in the past, taken what I've wanted and then turned my back without regret. But I've never needed to give this way, to make things good for a woman, to make her life happy. And I want to do that for you, Sasha. More than you can imagine, I want that. But I need your help. And I need *your* giving. The whole thing isn't one-sided anymore. That was why I had to know that you only wanted *me*. Because I only want you, babe. No one or nothing else.''

"Oh, Doug,'' Sasha murmured, her eyes awash with tears. "You make me feel so...special.''

"You are! Dear God, you are!'' Wrapping her in arms made of steel, he hugged her then. She half feared her ribs would crack, but she welcomed the pressure and returned it through arms coiled tightly around his neck. She held and held, and he did too. For the moment kisses were secondary—but only for the moment.

Tipping his head back, Doug smiled down at her, eyes shining, dazzling her with their brilliance. Then his mouth was on hers with the same hunger as earlier, yet with an openness that was loving and needing and aching combined. It seemed to go on forever, a dialogue of lips and tongues and teeth. Only reluctantly did they separate, and then to set about soothing the ache.

"Aren't you warm?'' Doug asked, kissing tiny dots of perspiration from her nose. When she nodded, he reached to the hem of her sweater and gently eased it over her head. Without pause he went to work on the buttons of her blouse, tossing the unwanted covering to the floor before releasing the catch of her bra. He bent his head then and found haven in the damp valley between her breasts, breathing in the sweet scent of her skin while she buried her face in his hair.

His lips were everywhere, on her throat, her ribs, the soft undersides of her breasts, then their crests. Sasha cried her delight when he opened his mouth on her nipple and drew it in, dabbling with the wet point of his tongue, then sucking so strongly that a shaft of raw heat sizzled to her loins. Eyes closed, holding his head tightly, she moaned and he released her, but only to slip to his knees and trail kisses to the hollow beneath her ribs while his fingers attacked the zipper of her jeans.

Then he was slow, tantalizingly slow, and she fought the urge to push him away and strip as quickly as he had. His hands inched the denim lower, taking her panties with them. His mouth worshiped each bit of flesh as it was revealed to his exultant gaze. His tongue found her navel and plunged. His lips dealt more gently with the soft ivory flesh of her belly. The fabric receded farther and in a burst of desire he peeled it to her thighs. Hands cupping the warm roundness of her bottom, he kissed the dark triangle of hair that protected her innermost secrets.

Sasha arched her back and whimpered, still clutching his head, fearing that her legs would give way. Her body quivered wildly, every muscle, every bone, every nerve end aflame. She felt more alive than she ever had, more needed, more cherished, and she wondered how she'd ever managed to put such feelings in words...and knew she hadn't. If her writing held emotion, it was the emotion born of dreams. This, though, was real, and that much more rapturous. Though she may have come close in her imaginings, she'd never truly known or expressed this exquisite emotional joy of being with a man she loved. And she did love him. As her clothes left her body, so all pretense left with it. There was no room for prevarication, no time for playing with words. To say that Doug was unique, that he was warm and caring and intelligent and charming and companionable, was only to say that she loved him.

"Oh, Doug," she breathed on a note of ecstasy, aware that her jeans had been tossed aside only when the man beneath her slowly stood. "Doug," she whispered, looking into his eyes then, needing to be as open as he. "I love you."

Had he been waiting for the words? Somehow she believed that even without them he'd have adored her without reservation, but the joy she saw in his eyes made the adoration that much more breathtaking.

His face said it all—the light in his eyes, the flush on his cheeks, the smile of awe on his lips. No words were needed. Nor were they offered. Lowering his head, he kissed her tenderly, then again, hunger momentarily taking second place to sheer devotion. He opened his eyes and lifted his head, and his gaze went to her hair.

"I've never seen it down," he said in a rasping murmur. "Do you know that? I've never seen it down."

Sasha watched in wonder as he reached for first one clasp then the other, tossed them aside, threaded his fingers through the thickness of her auburn tresses and very gently combed them down to her shoulders.

"Beautiful," he whispered, unable to take his eyes from the vibrant tangles. "Beautiful and wild and sexy. Do you know that?" His gaze returned to hers for a moment, then fell to her full breasts, her flat belly and finally that harbor he'd kissed so eloquently moments before. "You're beautiful, Sasha. Beautiful and warm and wonderful. And I think that if I don't make love to you now I'm going to die."

"Don't do that," she whispered back, a smile on her face. "If you die, I'll never know, will I?"

"Never know what?" he asked, wrapping his arms about the small of her back and drawing her intimately closer.

Her own arms settled around his lips, her hands pressing against the leanness of his buttocks. She didn't falter. "Never know what it's like to be made real love to," she breathed, entranced. "Never know what it's like to give you pleasure. Never know what it's like to feel you deep, deep inside me."

Doug sucked in a sudden breath. His body jerked, inflamed by her words. "Oh, God, I want you," he gasped, sweeping her into his arms and setting off in what direction Sasha neither knew nor cared as long as his strong arms were cradling her, holding her close.

Suddenly, almost comically, his tone changed. "Hell, the bed's not made. I never made the bed." His frustrated apology was offered on the threshold of his room.

Sasha grinned, finding his dismay all the more endearing. "We don't need it made."

"But I want you on clean sheets. Satin sheets. The finest."

"It's you I want. Not satin sheets." Her back came down on cool cotton, perhaps rumpled, but of a manly checked design. "And it's your bed I want to be in," she whispered, looking up at the face so close to hers, "not some sterile peacock showcase."

Doug chuckled and kissed her hard, lowering himself to her side while his hands began to reacquaint themselves with the body they'd never forget. He touched her everywhere, then followed with his mouth, licking her flesh, kissing it, nibbling here and there until she began to writhe with the desire he unleashed.

Breathing as hard as she, he finally raised himself to lie by her side, and turned her to face him. "Touch me again, babe. Please."

His pleading sent the flame higher and she yielded instantly, adoring his flesh as he had hers, feeling her own body weep in response. At last, her face a mere breath from his, her eyes riveted to the silver ones she so worshiped, she caressed him as intimately as she had before. She felt his fullness and his hardness, sensed him swell all the more in her grasp. Then she felt something else, a hand sizzling down her belly, finding her, opening her, stroking her with such gentle fire that she thought she'd drown in flame. She'd written steamy before, but nothing could compare with the imminent conflagration that threatened. Moaning softly, she arched onto his fingers, then the fingers were gone and she was on her back. Doug on his knees, spreading her thighs, giving thanks to the light of day that illuminated the portal of her sex.

Unashamed, she lay still, though the roughness of her breathing and the faint tremor of her limbs bespoke of the need he'd created, the need he'd have to fill. He came forward then, one hand lingering to feather stroke her a final time before joining its mate as a brace by her shoulders.

"You're ready for me," he whispered. "All wet and warm. You're not afraid, are you?"

She nodded. "I'm afraid you'll keep me waiting

longer." It was her turn to beg, but it was new and wondrous. "Please, Doug. I need you."

"And I love you," he said, holding her gaze as he slowly undulated his hips, moved closer, touched, gently entered, then penetrated completely. She held her breath, aware of a gliding, a slow filling, then the most heartrending sense of possession she'd ever dreamed. Who was the possessor? Who the possessed? One was the other, each was both. Their sighs of satisfaction were in perfect harmony.

"Oh, Doug," she whispered, wrapping her legs around his hips, her arms around his back, arching up from the bed to receive his kiss. He didn't move as he kissed her but used his tongue provocatively, inspiring her to do the same, while they both savored the sense of satisfaction down lower where their bodies were joined.

Then, slowly, he began to move, and what happened was pure fantasy to Sasha. With each thrust she rose hotter, higher. With each hungry twist she burned. She wanted to die and be reborn as part of this man, to have all of him, to devour him as she was being devoured by his magnificence. If this was what being loved and in love was about, she was more than willing to toss self-sufficiency to the winds. One couldn't be self-sufficient and have all this, this mind-boggling joining of minds and hearts and bodies that built a tension that coiled and knotted and was relieved by her writhing only to renew itself and soar onward.

"I love you, Sasha! I love you!" Doug cried, his face a mask of sweet pain that she saw for only a moment before, eyes shut tight against the unbearable agony of reaching, her body exploded into multitudinous fragments of flame. Seconds later Doug cried out again, this time from his own powerful climax, his body irrupting to quench her flame, succeeding in making it all the more grand as he collapsed atop her and held her close until the last of his shattering spasms subsided.

It was only later, long moments later, that either of them moved, and then it was Doug to roll to her side and Sasha to curl snugly against the damp warmth of his body. The air was rent with panting, then sighs. The sweet smell of their lovemaking lingered as a heady aura about them.

"Never before," Doug rasped. "I never knew..."

With a catlike grin of satisfaction, Sasha teased, "That should have been my line."

"Is it?"

"Yes."

Heads sharing a pillow, they looked into one another's eyes. "How do you feel?"

Her grin persisted. She couldn't have stifled it if she'd tried, which she wasn't about to. "Free. And warm. And tired. And happy."

"I'm glad," he crooned, smiling back.

"How do *you* feel?"

"Free. And warm. And tired. And happy."

"Free? I thought I was the one released from her fears."

"Oh, no. I had fears, too." He gently stroked the tangled mess of her hair. "I wondered if I could satisfy you. If I could give you what you deserved."

"You sure did, bub."

"I'm not kidding, Sasha." He was stone-sober. "I had no idea there were so many insecurities where the heart's concerned."

"You've a heart condition?" she asked, feeling far too giddy to think of being serious.

"You bet I do. And it's only partly relieved."

"Only partly?"

"Marry me, Sasha. Be my wife. Promise to spend the rest of your life with me."

His words took Sasha by storm. Wide-eyed, she stared at him, all giddiness suddenly gone. "Oh, Doug," she murmured sadly.

"What's 'Oh, Doug'? You said you love me."

"I do."

"Then marry me."

There they were again, those two gut-wrenching words. She took a sharp breath, her eyes pleading for something she couldn't quite fathom. "I—I don't know. It's so sudden."

He was up on an elbow then, single-minded and intense. "No more sudden than our falling in love. You've accepted that, haven't you?"

"Yes."

"Then why not marriage?"

Her face twisted painfully and she looked away. "Because I've been through it once before."

"With a jackass."

"Perhaps, but a jackass who took license to control from a bunch of meaningless marriage vows."

"Ours wouldn't be meaningless. We love each other. Did you ever love Sam?"

She rolled onto her back and stared at the ceiling. "No."

"You see? That'd be the difference."

It certainly was a difference. He had a point. But the fact remained that the thought of marriage unsettled her. Irrational? Perhaps. But until she worked it out...

Turning her head on the pillow, she faced Doug once more. "I need time," she pleaded. "Everything's happened so fast. Can't you give me time?"

"And do what in the meanwhile? See each other every once in a while? Date? Catch sex on the run?" He grunted in frustration, shot a glance at the window, then looked back. "Don't you see? I want you with me all the time. I want to spend every day with you and every night, all night."

"Can't we do that sometimes?"

"Oh, sure. And in the in-between times I'll sit here stewing, fearing that I may lose you. That's my insecurity, Sasha. And what about this crazy who's after you? What about him? How can I protect you if you're not mine to protect?"

She offered a faint gesture of dismissal. "Oh, it may be nothing. Really."

"Come on, Sasha," he growled. "Face facts."

"I am, and I know that I need more time!"

Doug stared at her, his eyes hard as stone. Then, before she could reach out, he rolled from the bed to his feet and headed for the door.

"Doug...?"

He didn't stop, and when her cry was swallowed in silence, she didn't follow him. This was a new side of Doug, a darker side, and she wasn't quite sure how to handle it.

8

Sasha tugged at the sheet to cover herself and lay quietly listening to the thunderous beating of her heart. She couldn't hear Doug, but then, did she really expect him to stomp around the living room in a temper?

Very slowly her eyes wandered and she took in her surroundings for the first time. Doug's bedroom was huge, made even more so by high vaulted ceilings painted a fresh beige as were the walls, and a multitude of windows. The carpeting was brown, as it had been in the other room, the furnishings slate gray and strictly contemporary, with a simplicity of line that broadcast masculine elegance. It was a fitting room for Doug, she decided, knowing that he'd have decorated it himself and admiring his skill.

Cocking her ear, she listened again. There was nothing but silence. Rolling to her side, she gathered the sheet to her breasts and recalled the wonder of what had happened earlier. Breathing deeply, she caught Doug's unique scent and felt the echo of a tremor deep within her. She loved him. And she loved what he'd done to her. But she was right, she knew, in demanding more time. Even now she felt slightly breathless at the thought of the turn her life had taken in barely ten days. Too fast. She felt caught up in a whirlwind of emotion. Yet there was so much more to the man that she still didn't know. And if she was to marry, to marry again, she had to know exactly what she was getting into. No longer was she a seventeen-year-old innocent. At the age of twenty-nine her eyes were open wide. And she had to look, to know, to be sure.

Until now, Doug had been the near-saint he'd thought Sean to be. But he was human. His stalking from the bedroom moments before was testimony to that fact. Human. Man. He'd been magnificent even as he'd strode away, tall, athletic of build, compelling and quite nude. Again she felt a quickening inside, and she shifted on the bed in a vain attempt to quell it.

He was hurt and frustrated. In a bad mood? Most probably. But, she mused, perhaps he had a right to be. Wouldn't she have been the slightest bit disappointed if he'd accepted her demand without a fight? If he cared for her as much as he claimed he did, he'd most naturally be upset. And she could accept that. She wasn't so starry-eyed as to believe that even two people deeply in love didn't have differences on occasion.

Hugging the pillow his head had shared with hers, she rolled to her other side and stared at the window. It was still raining out, drops creating a slow-changing pattern on the glass. Bad moods, petty differences notwithstanding, would he be there for her? This was the crux of her worry, the bottom line to her demand for time. Before she agreed to marry Doug she had to be certain she wouldn't be let down. She'd been so hurt once before, and then there had not even been a pretense of love in the relationship. But marriage, however farcical it might be, implied that kind of commitment. And loving Doug as she did, she couldn't bear the thought of coming to count on him, then losing.

He'd come through today. A slow, feline smile worked its way through her sober expression. He certainly had come through. He'd been home when she'd needed him, offering comfort and security. And when other needs had taken hold, he'd been there for her. He'd even put off his own work—that phone call her arrival had interrupted—to be with her.

Quite coincidentally at that moment the phone rang again. Out of habit she raised her head and speared a glance at the instrument beside the bed. This ringing was more distant, though. A business line in the den? The sound came again and was picked up midring. Smiling with the knowledge that he hadn't gone far, Sasha sat up. Then, strengthened by the love she felt and half-curious to see the rest of the house, she slipped from the bed.

A robe of thick chocolate-colored terry cloth hung inside the bathroom door. Reaching for it, she put it on. It fell to her knees; she imagined the midthigh point it would reach on Doug's hair-spattered legs. Feeling simultaneously lost in the volumes of fabric and deliciously cushioned, she loosely knotted the tie and rolled the sleeves. A quick glance in the mirror told her that her hair was unsalvageable. A double take told her that it was strangely sexy. Or was it the robe? Or the way she felt in the robe? Or the fact that the last body it had covered would have had to have been Doug's?

For a lingering minute she stared at herself, mildly stunned by what she saw. Her cheeks had a natural pink flush. Her hazel eyes seemed more green than usual. Her lips were moist and faintly puffed from erstwhile kisses. She looked very feminine. She *felt* very feminine. More than that. Enveloped so richly in Doug's thick robe, she seemed small, fragile, vulnerable. Strangely, though she thought she'd sworn off fragility and vulnerability years ago, she didn't mind.

Leaving the mirror, the bathroom, the bedroom behind, she silently made her way down the long hall she hadn't seen before to the living room she hadn't seen before. The lush brown carpet appeared to run through the entire house, as did beige walls and a thoroughly modern decor. The large living room, though, was furnished and accented in hunter green, rather than the gray of the bedroom, and while it looked every bit as masculine it seemed more…social. She smiled at the observation, thinking how irrelevant it was as she admired the sectional sofa, the glass-and-marble tables, the freestanding shelves that bore nothing at all, the unopened cartons at their foot.

Unopened cartons. So he really hadn't unpacked yet! Odd that a man in such a beautiful house would have put off such a chore. Odd. On second thought, not so. Typical. She smiled, and felt not disdain but fondness. For a man like Doug, so willing to give of himself, she would gladly do the unpacking, make the bed, do the laundry. In Sam's house it had been just another drudging task to perform. In Doug's it would be a privilege.

At the sound of a rising voice, she continued through the living room and entered a shorter hall from which branched the den. Pausing at its open door, she peered inside. Doug was at his desk, dressed now, though his shirt hung open. He looked quickly up when she appeared and she saw an instant's flicker of unsureness in his gaze. When he looked down again and continued talking, his voice was quieter.

Aware that he might want privacy, Sasha turned to leave, only to be waved back in by his sweeping gesture. Warmed, she slowly entered the room and looked around. Doug continued his conversation.

"What's wrong with Hasselfromm?...I know he's got other assignments, but he's the one I want.... Damn it, we've paid him enough in the past to expect some kind of preference. Offer him more. Give him some stock. He's the only model for this campaign. I want him."

Sasha let the discussion flow around her as she studied the den. So very like the rest of the house it was, yet different. This was the working room. Doug's large lacquered desk sat on one side, a drawing board on another. The easy chairs on which they'd sat earlier stood in the middle, their deep leather sheen almost identical to the carpet's hue. A long low table stood nearby, its top cluttered with open magazines and papers. One wall, that behind the desk, was sheer windows, another backed a long credenza atop which several smartly framed ad blowups were propped. The remaining walls, allowing for the door and a closet, held floor-to-ceiling shelving units of various depths and sizes, very obviously custom-made and as obviously bare but for an occasional book or sculpture. More conspicuously sat the cartons nearby, piled as high as three, even four in a bunch.

Curious, Sasha wandered to a stack of two, the topmost of which reached her waist and stood with its flaps open. Inside were books on fashion design and marketing. As well there should be, she mused, lifting first one out, then another, piling them in her arms and nonchalantly finding the shelf she thought to be most appropriate, setting them carefully upright. She returned to the carton, extracted several more volumes, flipped through one on the history of design, then placed them on the shelf with the others. She paused momentarily to arrange them by height before returning for another batch.

"Okay, Dan. See what he says to that. But I want him, remember that.... Fistran's lined up for the shoot, isn't he?... Good. Hey, what about that silk fabric? Did it come in?... Hell, what's it taking, a slow boat?... I know, but it should have been in two weeks ago."

Having filled one shelf, Sasha stood back to admire it, then shot a glance at Doug. His eyes were on the papers before him, brows drawn low with his frown, one hand fisted, the other rubbing the back of his neck. The casual muss of his hair did little to ease the air of tension surrounding him.

On silent cat's feet she walked around the desk, pushed his hand away and began to gently knead the taut muscles at his nape. Questioningly, he half turned, only to be urged forward again by knowing hands that then resumed their work.

Sasha took delight in her ministrations. Though his hair was thick and full it was well-shaped and trimmed. Her fingers brushed against the soft stubble at his nape and would have returned for a second velvety feel had not Doug's voice wavered sharply. She hadn't wanted to distract him, only make him more comfortable. Stoically keeping her attention on his muscles, she was rewarded when she felt them begin to relax.

Then the doorbell rang. Doug sent a sharp glance toward the hall, but it was Sasha who squeezed his shoulder and headed for the door. Only when she remembered what she was wearing did she come to a dead halt and slither an awkward grin toward Doug.

Covering the receiver, he murmured with a smile, "It's okay. Probably the mailman. Look outside. Anyone you don't recognize, give a yell."

Reassured first and foremost by his smile, she answered the door. It was indeed the mailman, mercifully one she'd never seen. She signed for two of the bundles, took the rest in her arms, backed the door shut and returned to dump the load on Doug's desk.

"Yeah, Dan, that's okay.... Well, let me know what he says. I'll call him myself if need be and twist his arm." He grinned at something his CEO said. "Only a figure of speech, Daniel. Only a figure of speech.... Sure. Talk with you later." He hung the phone up soundly, but rather than reaching for one of the packages that had arrived, he half rose from his chair to catch Sasha's hand and draw her around the desk again. Swiveling sideways, he imprisoned her between his thighs.

"It's nice to have you here," he said softly, his hands propped loosely on her hips.

"It's nice to be here," she answered, her wrists dangling over his shoulders.

He cast a glance at the shelf she'd filled. "You didn't have to do that."

"It's about time someone did. I think you need a caretaker, Douglas Donohue."

"I think so, too," he said, so humbly that she knew his mood was eased.

She hesitated for only an instant. "You're not mad at me?"

He knew she wasn't talking about the books. A look of gentle resignation gave his features a softer slant. "Of course I'm not mad. I can't have my way all the time, can I?" He arched a brow. "Not that I wouldn't like to force you to the altar, mind you. But that wouldn't be good for either of us. You need to be sure that marriage is what you want. I need to be sure that you're sure." One corner of his lips quirked upward. "In the meantime, you look sexy as hell." Drawing her closer, he pulled loose the tie and spread the robe to the side, then buried his face between her breasts. "Ahhhh—" he gave a muffled moan "—if a volcano erupted right now I could very happily stay this way for eternity."

Sasha laughed against his hair. "What a morbid thinker you are."

"Not morbid. Imaginative." He lifted his face and Sasha met his gaze, stroking the hair at the back of his head, as proud of her near-nakedness as she'd ever been. "I love you, Sasha. Do you love me?"

"I've said as much."

"Well, say it again."

"I love you, Doug."

"Mmmm." Spearing his hands inside the robe to her back, he crushed her to him and hugged her. "I can wait," he murmured gruffly. "If I'm a bear every once in a while and tear out of the room, you'll just have to understand. But I can wait. I can wait."

The phone couldn't. It jangled a second, a third time

before either Doug or Sasha noticed. At the fourth ring, Sasha spoke. "Doug? Aren't you going to answer it?"

"No," he murmured. "They'll call back."

"But it may be important."

"Nothing's so important as to take precedence over this."

"I didn't come here to disturb your work."

"Like hell you didn't," he teased against her stomach. "You came for a good lay, and you know it."

"Douglas!" Not sure whether to laugh or scold but definitely needing a show of dignity, she reached for the phone herself. "Good morning. Douglas Donohue Enterprises, Martha's Vineyard Headquarters. May I help you?" Her sing-song professionalism brought Doug's head slowly up. He was in the process of eyeing her askance when she covered the mouthpiece and whispered, "It's Sergio Martin?" She added a mouthed, "Sounds weird," before presenting the receiver to Doug.

He returned a mouthed, "He is," before donning his most commanding smile. "Sergio, my friend! Good to hear from you!"

Rolling her eyes skyward, Sasha squirmed from his grip, retied the robe, and returned to the cartons. By the time she'd completely emptied the first, what with skimming tables of contents here and there, she'd had a crash course on the history of clothing and clothiers. By that time she was also aware of Doug's returning tension. His grimace gave him away, where his voice had not.

"You're sure it has to be tomorrow?...I know, and I appreciate that. But I wasn't planning to be back in

the city for another week or two.... I understand....
No, no. It can be arranged." His lips thinned and he
scowled at the phone, though his voice retained its
cordial ring. "Fine. See you then."

This time when he hung up, Sasha stayed in front
of the desk. "What's wrong?" she asked softly.

"Damn!" Doug sat far back in his chair and swiveled to the side in disgust. "Just what I didn't want
to have to do."

"Go back to New York?"

He shot her a fast glance. "Mmm."

"Who's Sergio Martin?"

"My Italian coordinator. He was supposed to be in
the city for the month. I was going to meet with him
later. But he's got a family problem and has to cut his
trip short. Damn! But I didn't want him coming *here*."

Sensing an apology in the offing, Sasha felt all the
more sympathetic. "If it can't be helped, it can't.
When will you go?" The thought of his leaving the
Vineyard was a disturbing one.

"Tomorrow morning," he mumbled. With his elbows braced on the arms of the chair, fists pressed to
his mouth, head bent, he was obviously thinking.
Slowly he raised his head and swiveled back to face
her, a look of cautious hope on his face. "Come with
me, Sasha. We can fly down tomorrow. I'll have my
meeting. Then we can spend tomorrow night and the
weekend together. I promise to get you back here by
Sunday night. That way you can be around on Monday...."

Monday. She tensed, remembering things she'd
tried so to push from her mind. She looked down and
fumbled with the cord of the robe.

"It'd be good for you, Sasha," he went on, leaning forward in urgency. "Sitting here you'll only spend the time worrying."

"I was hoping to work," she said in a small voice. "That usually keeps my mind occupied."

"But I don't want you to work. I want you to be with me. Even if I weren't going to New York, I'd want you to stay here. I'm not sure how safe your place is."

Another dilemma, also far from solved. Sasha helplessly met his gaze. "I can't go into hiding. I mean, if someone's after me, he can find me wherever I go. Those barrels are a point in fact. I wasn't even at home then."

"But I was there. And if you come to New York with me, I'll be there. When we get back, you can stay here with me."

"I have to work. I can't work here."

"Why not?"

"I'd—I'd be distracted."

"Not if I'm working," he reasoned. "Try again."

"My computer."

"I'll bring it over."

"But my house! I love my house!"

"Don't you like mine?"

"Of course I like yours," she wailed, casting a sweeping glance around the room. "It's light and beautiful and—"

"Large enough for both of us. There's even a den you can have all to yourself. I mean, what the hell, Sasha. When we're married—"

"Doug!" she whispered, shaking her head in confusion. "I haven't said I'll marry you."

"But you will. In time." His smugness faded when he sensed imminent rebellion. "And you've got that, Sasha. I can wait. I told you that before. I can wait."

Knowing now how her clothes felt swirling round and round in the washer, Sasha sighed, blew her bangs from her brow and turned, sinking into one of the nearby easy chairs. Doug's voice came quietly from his desk.

"Will you come, babe? Tomorrow. To New York. With me." When she remained silent, staring at her hands, he sugared the deal. "I promise I won't mention marriage again. Not until you bring it up. And when we come back we'll reach some kind of amicable agreement on living conditions. Does that sound fair?"

It did. Oh, it did. For as much as she loved her house, she loved Doug more. The thought of spending time with him was infinitely pleasing...and perhaps just what she'd need if she ever hoped to find the answer she sought to that one lingering question.

"Sasha?"

As she'd been thinking, he'd come from the desk to squat by her side. She lifted her gaze to encounter the raw need, the vulnerability that could sway her each and every time.

"I'll come," she agreed softly, then manufactured a scowl. "But if my career's shot to hell because I'm so distracted that I can't get back into my book, it'll be your fault." As she spoke, she poked a finger against his chest. He deftly captured it and brought her hand to his lips, then called her bluff in a muffled tone.

"I could get your machine now and let you get to work."

"No!"

"Why not? I've got all this mail to go through and there's probably a tape from my secretary to listen to and then a score of letters to dictate and send back."

"I'm not in the mood," she said crossly. "And besides, if I'm going to spend any time *here* I want those cartons unpacked."

"Aw, Sasha, they'll wait. Unpacking is a drag."

"You work. I'll unpack."

"I can't let you do that."

Her tone softened. "But I want to. It's fun learning about all your little treasures. You do want me to get to know you, don't you?"

"Of course, but—"

"Then it's settled," she declared, bounding up before an openmouthed Doug and heading toward another carton. No more than halfway there, though, she stopped in her tracks and began to look around, puzzled.

"What's wrong?"

"My clothes. They were—" she pointed to the spot on the floor where she thought they'd landed once upon a time "—there."

Doug stood, drawing himself to his full height. "Now they're there." He pointed to a small shelf behind the desk upon which her clothes were neatly folded. "I may hate unpacking and be lazy about making my bed, but when it comes to clothes, I have the utmost respect."

"Figures," she said, but she couldn't be angry. "Does that mean I won't find piles of laundry waiting in another room?"

He went beet red and grimaced. "Well, I don't

know...there may, uh, be some things on top of the washer...."

"Um-hmm."

"But you don't have to do them," he was quick to advise.

She sent him a feminine smile and turned to retrieve her clothes. "Of course not," she murmured as she set off quite happily for the bedroom.

By midafternoon she'd changed the sheets and made the bed, done two full loads of laundry, made lunch for them both and put a stew on to cook for dinner. She'd unpacked four cartons in the den and three more in the living room, admiring each and every item along the way, and she'd watched Doug work with pride she couldn't fathom.

For the most part she simply eavesdropped as he talked on the phone or spoke into his tiny tape recorder. She couldn't help but straighten and look his way, though, when he played the tape his secretary had sent. It was primarily a rundown on calls that had come in, on correspondence he didn't have to bother to read, on appointments set for his future trips to New York. At its end was something else.

"Oh, and Doug," the pleasant voice added, "Lisa thinks you're a bum. I'm afraid she's taking your exit pretty hard. Maybe you could put in a gentle word while you're here? Ta-ta." The recorder clicked off with a deafening thud.

"What was *that?*" Sasha asked, more bemused than threatened.

Doug had the good grace to look uncomfortable.

"That was my smart ass of a secretary putting in her two bits about my private life."

"Who's Lisa?"

"Her sister. We dated for a while."

Sasha gave an exaggerated nod. "Ah. I see. So…will you?"

"Will I what?"

"Put in a gentle word while you're there?"

"To Lisa? I've already put in as many gentle words as I can." He shook his head. "The woman won't let a dead dog lie."

Crossing her arms over her breasts, Sasha leaned against the arm of a chair. "What's she like?"

Doug stretched back in his chair, folded his hands across his stomach and sighed. "She's very pretty. And very nice. But not terribly bright. And she's a clinger."

"You don't like that? Some men would."

"I suppose I did at one point. In the big ego days." He widened his eyes for emphasis as he drawled the words in self-mockery. "But those days are gone. The woman I want now can stand on her own two feet. She's got a successful career and prides herself on being selfsufficient. She's independent, sometimes too much so. But I love her, faults and all."

Silently bidden by his gaze, Sasha came to stand before him, her hands on his shoulders, her knees braced against his. "I'm not sure whether to be flattered or offended."

"The first," he declared, then mistook her deep, happy sigh for one of fatigue. "You must be beat. You've worked hard today."

"I've had fun. You know, it's strange," she began

softly, raising her eyes to the window beyond which the ocean thrashed in the rain. "I used to resent doing things for Sam. I mean, I had to do everything around the house, and then some. I felt like a slave. But today was different. Maybe it's the fact that I have a career of my own. Self-respect. I had none then." She returned her gaze to his face, her eyes glowing with feeling. "Maybe it's the fact that I love you. Doing for you is...nice. Then again," she cautioned, lest his head grow too big, "maybe it's that I have a choice. That makes all the difference in the world." She reached out on impulse and brushed the hair from his brow. It was an exquisitely gentle gesture, touching Doug at his core.

"You'll always have the choice here, Sasha. Even if I'm not good at doing things, I'll try." He'd already showed her that the morning he'd fixed breakfast in her kitchen. "And when you're busy with your writing, we could hire someone to help. I want things to be as easy, as enjoyable, as rewarding for you as possible."

Sasha beamed. "You're a sweet man, Doug Donohue."

"Humph. I do believe you're the first person to describe me in quite that way. I'm not sure whether to be flattered or offended."

"The first," she said, echoing his own words with a grin. At the pressure of his fingers on her back, she leaned forward to receive his kiss. It was filled with love and sincerity, and was very sweet indeed.

And it was only the beginning. After a delightfully intimate dinner at his house, they returned to hers, where she packed a bag and closed things up while

Doug saw to renailing the stair that had been tampered with. Back at his house, atop his clean checkered sheets, they made love again, slowly, gloriously. With his greatest urgency released that morning, Doug was more tender than ever, the epitome of selflessness even at the height of his passion, worshiping Sasha's body in ways she'd once have thought sinful but discovered to be profoundly erotic. It was all in the approach, in the state of mind that in turn primed the body. Where love was involved there were no bounds, she decided quite joyously before falling into a deep, deep sleep in Doug's strong arms.

New York was startlingly wonderful given the fact that in the years she'd lived there Sasha had developed a strong aversion to frantic crowds, looming skyscrapers and taxis. With Doug by her side, all was different. She was oblivious to the crowds, uncowed by the skyscrapers, and aware of taxis only as places to steal a kiss on the sly.

Though the nip in the air signaled winter's approach, they spent hours walking the avenues arm in arm, stopping now and again to window-shop, doing touristy things neither would have dreamed of doing before. They soared to the top of the World Trade Center, took a hansom ride in the park, paid their respects to the Statue of Liberty. If Doug was wowed by the sight of Sasha in a dress, she was no less impressed by him in a suit. They ate well, slept well and made love particularly well.

There was only one snag to the weekend and that was the fact that when it ended Sasha would have to face two issues she desperately wished to avoid. The first was the matter of her mother, whose surgery was to take place on Monday morning. The second was the matter of the deranged faceless someone who was systematically plotting her harm.

Doug faced both of these, plus another. He had no idea how to get Sasha to finally say yes. In the time they spent together his love for her grew to frightening proportions, such that the thought of ever losing her sent him into a cold sweat. At every opportunity he did what he could to prove his love, no effort at all since the feeling was every bit there. But what it would take to secure that final agreement on her part—that was where he was stymied. He'd promised her time, and he'd give her that. But, Lord, he was impatient.

They were a straight-faced duo returning to Martha's Vineyard on Sunday evening. Mindful that Sasha would want to be near the phone on Monday, they spent the night at her house after thoroughly searching it to make sure all was in place. Sasha found it a novelty having Doug there, watching him shave before her mirror, do sit-ups on her rug, virilely stretch his bronzed body on her large white bed. He distracted her from more somber thoughts with the sheer force of his presence, the fiery dominance of his lovemaking. But Monday morning came, as Sasha knew it would, and she was tense.

While Doug read the paper, then pretended to doze, Sasha made ceremony of writing. The phone rang twice, one call from Maggie who, after trying her all weekend, had been worried, the second from the office-supply store to tell her that the computer paper she'd ordered was in. Both times she jumped a mile. Both times Doug was alert and as tense as she.

By the time noon arrived she'd produced nothing worth saving. Turning the machine off with a muffled oath, she went to Doug, took the newspaper from his knees and slipped down onto his lap, then slid her arms around his waist and rested her head on his chest.

"Oh, Doug," she murmured wearily. "I feel so helpless."

Rising quickly from his half nap, he traced her spine, then caressed her back with his palms. "It's only natural."

"Maybe I should have flown up there."

"Would you have felt any less helpless then?"

She sighed. "No, I suppose not."

"Then there's nothing to do but wait." He pressed a warm kiss to her bangs, then, bending his head farther, the bridge of her nose. She sighed again and yielded to his comfort, only to push herself to her feet after several moments and head for the phone.

"I'm trying Vicky."

"She may not be home yet."

"Then I'll call the hospital."

"I doubt they'll give you the information you want."

"I've got to do something!" she cried, lifting the receiver and punching out Vicky's number.

Doug was right. Vicky wasn't home. And a call to the hospital merely said that Natalie Blake was in the recovery room.

"At least she made it through surgery," Sasha breathed shakily.

"You never doubted that. Come here, babe." Docilely she returned to Doug's outstretched arms. "Ya' know," he suggested softly, "I do think you ought to consider going back for a visit." When she opened her mouth to protest, he sped on. "Not necessarily right away, assuming your mother's all right. But in time. I mean, look at you, babe. You're a nervous wreck worrying about your mother's condition and you haven't even seen the woman in years. You care."

"Of course I care," Sasha responded thoughtfully. "And it's because I care that it's so hard for me to go back. I hurt when I think of them. I want their acceptance and respect, not another rejection."

"Who says they'll reject you now?"

"I say. You don't know them, Doug. They're dogmatic as the day is long. They're not going to change. Not at this late date. If they'd wanted to patch things up over the years, they could have."

"Perhaps they're afraid."

"Afraid? Of *me*?" She gave a dry laugh. "They were never afraid to tell me what they thought of me then."

"That was then. This is now. And you happen to be an internationally known writer who is sophisticated in what may be a threatening way to them. Perhaps they feel that *they're* the ones who won't fit in."

"Humph. I doubt that. They go through life with blinders on. I doubt they know what they've missed."

"Sasha," Doug chided softly, "where's your generosity?"

She raised her head to look at him, then bowed it, ashamed. "I don't know, Doug. I just don't know. It's become such an emotional issue with me. Strange, I never really dwelt on it before. Maybe that's why it's boiling over now."

"Maybe. But I'm glad it is. You've got to settle it,

babe. After all, you said it yourself. The issue is there. It's not going away. At some point or another, something's got to give.''

Tipping her head back in the crook of his shoulder, she slanted him a curious stare. "Have you always had these analytic tendencies?" she asked softly.

He shook his head with a smile. "Only since I've met you, and it's because I care that I want things settled. More than anything in the world I want you to be happy. I don't want any shadows hanging over us when we're—'' He caught himself just in time. "Sorry about that,'' he murmured, though he really wasn't. He meant what he'd said and he knew she'd heard the word he hadn't. "What if I went up there with you?''

Sasha chuckled lightly. "That would be great. Mom and Dad, I'd like you to meet my lover, Doug Donohue. They'd die. I mean, they'd really die.''

"You could always tell them we were engaged,'' he dared, quite expecting Sasha to come down on top of him. Instead, she gave him a high laugh.

"Then they'd *know* I was beyond hope. No offense intended,'' she added as a pert aside, "but you're from that sinful world, too. A designer of men's haut couture?'' The accent she drawled into the words through pursed lips would have been funny had it not been blatant evidence of her highly emotional state. "They'd assume you were gay,'' she announced baldly, then broke into wild laughter. "They sh-should only know how wr-wrong they'd be!'' she gasped. "They should only know what we've done in bed! H-how good you are!'' Suddenly her laughter dissolved into tears and Doug held her very tightly.

"Don't go hysterical on me, babe," he growled. "Everything's going to be all right."

"Oh, Doug," she said, sniffling against his sweater, "if only I didn't feel s-so guilty about it. I mean, life has been good to me these past f-few years. And you're right. I should be more generous. I should feel sorry for them. But instead I'm angry. Why?"

"Because they're your parents. Because despite everything you love them. Because you're hurt and frustrated and confused."

"So what do I do?"

"You calm down and try Vicky again. It's the waiting that's always the worst. Once we know what's what, we can think about what you ought to do."

"What's what" was very good news indeed. After trying Vicky a second time, then finally reaching her on a third, Sasha learned not only that her mother had come through the surgery well, but that an open exploration had revealed no spreading of the disease. Mild radiation treatment was being considered as a precaution, but the prognosis was excellent for Natalie Blake's full recovery.

Reassured of her mother's well-being and feeling slightly ashamed of her own emotional display, Sasha gave Doug no argument when he insisted she pack up her computer and more clothes and stay at his house for a while. She left his number with Vicky in case of emergency, with no explanation other than a general if-you-phone-me-and-there's-no-answer-try-this kind of thing, locked up the house and returned with Doug to his ocean-front retreat.

The next few weeks were strangely peaceful and very happy ones for Sasha. She and Doug were constantly together, if not in the same room of his house then within easy calling distance. To Sasha's amazement, both her computer and her concentration survived transplantation. Comfortably set up in Doug's spare den, she found plenty to write, and though she'd begun to have her doubts about ever submitting this particular manuscript for publication, the story sped along.

"Tell me about it," Doug said one night as they lay naked together in his bed. "I mean, you've been typing away there for days and all I get to see is the flash of a skimpy synopsis you wrote months ago."

Sasha snuggled closer to the body that was now like her second skin. She rubbed her cheek against the warm hair on his chest, slid her arm over his ribs to rest on one leanly masculine hip, tucked her leg down between his, sealing her lower self in intimate collusion with his thigh.

"It's a lovely story," she began lazily, gazing up past his strong chin and nose to his eyes. "My hero and heroine meet quite by accident, fall in love and live happily ever after."

Doug gave her a squeeze. "Even the synopsis said more than that. Come on. Give."

"Naw. Romance always suffers in the retelling. You'll just have to read it some day."

"Have you decided on a name?"

She hadn't, until that moment. Craning her neck, she placed a soft kiss on his cheek. "I think I'll call it *Bronze Mystique*."

"*Bronze Mystique?*"

"Mmmm. *Bronze* for the very masculine color of

the hero's skin—'' she brushed her nose against Doug's ''—and *Mystique* for the heroine's unbelievable fascination with him.'' Her gaze slid up to lock with the intent silver one above her. ''She's never known a man like him before, and there are times when she can't begin to fathom the extent of her feelings for him.''

''She loves him, though.''

''Of course. Wildly and to distraction.''

''Will she marry him?''

Sasha took a breath. ''In time, I think. But first she's got to work out one or two last things for herself.''

''What if he gets tired waiting?''

''He won't.''

''Why not?''

''Because he's as fascinated with her as she is with him. And besides, there's got to be a happy ending. Isn't that the way it works?''

''I hope so,'' Doug murmured, then kissed her tenderly.

Whoever the villain was in Sasha's life, he was making himself scarce. She couldn't quite understand it, other than to assume that his original plans had been thwarted by Doug's continual presence. As the days passed, she began to wonder if he'd simply given up. Yet she couldn't help but think of him from time to time. And she couldn't help but imagine what would happen if he was simply lying low and revising his plot.

More and more, she found herself thinking of marriage. Living with Doug on a day-to-day basis proved to be almost idyllic. True, there were times when he was tense, when his mood was lighter or darker. But he was ever attuned to her, and she could find little to fault with his love.

Often while she worked he did the same in his den. On more than one occasion he sat quietly in hers, a pad of paper on his lap, a pencil in his hand, looking at her, turning his attention to the paper, looking up again. When on one such occasion her curiosity was piqued, she slapped a finger to the save button and whirled around in her seat.

"What *are* you doing, Douglas?" she demanded, materializing at his shoulder before he could hide the sketch he'd been making.

"Aw, nothing really. Just doodling."

She reached down and stole the pad from him. "You've been so busy. Let me see. Hey…" She studied the top sketch, then flipped the pad back to find a dozen different drawings. "But these are women's clothes."

"Do you like them?"

"They're gorgeous," and they were. Casual clothes, slacks, sweaters, blouses with a sporty kind of femininity about them, smart business ensembles, formal wear that was soft and chic. "I love them! But…you only do men's things."

He cocked his head with modest smugness. "That doesn't mean I can't try something new."

Her eyes widened. "Are you going to? I mean, are you thinking of starting a line for women?"

"I wasn't…until I started sitting here looking at you." He smirked. "God only knows I've undressed you enough. I think I'd like a chance to switch it around." Squeezing over to make room, he pulled her down onto the chair beside him. "What do you think?

Wouldn't you like to have a D D on your breast?"
He raised a finger to the spot where an insignia might
be and traced a tiny circle there.

"I've already *got* a D D on my breast," Sasha whispered naughtily. She caught his finger to stop its sweet
torment and brought it to her lips. "But I'd love to
wear your clothes! A new line...that's exciting!"

They spent the rest of the afternoon talking about
it, until the excitement and the nearness made talk irrelevant. They made love there on the chair in her den,
then showered together and took a ride into town for
a quick dinner, stopping only for a quart of Sasha's
favorite homemade ice-cream—a heavenly butter
crunch—on the way home. Then they settled in for a
quiet evening listening to music in the living room.
They talked softly from time to time, the atmosphere
one of peace and contentment. When Doug received
a late call from a friend, Sasha stole to the kitchen for
a spoonful of ice cream. She returned with one for
Doug; when he shook his head, she licked the spoon
clean, dropped it back in the kitchen, then retired to
the bedroom to wait for him.

He wasn't long, but she found herself feeling
strangely hollow. When he finally joined her, stripping
and taking her into his arms, she breathed a sigh of
relief. When the hollow remained, she simply pushed
it from mind, immersing herself in Doug's lovemaking
until they'd both reached dizzying heights and fallen
slowly back to earth.

Strangely, her dizziness remained, yet she dozed.
When Doug woke her less than half an hour later, her
body was covered with sweat.

"Are you all right, babe?" he asked, concern written over his features. "You feel hot."

It took her a minute to focus. "I don't know," she murmured. "I feel weird."

"Weird like how?"

"Like dizzy. And...crampy."

"You had your period last week."

"I know, but..." She tried to sit up and her stomach churned. "Oh, God," she moaned, then bolted from bed and made it to the bathroom in time to be violently sick.

Doug was right beside her, holding her head, bracing her quivering limbs, propping her on the commode when she'd finished and bathing her with a cool cloth.

"Any better?" he asked at last. She looked deathly pale despite her body's heat.

"I think so. Must be a bug."

He carried her back to bed and let it go at that, but he was awake long after she'd fallen asleep, watching her, relieved when her forehead cooled and her breathing deepened. Only then did he get up, throw on his robe and head for the kitchen.

9

He was wide awake, propped upright in bed, when Sasha opened her eyes the next morning. "How do you feel?" he asked cautiously.

"Fine." Something about him brought her quickly awake. "*You* look awful. Didn't you sleep? You're not coming down with whatever it was I had, are you?"

"I doubt it," he declared with such conviction that she gave him a closer look.

"What do you mean?" she murmured timidly. Studying his taut expression, she had the fleeting impression that the past few weeks had been the calm before the storm. "What's wrong, Doug?"

The muscle of his jaw worked once. "That ice cream you ate last night? I do believe it was poisoned."

"Poisoned? You've got to be kidding!"

"I'm not." His eyes were the texture of slate. "I took a good look at it last night after you fell asleep."

"I saw it, too. It looked fine!"

"Did you happen to catch the tiny pinhole on the side of the carton just below the rim of the lid?"

She blanched. "Oh, my God!"

"Someone injected something into that tub."

She shook her head in stunned denial. "No...oh, no...."

"Come on, babe. Look at the facts. You were fine before that. Your health is excellent. You have one spoonful, two spoonfuls of that stuff, then you're sick."

"Oh, Doug," she whispered, her eyes filling with tears.

"It can't be anything else, Sasha. The only thing I can't figure out is where he got the idea. I've read every one of your books. There's nothing about ice-cream poisoning in any of them."

She bit her lip and sat up, clutching her stomach, rocking back and forth. One by one tears trickled down her cheeks.

"It hurts again?" Doug asked, leaning forward to give her support.

She shook her head. "Not here," she whimpered, pointing to her stomach. Then she pointed to her head. "Here. Oh, God! Oh, my God!"

His arms went around her, trembling but holding her steady. "What is it?"

"Oh, Doug. I *did* write that."

"But where? I haven't—"

"In this book. This new one. I mean, I haven't actually written the scene, but it was in the synopsis. Oh, my God!"

Doug looked away, his eyes darting from side to side. "The synopsis. I didn't think." Then he looked back at Sasha. "Who's seen it?"

"Diane. Diane...and my editor. Maybe some others at M.P.I."

"Anyone else?"

"Oh, God," she cried, burying her face in her hands.

"Who, Sasha? It's important!"

The eyes she raised were wet, frightened and held an agony beyond belief. "Simon," she breathed. "Diane told Simon about it! But—" her expression turned pleading "—it couldn't be! It just couldn't be! We were so close there for a while! He was like a big brother. I still think of him as my mentor." Her mind wandered for an instant to the plot of *Bronze Mystique*. The villain there had been the hero's mentor, a man made vengeful by jealousy and suspicion. She slowly shook her head. "He's not the suspicious type. He's cocksure of himself and adventurous and unconventional. And I've never taken an idea from him. I'm sure of it!"

"But he hasn't sold anything lately."

"No. Just his first."

"So you've soundly eclipsed him."

"But he's doing other things. Diane said so."

"That does mean he can't be jealous." Another thought came. "You said he had a flair for the dramatic. And that he used to disguise himself and play different roles. Is it possible, just possible, that you may have seen him around the island and not recognized him?"

"Oh, Doug, anything's possible! But he wouldn't! Simon loved me in his way. I'm sure of it."

"Maybe his way was different from the way you think," Doug suggested quietly.

Sasha was instantly wary. "What do you mean?"

"Maybe he loved you. Really loved you, while you thought of him as a brother and mentor. Maybe he wanted more. Did you ever get that feeling?"

"Of course. But he knew what I'd been through and

that I wasn't looking for that type of involvement. He fully accepted it.''

"Which doesn't mean that, as the years passed, he didn't think of it again. If his career had gone sour while yours soared, and he saw you getting involved with me—"

"But all this started *before* I met you."

"True," Doug admitted. He was pensive for a moment. "But suppose, just suppose, that his mind was warped enough to bring him down here with mischief in mind. Those early things were more frightening than harmful. On second thought," he added with a grimace, "you could have been killed on that cycle." He took a breath. "But suppose he only intended to scare you, to play a sick game. Then he saw us together and got really angry. Hell, Sasha, poison is something else! Lucky you only had a little of the stuff!''

"Lucky you didn't have any!"

"Damn it, I don't care about *me*. You were the one who was sick! But come to think of it, if the ice cream *was* poisoned, he had us both in mind, which makes it my affair as well. And *I* say we call the police!''

"Oh, Doug, I don't know. If it *was* Simon—and I still can't accept that it was—he needs psychiatric help, not criminal detention.''

"That's fine for you to say now, babe, but what if you'd eaten a whole dish of that stuff. What if you'd been *really* sick. What if you'd died? I agree that he needs psychiatric help, but first we've got to find him.''

"If it is him." She frowned, trying to clear her head. "I keep trying to think back to the ice-cream parlor. There were only a handful of people in there. And two guys behind the counter."

"How was it going to work in *Bronze Mystique?*"

"The villain was going to be one of those behind the counter." She caught her breath. "In disguise."

Doug nodded, his point well made. "One of those fellows was young, the other more middle-aged. How old is Simon?"

"In his early forties, I guess. But that man was sandy haired. And Simon is dark."

"But adept at disguise. How about the height and the build."

"About...right, I guess," she admitted miserably. "But Simon wouldn't! I know he wouldn't!"

Feeling that she'd had enough for the moment, Doug hugged her. "Okay, Sasha. Just relax. I want you to have a nice long bath while I make a few calls and find out how we go about having that ice-cream carton analyzed. Maybe it was just a bug. There's always that chance."

Much as she wanted to believe it, Doug had planted too many ideas in her mind. And the coincidence with her plot was far too startling to ignore. Obeying him without further fuss, she relaxed as long as she could in his large sunken tub before climbing out and toweling herself dry. She'd barely wrapped the towel about her when Doug joined her in the warm, steamy room.

"Well?" she asked timidly.

He took her by the shoulders and looked her gently in the eye. "The police will take a look at it."

"The police? You didn't, Doug!"

"I had to, babe. For your sake...and mine. If anything happens to you..." He shuddered and pulled her into his embrace. "I can't bear the thought."

"You didn't...you didn't tell them..."

"No. I didn't mention Simon's name. I simply said you'd been violently ill and that I wanted the ice cream checked. They'll stop by for it in a little while. I think the hospital has a lab they can use."

Sasha sagged against him with a sigh. It was done. Perhaps, despite her protests, she felt a little relieved. After all, if the ice cream was found to be untainted, the police would fade out as quickly as they'd been brought in. If not... She winced. Maybe Doug was right. Simon—or whoever—had to be found. She was no longer the only one endangered. And if anything happened to *Doug*—she couldn't bear the thought!

Within an hour two officers were at Doug's door to pick up the container of ice cream. Sasha stayed in the background, curled in a chair, while Doug talked with them. When he returned, he swooped down and took her hand.

"Come on. Put on a skirt. We're going to Boston."

"Boston? At a time like this?"

"What better time could there be?" he asked, a gleam in his eye. "The police are at work and there's nothing we can do until we hear from them. Don't tell me you'd be able to concentrate on work today."

"I suppose not."

"It's settled then. Let's go." He had her clasped to his side and on her way to the bedroom before she could think of further excuse. "Something warm and pretty. We'll have a day on the town."

To her astonishment they did just that. To her astonishment she had fun. Doug kept her busy walking through the Marketplace, asking her opinion on pieces of art in various galleries, charming her with witty observations, regaling her with humorous anecdotes of one experience or another he'd had in his life. He was prone to self-mockery in a way she found endearing, but the modest pride he took in his accomplishments was unmistakable and contagious.

By the time they returned to the Vineyard it was late afternoon and a light blanket of clouds billowed through the skies. It was warm, surprisingly so for early December, a rare gift. ''How about a quick trip to the cliffs?'' he asked, tucking her back into the car they'd left at the airport.

''Now?''

''Why not?'' He glanced at the skies. ''It's been a nice day. The rain will hold off for a little while longer. Besides,'' he added more softly, ''I don't think I'm ready to go back to the house yet. Let's prolong the fun…just a little?''

How could she deny him, when she felt the same. ''Okay,'' she said with a smile.

Unfortunately the weather didn't cooperate. By the time they arrived at the Gay Head cliffs a light sprinkle misted the windshield. But Doug was determined.

''Wait here,'' he ordered, taking his keys and opening the trunk of the car. He extracted a large piece of what appeared to be canvas and, when unfolded, proved to be an oversized poncho.

''Designer, no less,'' Sasha quipped as he pulled it over his head and opened her door. ''That'll keep you dry, but what about me?'' All he had to do was to extend one arm and produce a rakish grin and she understood. ''This is absurd, Doug,'' she said, but she scampered under the poncho nonetheless and managed, with his help, to squeeze her head through the same opening as his. "A two-headed monster." She sent a glance around. "Let's hope no one's watching."

"No one's watching. Look." They both did. "The place is deserted. No one else is crazy enough to be outside in the rain on a balmy December day."

"Sounds romantic," she drawled, feeling lightheaded as sin. Doug's wandering hands did nothing to quell her mood.

"Most definitely," he replied in a deep husky tone that promised more to come. For the moment, though, he drew his arm back to her shoulder and glued her to his side.

The cliffs, as always, were breathtaking in their multicolored cloak of salmon and mocha and white. Doug held her carefully while they made their way through the damp grass above, down onto the clay itself, then farther, weaving along jagged outcrops and into valleys.

"This isn't swell with high heels on," Sasha observed as she tottered and clung more tightly to his waist.

"Yeah, but without them your head wouldn't clear the neckline of this thing. And anyway, if you fall, it's against me. Not so bad, hmm?"

"Not bad at all," she mused happily. The rain brought a fine sheen to their faces and hair, but otherwise they were warm and quite protected beneath the poncho.

Guiding her around one jagged crevice and down into another, he found just the right spot. It was a cozy nook, receding slightly into the cliff, just big enough to hold them both and offer a spectacular view of the sea. Nestling in as far as he could, Doug eased them down.

"There. Comfortable?"

She tipped up her head and kissed his jaw. "Mmm."

"Look." His eyes led the way. "It's beautiful, isn't it?"

"Yes. But I'm glad I'm up here. Those whitecaps look cold."

He tightened his arms around her and for long moments they simply sat as one, admiring nature's gentle fury. When his hand found its way to her breast, she took a deep breath and sighed. "Oh, Doug. This has been a lovely day. I'm not quite sure how you did it, but you did it."

"I'm glad, babe," he crooned, then bent his head and took her lips in a kiss that was warm and wet and as furiously gentle as the sea. His tongue traced the even line of her teeth, then plunged farther in search of her essence. Meanwhile his fingers did highly erotic things to her nipple, which thrust forward through a layer of cashmere in response.

He could arouse her. Always. Whether simply by standing straight and tall in an art gallery, brushing his thigh against hers beneath cover of a tablecloth in a restaurant, rubbing his thumb to her palm in the middle of a cobblestoned street. Now, in the middle of God's country, her breath came faster and she twisted to put her arms around his neck. Deftly he shifted her until she was on his lap facing him, her knees strad-

dling his thighs. When he put both hands on her bottom and crushed her closer, she moaned.

"Doug, this is indecent!" she whispered hoarsely,
but her legs clung.

"No one can see." He grinned, returning both
hands to her breasts, squeezing them, taunting them,
brushing his fingers against their crests until the fire
beneath her was unmistakable. His eyes glowed into
hers. "I love the feel of your body. So warm and firm
and aroused all the time." Slipping his hands beneath
the hem of her sweater, he pushed the fabric high on
her chest. Then his fingers slid under the lace of her
bra, tormenting her until she strained upward. Only
then did he release the catch, freeing her hot breasts
to spill into his palms.

"You shouldn't," she whispered against his lips.

"But it feels good, doesn't it," he whispered back,
kissing her again in declaration of his growing hunger.
She could feel that hunger, both in herself and in him.
Retaliating against his intimate tugging of her nipples,
she snaked her hand between their bodies and touched
him, stroked him, felt him grow until the fine wool
fabric of his slacks was sorely tested.

"Oh, yes," she breathed, against his mouth, "it
feels good. I want—" The words were sealed into her
mouth when he kissed her more forcefully, and though
his hands left her breasts, the position they took up at
her hips and the movement they directed did nothing
to ease the physical longing. "We've got to stop,
Doug," she whispered roughly. Her body was aflame
with need of his, a flame that seemed to have grown
hotter day by day. If either of them had thought their
recent freedom to love would have taken the edge off

their hunger, they were mistaken. Perhaps it was the late night's misadventure, perhaps this day of public restraint, but whatever, their desire at the moment was beyond bounds.

"Let's go home," she whispered even as she arched her hips and sought his hardness.

"Oh, no," he rasped, shoving her skirt to her waist.

"Doug!"

"Shhhh. Easy does it." He slid a finger into the inner leg of her panties and found her unerringly. She cried out, then held her breath, only the occasional animal murmur coming from her throat. Arms around his neck once again, she raised herself slightly to give him room.

"Oh, please, no. Let's go home. I need you, Doug. Not your finger. *You!*"

"You'll have me," he stated, his voice hoarse and uneven as he began to wriggle beneath her.

"What're you doing?" she cried dazedly.

"Trying," he grunted once, then again, "to get these damned pants down."

She looked at him round-eyed and whispered a conspiratorial, "Here?"

His expression held the same urgency she felt in his body, in her own. "Yes, here," he gritted, rolling his hips from side to side as he worked his open pants to his thighs.

"Doug, we can't!" she croaked, but already his fingers pulled at the waistband of her panties, and elbows braced on his shoulders, she helped him. She had only time to free one leg from the silk when he brought her back down. Slowly, surely, he entered her, filling her as fully as she'd ever been filled before.

"I'll never get enough of you," he gritted, his hands at her hips, lifting her, lowering her, letting her feel his throbbing as he felt her sheathing. "I love you, babe. God, I love you!"

Their lips met then, tongues stroking in mime of that lower motion. And Sasha knew that just as each time they made love it was better and better, the physical was only half of it. The other half was the sheer joy they found in one another, which seemed so perfect it frightened her. But she loved him more than life itself. And the passion she showed him said as much.

In tandem, as the waves below thrashed against the rock, they reached a shuddering climax. Then they clung to each other as the waves subsided, and whispered soft words of love and praise. How long they sat there in their hidden nook, locked together in the most intimate of embraces beneath the sheltering cover of the poncho, they didn't know. Time had no meaning. Nor did place. It was only an increase in the rain that finally bid them repair their clothing and begin the trip back to the house.

It was indeed poison. The lab technician had given it a fancy name, one the police repeated but which was foreign to Sasha. But then, that wasn't surprising. She hadn't mentioned specifics in her proposal.

At the prodding of the police and Doug's gentle insistence, Sasha related the sequence of events that led her to believe mischief was in the works on the island. With reluctance she told what she could about Simon, though her descriptions were heavily interspersed with denial.

"It couldn't be him," she repeated time and again, while Doug tried to reassure her that nothing would be done unless there was sufficient evidence to warrant it. When she stated that Simon was probably at home in Maine, the police suggested she try to call him. Again reluctantly, she did so. When no one answered the phone, she tried to rationalize. "He's into different things all the time. The latest was deep-sea diving. He's probably somewhere down in the Caribbean," she offered prayerfully.

"Could be," one of the officers said, but he made copious notes nonetheless.

At Doug's urging, the police agreed to keep their investigation as quiet as possible. Their approach, they claimed, would be simply to look for strange faces on the island. Their first stop would undoubtedly be the ice-cream store.

Left alone with Doug at last, Sasha reeled uncertainly. To have slid from such heights of passion on the cliffs to the doldrums the instant they'd returned, finding the police at their doorstep, was unsettling. Even more so was the waiting that commenced.

Both Sasha and Doug were tense. Though life went on, outwardly normal and blatantly uneventful for the next few days, they were cautious, watchful. Sasha called her sister several times, satisfied when told that her mother was recovering nicely, then was going home. She sent another note, this one addressed to the farm and more chatty than the other had been. Agreeing with Doug that at some point she'd have to visit, she paved the way with small talk about her house on the island and about her work.

Her work was another matter. Sasha wrote nearly

every day, but *Bronze Mystique* was proving to be more a diary than a work of fiction. When her heroine brooded on her love for her hero, it was Sasha's feelings about Doug that lit the screen. When her heroine contemplated the future, it was Sasha's feelings about marrying Doug that achieved outlet. When, in those darker moments, her heroine wrestled with thoughts of the mysterious being who stalked her, it was Sasha's fears that were aired. Anticipation of the climactic scene in the book was what made Sasha particularly uneasy. The heroine, as per Sasha's proposal, was to be kidnapped and buried alive in a coffin-sized box with nothing but an air pipe to keep her alive. It would be a terrifying experience from which, of course, the hero would rescue her. Of course. And there would, indeed, be a happy ending. It was at this point that Sasha began to pray.

The balmy weather continued. Sasha and Doug took long walks on the beach, holding hands, silently contemplating the tide, waiting, waiting for the villain's next move. As mindful as her of the ending of *Bronze Mystique,* Doug was reluctant to let Sasha out of his sight for more than a few minutes at a stretch, and then only when necessity demanded it.

The police had dutifully interrogated the young man who'd been working at the ice-cream shop, only to learn that he was an off-islander working part-time who had thought nothing about an older man with an air of authority popping in to help. The young man had simply assumed him to be the owner's partner. But the older one had come and gone quickly, leaving no concrete clue to his identity. And he'd never shown up again.

Slowly the agony of waiting began to take its toll. Furious at feeling so helpless, Doug grew testy. He wanted to steal Sasha back to New York or to some other hideaway where he might keep her safe. But as the police had pointed out, that might either prolong the inevitable or, worse, land the couple in an even more vulnerable situation than their present one. At least the population of the Vineyard was small and somewhat watchable. Unfortunately there were no less than a dozen eccentrics, recent *and* not-so-recent arrivals on the island, who might be their man.

It was late on a Thursday afternoon when Doug stalked into Sasha's den and eyed her idle form. "Come on, babe. Let's go into town. We need a change of scenery and the refrigerator's getting bare."

"You go," she mumbled without turning, as tightly strung as he.

"Not without you. I'm not leaving you here."

"Oh, please, Doug," she blurted out. "I'm not a child who needs constant baby-sitting." She propped her chin on her fist and stared at the blank screen before her. "Nothing's going to happen. I'll be all right."

He came forward in two angry strides. "You're coming with me."

"I'm not."

"Sasha..." he warned quietly.

She turned to throw him a livid glare. "Damn it, you can't order me around! I'm tired of being guarded! I feel as though I'm under house arrest! Well, you know what? I hope the guy *does* attack! I can't take this much longer!"

Doug's eyes narrowed. "My company's that much of a punishment?"

"That's not it, and you know it! But I see no reason why we can't be apart for all of an hour!" Her eyes flashed. "I'm not going into town. Period."

Hating herself for her tone, feeling ungrateful and unloving and angry and frustrated, she gritted her teeth and turned back to her screen.

A day before, a week before, Doug might have been understanding. But his anger and frustration matched hers and he was in no mood to be solicitous.

"Fine. You stay here. I'll see you later."

Without further word, he stormed from the room and the house, leaving rubber on the drive as he spun the Maserati around and off. Only then did Sasha bury her face in her hands and wonder how she could have been so cruel to the man she loved, to the man who was going through so much because of her. And *it was her fault.* Someone was after *her*—and after Doug whose sole crime was loving her. It wasn't fair, damn it! It wasn't fair!

Surging from her seat in irritation, she grabbed her coat and headed for the beach. She needed a change of scenery too, and though a ride into town with Doug would have been nice, had she not been so ill-tempered as to refuse him, the beach would be some solace. It had to be. When Doug returned, she owed him an apology.

It had been a sunny day, but already the skies were beginning to darken with scattered clouds and the setting sun. The days were so short at this time of year, she mused. Life was so short. So why was she putting Doug off when, in her heart, she knew she wanted to marry him? What was she waiting for? Some sort of divine intervention? Some mystical revelation of the future?

No one knew what the future held, least of all her and Doug. Were there ever guarantees? Doug had done everything in his power to convince her of his love. Could she continue to punish him for something Sam Webster had done over ten years ago? Could she continue to punish herself?

The tide was low. Walking slowly, head down, she made her way far out across the damp sand, her sneakers leaving the ghost of a trail along intricately patterned ridges, between scattered clusters of seaweed. By the water's edge, she stopped to study the lapping foam, then the far horizon. There was something lulling about the constancy of the surf, lulling as Doug's arms, as his gentle voice, as his love. When she'd heard the Maserati roar off, she'd felt alone as she hadn't felt in weeks. Was this what life without Doug would be like, this gnawing emptiness? He'd given so much of himself. Wasn't it time she reciprocated? Wasn't it time she decided to take that chance on the future? Didn't she owe it to Doug? Didn't she owe it to *herself*?

After agonizing for weeks, the decision was simply made. Feeling suddenly lighthearted, Sasha turned to retrace her steps. The air had chilled noticeably since she'd been out. Her skin prickled.

She'd taken no more than two steps when she swayed. Dizzy, she shook her head and tried to walk on, but her legs felt strangely stiff and uncooperative. Lighthearted...light-headed? Too many emotions, she thought. Too much cold. It was, after all, December, and getting darker, darker....

Senselessness came fast and she crumpled onto the wet sand. Only then did the distant figure on the cliff lower his gun, take a long swig from his pocket flask and retreat.

A circuitous drive around the island had done little to curb Doug's anger. When he'd finally headed into town, he'd been hell-bent on satisfaction. The Maserati screeched to a halt in front of the police station and he was out in a minute, storming into the building. By a coincidence not surprising giving the limited size of the Vineyard's department, the officer on duty was one of the two who had dealt with the poisoned ice cream. Doug had been prepared to spill his guts regardless of whom he found there.

"All right, officer," he gritted, planting his elbows firmly on the high desk. "I think we've pussyfooted around enough. You've got that woman and me out there like sitting ducks and it's about time we do something."

The policeman raised his eyes from the form on which he'd been idly drawing. Though life on the Vineyard was usually quiet, particularly in this off-season, he'd had years enough of dealing with temperamental residents to be perfectly calm before Doug.

"Just what do you propose we do, Mr. Donovan?"

"Donohue. It's Donohue. And I propose we—you—start bringing people in and questioning them."

"Bringing *who* in?"

"Suspects! You said there were a number of people new to the island!"

The officer laughed. "Great. I should alienate citizens who've come here for peace and quiet? How would *you* have taken that sort of thing, Mr. Donohue?"

"*I* didn't come here with the express purpose of terrorizing an innocent woman!"

"No, and neither did any of the others, to our knowledge."

Doug's eyes hardened all the more. "Are you suggesting that we imagined that ice-cream incident?"

"Of course not. We've got the lab report on it. It was poison, all right. But we can't just go out and corral a bunch of law-abiding people without any evidence pointing to one or the other. All we can do is to keep our eyes open. We're doing that."

Doug's gaze dropped to the officer's doodles and he uttered a tight-lipped, "Yeah. So I see."

"Look. Someone has to be here. We can't leave the office unattended. But there are other guys on the streets. Take my word for it. You're not being forgotten."

"But how long must we wait?" Doug growled. "I mean, we're going crazy. *You* were the one who told us to hang around here. But nothing's happening." He slapped his hand on the desk and looked away. "This is ridiculous!"

"If nothing's happening, good. Maybe your fellow's begun to realize that he won't get away with whatever he's trying to do. Maybe he's left."

"Who's left?" Doug asked pointedly. "Any of those eccentrics you mentioned?"

The policeman took a deep breath. "I can't tell you that, Mr. Donohue. We have no way of monitoring every coming and going. People arrive on the ferry for the day, they leave. There are flights in and out. For every private boat that docks, another shoves off. All I can say is that we're trying to keep on top of anything strange. If this person is as demented as you believe, he's bound to tip his hand somewhere along the line.''

What had started as an excuse in patient indulgence on the officer's part had become a staring contest between him and Doug. Neither was backing down.

"Sure," Doug seethed. "But what if it's too late?"

"We're doing everything we can."

Doug took a breath, ready to further lambaste his opponent, then he realized the futility of it all. With a look that promised harm if any was done to Sasha, he whirled on his heel and left. Hands on his hips, he stood beside the Maserati breathing hard in the cool night air for several minutes before slamming into the car and starting off.

The grocery store benefited from his frustration, since he threw one item after the next into his cart with hardly an awareness of what he bought. Three bundles sat beside him in the seat when he realized that he was still in no mood to return to Sasha. She needed his support, not his misdirected anger. Swerving onto the main street of town, he drove a block, then pulled the car sharply over and parked it. A bench stood nearby. He stalked toward it and sat, hands jammed in his pockets, legs sprawled carelessly before him.

It was dark. Cars moved slowly along the streets, echoing the leisurely pace of the pedestrians who passed. The tempo there was slow. Why then was he in such a turmoil?

Answers came to him in rapid succession. Love. He was a novice at it and it had thrown him for a loop. Sasha. He wanted her so badly that he didn't know what to do. Simon Tripoli, damn him. Making their existence miserable, complicating things. Who in the hell did he think he was to be able to control their lives this way?

Inhaling deeply, Doug let his head fall back, then he brought it forward with a remorseful sigh. It was his own frustration, and he'd taken it out on Sasha as though it had all been *her* fault. He'd stormed from the house as if she'd personally rejected him.

Now he had to look at things from her side. She'd given so much, she truly had. She'd admitted her love, she'd asked for time, she'd even so much as hinted that she would marry him one day. Could he fault her that she was cautious? Could he fault her that she was as tense as he with the knowledge that that maniac was on her trail? Oh, she hadn't yet fully agreed that it might be Simon, but Doug knew that much of her agonizing related to that distinct probability.

And he'd left her alone. He'd left her alone to stew...just when she needed him the most!

Deeply engrossed in his guilt, he bounded from the bench and ran smack into a man who'd approached. "Whoa," the man said. "Where're ya goin' so fast?"

The smell of whiskey was as telling as the slow slur of his words. A drunkard, Doug mused. Just his luck.

"Excuse me," he gritted quietly, intending to sidestep the man. "The bench is all yours."

But when he would have continued toward his car,

the man's sheer bulk restrained him. Though comparable to himself in height, Doug saw at a glance that it was multiple layers of jerseys, shirts and a loud plaid wool jacket that gave the deception of bulk in the drunkard, rather than muscle itself.

"All 'lone? Wha' fun'd thad be? Come sit wi' me a bit. We'll talk."

"I'm sorry. I've got to run," Doug said, making another attempt at escape, only to be snagged by one steely arm.

"'S too late," the man mumbled, and something about him drew Doug's closer scrutiny. Dark haired, with the thick stubble of a beard on his jaw, he could easily pass as a vagrant. Yet his clothes weren't quite worn enough or dirty enough. And the flask he raised to his lips was a far cry from the brown-bagged bottle a vagrant would carry.

"What?" Doug asked tightly, his every sense suddenly razor sharp.

The man seemed to be focusing on a distant dot in the dark. "'S too late. Ya can't have her."

"What?"

"If I can't have her, you can't." He took another drink. Something caught Doug's eye. On impulse, he grabbed the flask from the man's unsuspecting hands and turned it toward the dim light of a nearby streetlamp. A second after he'd absorbed the initials on the side of the flask he threw the metal to the pavement.

"Wha—?" The drunkard hadn't finished his first word before Doug seized him by the collar and threw him down against the bench with a rigid knee pressed to his stomach.

"Where is she, you creep?"

"Ya can't have her."

Doug shook him. "Where is she? What've you done to her?" His heart pounded in terror, but his body was coiled, a tool of potential murder.

"I wanted 'er…I wanted 'er an' she left…an' she's gotten so high and mighty thad she ne'r called…." From a wail to a growl, he widened his red-rimmed eyes on Doug. "Well, you can't have 'er! She's gone! I took care a' that. You won't have 'er!"

"Where is she, you bastard!" Doug roared, shaking Simon again and again out of sheer helplessness. One part of him told him to try to find Sasha; the other knew it might be futile without this man's help.

"Gone," the other gulped, seeming to collapse spinelessly.

"Tell me! Tell me, or so help me I'll personally see that you spend every last day of your life in prison. I don't give a damn if you're sick or not. You'll rot in hell if you don't tell me what you've done!"

A new voice joined the fray and hands hauled Doug from the sprawled form beneath him. "Hey! What's going on here?"

Doug fought with all his strength to get back to the man who held the only answer he wanted. "That bastard's done something to my girl," he gritted, struggling to free himself from the restraining arms.

"Donohue?" the policeman asked. "That you?"

Panting furiously, Doug looked back. "Yeah. It's me. And that's Simon Tripoli, the man you should have found days ago! He's done something to Sasha and he won't tell me what."

Sensing the urgency of the situation, the officer abruptly released Doug's arms and leaned over Simon.

"Okay, bud. You're in trouble enough. Things would go better for you if you gave us some hints. Where is she?"

Simon shrugged and rolled his head, then craned his neck and looked for his flask. "She's nice an' peaceful. Ri' near home. Where's my whiskey?"

"Damn your whiskey!" Doug hollered and would have lunged again had not the policeman set a preventative hand flat on his chest.

"Come on, Tripoli. Where is she?" Doug retrieved the flask and held it just out of his reach.

"She's on the beach."

"What beach?" Doug growled.

"Yours."

"What did you do to her?" he demanded, waving the flask before the other man's nose.

"Nothin' much."

The policeman took over, placing a threatening knee at Simon's groin and beginning to apply a slow, slow pressure. "What? Exactly."

Simon made a face of annoyance. "A dart. Tranquilizer. The tide's comin' in." He grunted when the officer leaned forward, but the eyes that went to Doug's were defiant and without fear. "You can't have 'er, Donohue! You can't have 'er!"

Doug didn't stay long enough to hear the continuing tirade. Ramming the flask toward the bench, he turned and bolted for his car, driving like a man demented which he was in a way. If anything happened to Sasha...if anything happened...

When the windshield blurred, he swore and batted on the wipers, only to realize that it was his own eyes that were filled with tears. Sniffling, he mopped his face with the back of his hand and drove on, willing himself to be cool, willing the road to shorten, willing the tide to stay out, willing Sasha to wake up before it was too late.

Hands in a death grip on the wheel, he drove like a maniac, caring little if a police escort joined the race. But the only other cars on the road passed in a whir on the opposite side, or slammed on their brakes to yield to the whizzing Maserati.

The beach. He had to get to the beach. He had to get to Sasha. Damn, where was the moon when he needed it? Would he be able to find her? If he did, he'd take her on any terms he could. Marriage? To hell with it! If he could simply be *with* her....

Taking the turn onto his private road at a madman's pace, he jounced over ruts he'd never seen before. At his house he slammed on the brakes and burst from the car, leaving the door wide open.

At a full run, a nervous sweat pouring from his skin, he raced down the embankment, over ragged cliffs, ever downward. He tripped once and slid several yards, then pulled himself up and tore on. His eyes were trained on the beach, his pulse pounding as thunderously as the tide.

When he reached the level sand he stopped, gasping, squinting frantically toward the water for a form, any form. He paced to the left and the right as he searched.

"Where are you?" he gritted. "Where are you? Damn it, Sasha, where are you?" Then he raised his voice in a mournful wail. "Sasha! Saaaashaaa!" He ran forward into the surf, heedless of the frigid water that soaked his sneakers and jeans. "Saaaashaaa!"

10

Sasha came to slowly, feeling cold and numb and disoriented. She was sprawled on the wet sand, her cheek to the coarse grains. One hand lay across a strand of seaweed, the other was pinned beneath her. It was the foot that lay in the rising water, though, that jarred her to awareness.

Pushing herself up, she pressed a hand to her head and looked around in confusion. There was water...everywhere, save the small sandbar on which she'd apparently fallen. But...what had happened? She recalled having started back toward shore, feeling dizzy, falling...

Looking frantically about the ink-black sea, she gasped. Then she hugged her knees to her chest and tried to still her thudding heart. Where was shore? She was sure she faced it, but everything was so dark, so forbidding, so threatening.

Gradually understanding dawned and she realized that while she'd been unconscious the tide had come in. How long had it been? She didn't have a watch, though she doubted she'd have been able to read one anyway. It was dark, so dark. She could barely make out the vague outline of the cliffs, much less the house. And it was cold. All balminess had gone with the light of day. She was chilled to the bone.

She'd have to swim. That was all there was to it. With a great effort she pushed herself to her feet, only to find she was dizzy and frighteningly weak. Numb and oddly divorced from the rest of her body, her legs wobbled. She glanced in bewilderment at the encircling waves, then the shore. She had no choice. Even as she stood, her small hill of sand seemed to shrink. The water couldn't be that deep, she reasoned in a desperate attempt to encourage herself. She'd been unaware of any major slopes in the sand when she'd wandered earlier. But then, her mind had been on Doug. As it was, she couldn't believe she'd come out so far!

She took a step, swayed and crumbled to her knees, only to have her jeans become soaked within minutes. Of course. *This was what he'd planned.* If her legs wouldn't work and her head spun each time she tried to move, how could she possibly swim to shore? If she stayed there she would die of exposure or fright, unless of course she simply passed out and drowned the easy way.

But she wouldn't. She had to get in…there was something she had to say to Doug…there was too much to live for!

Swallowing a growing wave of panic, she struggled to her feet again. Her teeth chattered; her fingers were wet and frigid. She took one tentative step, then another. When the waves saturated her sneakers, she was momentarily paralyzed. But she tugged her coat around her and took another step. Head ablaze with an icy inferno of lights, she tottered; then, even as her mind screamed in protest, she sank helplessly into the waves. Too frightened to cry, she was shaken by dry

sobs of terror. Doug! She had to get to Doug! She had
to see Doug!

On hands and knees she crept forward, but each
inch brought the water higher on her body and her
clothing began to weigh her down. Doug. Doug.
Where was he? *Help me, Doug! Please help me!*
Rocking back and forth on her knees, she prayed
softly. Then, above the ocean's din, she heard a voice
in answer.

"Saaashaaa!"

It was distant. Imagination? Hallucination?

"Saaashaaa!"

She puckered up her face and screamed with all her
might. "Doug!" She screamed a second time, drawing
from hidden reserves, not caring if she was left with
nothing. "Douuuuugggg!"

At the sound of her voice, Doug's heart nearly exploded. His eyes riveted in the direction from which
she'd yelled and even as he began to run down the
beach he was kicking off his shoes, dropping his
jacket, scrambling out of his jeans. When he hit the
water he wore nothing but his shirt and briefs, yet his
blood was pounding too fast to allow for the cold.

"Sasha! Yell again! I can't see you!"

Frightened and weak, she cried his name again, but
her voice seemed to drown in the waves the instant
she opened her mouth. Again and again she tried,
shaking uncontrollably, though mindful of nothing but
that Doug had come. She'd needed him and he'd
come. She knew that if she passed out and died in that
instant it would be with the conviction that he'd loved
her that much.

The thought gave her strength. "Doug!" she

screamed, head up though she was doubled over holding herself. "I'm here! Here, Doug!"

At last he saw her, farther east then he'd expected, a faint shadow on a frighteningly small piece of sand. Running through the shallow waves, he dived forward and swam, arms and legs miraculously endowed with the superhuman strength needed to counter the onrush of the waves.

Though Doug was the one making the exertion, it was Sasha who gasped for air. It was so cold and he was swimming against the tide. If anything happened to him...

"Oh, Doug," she cried softly. "Come on, Doug. Come on."

He stroked steadily, shortening the distance between them until the water grew shallow again and he was able to stumble to his feet and run the last few yards. Then he was on Sasha's tiny island, taking her into his arms, crushing her to his wet frame.

"Thank God," he murmured brokenly, his face buried in her hair. "Thank God you're all right."

Sasha clung to him as to life itself. "I was so frightened.... I c-couldn't stand...and it's s-so dark....''

"It's all right, babe. I'm here. I'll take you back with me now." Mindful of what lay ahead and of the continued urgency of the situation, he set her back on her haunches and quickly began to unbutton her coat. "This will be more heavy than warm." He tore the jacket off and let it fall, then reached for her feet and discarded her sodden sneakers. The wool sweater went too, along with the jeans. "Hold your breath and try to relax, babe. Let me do the work. It'll be cold."

She nodded, but she was already so cold that the

temperature of the water held little impact on her.
Doug carried her until the waves reached his ribs, then
he plunged them both in and, one arm around her
waist, stroked steadily toward shore. Arms looped
around his neck, Sasha could feel the extent of his
exertion, but he forced himself on, bringing them
closer, closer to the beach. When he could more easily
wade again, he scooped her up in his arms and began
to run through the surf, at last reaching the beach,
stopping only to get his bearings before heading
straight for the house.

Sasha was never to know whether she'd passed out
again or simply been so numbed by the cold that her
senses went on hold. The next thing she knew, though,
she was in Doug's house, in his tiled shower, being
held upright by his strong arms while the warmest,
most deliciously welcome water hit her skin.

Above her, Doug's face was a mask of worry.
Throwing her arms around his neck, she burrowed into
his neck and hung on until the lump in her throat allowed for speech. "I love you so much, Doug," she
murmured through her tears. "I love you." She
clutched him harder and was rewarded by a corresponding tightening of his arms about her back.
"Don't ever leave me again. Please don't leave me."

"Shhhhh," he soothed, threading unsteady fingers
through her hair, brushing it back from her face and
kissing her forehead. "It's all right. I'm not going anywhere." Slipping his thigh between hers to brace her
against the shower wall, he gently stripped off her
blouse, her bra, then her panties and socks. Removing
his own, he took her back in his arms, hugged her,
rocked her beneath the regenerative spray. "Shhhh,"

he crooned again, as much for her benefit as for his own as slow tears trickled one by one down his cheeks.

Sasha cried freely, whispering his name between sobs. With her thawing came the full awareness of what had happened, and she was overwhelmed by the force of divergent emotions. By the time she began to calm, a thick steam filled the stall. Turning the water off, Doug reached for a towel, wrapped it warmly around Sasha, took one for himself, then led her into the bedroom where his heavy quilt awaited.

"Warm enough, babe?" he asked, softly, his face inches from hers, torso flush with hers, arms and legs intertwined with hers. He tucked the quilt more tightly around them.

She smiled and sighed a breathy, "Yes," then sent him a look of remembered terror. "I was so scared and confused," she whispered, round-eyed. "I kept trying to stand but my legs wouldn't hold me. I was dizzy and cold. If you hadn't come—"

Doug's warm finger sealed the words at her lips. "I did come. That's the important thing."

She breathed a ragged acknowledgment and simply held him for a minute, reassured by his strength and the warmth of his long lean body. Then she forced herself to speak. There was so much to be said. "Doug?"

"What, babe?"

"I...I guess it had to have been Simon." When Doug simply stared at her, she went on. "I know I resisted the idea for a long time, and I suppose if I'd been more open to it I might have been able to help locate him. But I'm sure it was him. The MO is too distinct.''

"MO? What do you mean?''

''The technique. Simon used it in his book, that first one, the only one that sold. He waited until I was as far out as I could get, then hit me with a tranquilizer dart.'' She paused, bit her lip. ''I know he's out there somewhere. Maybe in the light of day if we got the police and went looking...?''

"No need,'' Doug said softly. ''They've got him.''

Her breath caught in her throat. ''What do you mean? If they've got him, then who did this tonight?''

"Simon did...before he came into town and got drunk.''

"Got drunk? You saw him?''

Doug nodded, his nose rubbing against hers. Now that it was over and Sasha was safe, he felt no anger, but rather a strange pity for Simon. ''He's a sick man, Sasha, and what he tried to do to you, to us, was wrong. But he's suffering. After he shot that dart at you, he tried to bury it all in a bottle. When that didn't quite work, he actually stopped me and told me about it.''

"He *what?*''

With an indulgent smile, Doug backtracked a bit. ''After I left the house, I stormed around the island for a while, went to the police station and gave the officer on duty a piece of my mind, blitzed my way through the market, then found a bench in town and sat down to gather my wits. I had finally reached a grand conclusion and had got up to come home to you when he approached. He obviously knew who I was. When he started to talk, I realized he knew something about you. Then I saw the flask he was drinking from—with the initials S.T. on the front. That was when I got a little, uh, rough.''

"What did you do?" Sasha asked, alarmed.

"Not much. Oh, I threatened, but the police came around and hauled me off before I could do any damage. Between the good officer and myself, though, we managed to get the information we wanted. That was when I came after you."

Sasha closed her eyes and moaned softly. "And the police took Simon?"

"Yes. They'll keep him in custody." When she winced, he stroked her arm. "They have to, babe. Don't you see? He needs help. Tomorrow morning he'll most likely be sent to a hospital for evaluation. But he can't be let out on the streets. Not after what he's done."

"But *why*, Doug?" she cried, eyes awash with tears. "Why did he *do* all these things?"

"For many of the reasons we suspected. Jealousy—of you and your career, of me and our love. His belief that you'd abandoned him. There are probably a whole slew of other things totally unrelated to you that brought him to this state. The important thing is that he get the help he needs."

Tears spilled down her cheeks. "Oh, Doug, I'm sorry. It's partly my fault. I should have kept in touch with him."

"Don't blame yourself, babe. That was only a small part of the problem. The fact is that you surpassed him both personally and professionally. It's possible he couldn't take the turnaround."

"Well, then," she said, sniffling. "I'm sorry for

being so stubborn about him. And I'm sorry for what I said to you before, Doug. I was cranky and upset. I shouldn't have—''

"I'm the one who should apologize, Sasha. I was imperious and insensitive. I was upset, too, but you didn't deserve that—''

This time it was her finger that stoppered the words at his lips. "I love you, Doug. I should have understood, rather than send you off and then run out of the house like an idiot.''

His gaze narrowed. "Why did you do that? You have to admit that it was a pretty stupid thing to do given the fact that a madman was on the loose. What were you doing on the beach?''

"Same thing you were doing driving around the island. Calming down. Thinking. Putting things into perspective. I had finally reached a momentous decision and was starting back here to wait for you when Simon's dart knocked me out.'' Her voice softened to a sweet whisper. "I owe you my life, Doug Donohue. Do you know that?''

"You don't owe me anything,'' he said with a sudden gruffness. "If I hadn't arrived, you'd have swam to shore yourself. You're a pretty self-sufficient lady, Sasha.''

"Not that self-sufficient,'' she argued gently. "My knees wouldn't work and I was dizzy. I could never have made it to shore myself. And anyway,'' she mused more soberly, "self-sufficiency has taken on a different light since I've met you.''

"Oh?'' he asked cautiously.

"Yes.'' Her fingers found their favorite niche against his spine at the small of his back. "It's lost some of its glow. I used to think that it was the most important thing in my life. Not that I'm denying its importance now. But...there are other things that matter more."

"Like?"

Facing his beloved bronze visage, she didn't hesitate. "Like my love for you, my need for you. The joy I get doing for you, sharing with you." She glanced down for an instant. "And the future."

"What about the future?"

"Is—is that proposal still open?" She heard herself say the words, then held her breath while Doug stared at her. When his lips thinned, her heart constricted.

"You mean to say that you'd marry me because I saved your life? You'd marry me out of gratitude— stemming from another man's connivances?" He set several inches between them. "No way, Sasha. I don't want marriage on grounds like those. In a way that was what I'd decided on the bench in town just before I bumped into your friend." His eyes darkened to a gleaming charcoal gray. "I love you. I want to spend the rest of my life with you." His voice gentled. "But I'll take you on your terms, regardless of what they are. If you don't want marriage, so be it. Because if you're not happy, I'm not happy. It's as simple as that."

As quickly as those cold fingers had closed around her heart, they warmed and began a heady massage. Sasha smiled slowly. "But I'd made a decision, too, remember? *Before* Simon's dart hit. I'd decided that you were everything I'd always wanted in a man, a lover, a husband, and that I was hurting both of us by letting my experience with Sam hold me back." Her voice, too, gentled, and she followed her fingers as they wove through the rich vibrancy of his hair. "I love you so much that I sometimes think I'm just wishing it to be so. I've lived so long on wishes, I guess. It's hard to believe this one's come true."

"It has, babe. Believe me. It has."

"Then you'll marry me?"

His eyes danced. "If that's what makes you happy."

"But what makes *you* happy?"

"Your marrying me. Will you?"

"Yes. Oh, yes."

"No more doubts?"

She shook her head. Though tears glistened in her eyes, a brilliant smile lit her face. "I love you," she whispered.

"I love you," he echoed through a tremulous smile, then cautioned her more playfully, "But this isn't a happy ending, ya' know."

"I know." She glowed. "It's a happy beginning. Right?"

"Smart lady," he said, and turned the first page.

Several days later, before a local justice of the peace, Sasha and Doug were married. It was a brief ceremony made beautiful by its very simplicity. With neither family nor friends present, it was a statement of the very private nature of their relationship. They married for neither money nor business nor family convenience nor tradition, but rather because they loved each other. Very simply. They loved each other.

A week later, Sasha brought Doug to Maine to meet her parents, who, though very definitely of Grant

Wood's "American Gothic" school, had as definitely begun to mellow. Not that there were open arms and tears and smiles of excitement all around, but then Sasha hadn't expected that. Rather, as an initial wariness gradually eased, the visit became a pleasant one. There was talk of Natalie's improving health, of the farm, of Doug's work and of Sasha's—the last with a quiet if cautious respect on the part of the elder Blakes. It was a beginning. Sasha couldn't ask for more. Besides, she was intrigued by her mother, who, under the guise of following doctor's orders, let her father putter around fixing lunch. There was something about that ghost of a smile on Natalie Blake's face that held hope.

Simon Tripoli was indicted on multiple counts of attempted murder. Though Sasha might have herself chosen to drop the charges, the matter had been taken out of her hands with the involvement of the police. Thanks largely to the lawyer Doug brought in from New York, the defendant was found not guilty by reason of insanity and was placed in a private hospital for the care he so badly needed.

Donohue for Women took off like a house afire, from drawing board to sewing room to runway to boutique. More willingly than he ever had, Doug promoted the line nationwide, each new city an adventure with Sasha by his side. At Sasha's request, M.P.I. coordinated her publicity tours to coincide with Doug's, a practice so satisfactory to author and publisher alike that when her sixth and most critically acclaimed novel, *Scheherezade Sunday*, made its debut it received the finest send-off ever.

Bronze Mystique never made it to press. On the day

of their wedding, Sasha gave it to Doug, who promptly had it bound in leather and set it on the nightstand by their bed to be read only on special occasions when they were alone, together and naked. It became quickly dog-eared, for he found himself rereading various portions on the sly from time to time, just as she did. It was a diary, a treatise on trust and understanding and patience, as well as on jealousy and suspicion and fear. It was a story of the heart's victory. And it held the promise of love for a world of tomorrows.

Take 3 of "The Best of the Best™" Novels FREE

Plus get a FREE surprise gift!

Don't miss this chance to get these popular titles
from *New York Times* bestselling author

BARBARA DELINSKY